In strange orbits
Volume 1

Ramón Somoza

© 2016 Ramón Somoza García.
1st edition
Published by: Editorial Dragón
ISBN: 978-84-15981-41-1
Cover: Alexia Jorques Castelló
Translation: Ramón Somoza
Original title: "En órbitas extrañas – volumen 1"

To my children:

Alan-Carlos, Irving-Ángel and Cristian-Jorge

Table of Contents

Preface

This book is the first volume of the SF saga "In strange orbits". Actually, I had not planned to publish Tanit's history in book form, but several readers asked me to publish it on paper, and not only as an e-book. As the individual novellas are too short for traditional publishing, I decided to make a compilation and publish every five stories as a separate volume. I did consider publishing it every ten stories, but that would require that my readers would have to wait too long between two books.

"In strange orbits" is a series of novellas about a little girl that due to an accident on a starship will be forced to survive alone in interstellar space. She is a genius, but she has a certain tendency to run into trouble… especially because she assumes that everything works like in a human society.

This first volume covers the first five episodes of the series, such as they were published. I toyed with the idea of partially rewriting the stories so as to smooth the transition between the different chapters, but I finally rejected the idea. The main reason was that it would be unfair to the readers that bought the different novellas separately, but also because the episodes are clearly sequential. If you find that there is some repetition between the different chapters, this is the reason.

Each chapter of this book is a different episode, which covers a complete adventure. You can read the book in one go or chapter by chapter. Unless you have a lot of time, I recommend the second.

For those readers that meet Tanit for the first time, I hope that you enjoy her adventures.

Ramón Somoza

The lost girl

"Our job is to be in strange orbits," laughs my father. "But this time the orbit couldn't be more common. I've lost count of the times that I've orbited Earth."

I look with curiosity through the window. It's very exciting to see the blue and white planet that is humanity's cradle. Nothing would please me more than visiting it; I've never been to Earth, I always lived on Mars, the red planet. But it won't be possible. As soon as the colonists embark, our starship will depart for Thuis, where mom is waiting for us.

It wasn't easy for mom, nor was it for me. She left with the first consignment of colonists to that planet orbiting a red dwarf in the Dorado constellation. A planet that is very similar to Earth, they tell me, though with a somewhat higher gravity. It's the second planet that human beings have colonized outside the solar system.

Mom, of course, had to go. There is no greater expert in exobiology than mom within the solar system, and her presence was essential for this colonization. When they colonized Zeta, the whole colony went to the verge of annihilation due to the ecosystem they encountered. A wildlife so strange that they had no clue what they were facing. The Ministry of Colonization learned the lesson: You simply can't establish a settlement in a new world unless you know the planet's biology.

So I had to stay with Aunt Ethel. No kids with a first colonization; it's far too dangerous. And daddy could not take care of me, he's an exploration pilot. Actually it was him who discovered Thuis. When he landed, he was also the one that gave it its name, in Dutch: Thuis, the home. He said that if he ever retired, it would be there, as that would be like being home. After seeing the holograms he came back with, I understand why he said that. That was also the main reason why mom agreed to go, leaving me behind with only eight years. Mars is terraformed, but even so it is a tough planet to live on. On the other hand, they say Thuis is even better than Earth ever was. My parents believe it will be a great place for me. It better be. Because it has stolen my mother from me for more than two years.

I suppose I'm pretty weird, even for Mars. For starters, I'm white and blond. Dad is of Dutch origin, mom is a mixture of Swedish, Canadian, Austrian and Spanish, her parents came directly from Earth. Not like anything of the race melting pot on Mars. But I am also small for Mars, where the lower gravity makes that people are taller than on Earth. I am slightly taller than a girl of my age on Earth, that is, slightly more than fifty-nine inches. But all my friends are between eight and twelve inches taller than I am.

Probably it makes sense. It's almost three years that I carry the equivalent of three times my weight; I use a gravity intensifier. It's very uncomfortable, but it's necessary if I want to see mom again. Given that the Martian gravity is 38% that of Earth, I would not even be able to stand upright once I arrived at Thuis, so I've been preparing for that. My friends on Mars are far more agile than I am, since they weigh only one third of what I appear to weigh. On the other side, I am far stronger. Not even the big boys dare to mess with me. The last one who tried ended up with a broken bone, and I had not even intended to hurt him. I am not as fragile as they are. In reality, I am not fragile at all. That's what happens when you live permanently with 1.3 g. On this ship, with just one Earth gravity, I feel pretty light. It's for that reason that I have to pay attention to my movements; I tend to apply too much force.

Oh, and if that wasn't enough, I passed the colonist training. You can't colonize a planet without that training; no matter how paradisiacal a planet may look, survival is essential. We must know how to survive. At slightly less than fifty light-years from Earth, nobody will be able to help us if there is a problem, if there is some danger, if a catastrophe occurs. A starship will take six months to reach us, supposing that there is one available when the distress message is received. If we can't help ourselves, we will be dead by the time help arrives. But by now I can take care of myself. I know how to fight, to hunt, to plant, to build a house, to splint a bone, I even know how to assist in childbirth or perform an appendectomy. The colonist training is not exactly easy, and they did not reduce the requirements just because I am a girl. I have complied with the whole program, exactly the same one that an adult has to go through.

I leave with the third colonization wave, but I am still the only girl. They will not start admitting children until the fifth or sixth colonization wave, once the planet is sufficiently secure. But in my case they had to make an exception. It's not just that mom is essential for the colony. Or that I am the only minor that has managed to finish the colonist training. It helps that my IQ qualifies me as a genius. And that I have finished the university studies in Astrobiology, with the specialty of Exobiology, which makes me a very valuable asset for the colony. In fact, I'll become mom's assistant. I am the youngest astrobiologist in history, which fills me with pride.

The fact that I'm so young has an additional advantage: They will not freeze me. I will travel on the starship with the crew, instead of inside a frozen coffin with the rest of the colonists. And given that daddy is the first officer, I will travel with him. I don't have so many opportunities to be with dad, he spends months exploring far from the solar system.

I point towards space, to a small dot floating over the curvature of Earth.

"I suppose that's Beta Station, isn't it? Since it's at L2..."

Dad laughs.

"That's correct, my little genius. I guess you're the only girl who can identify the space stations by the Lagrange points where they're located."

I shrug, somewhat uncomfortable by his flattery.

"Daddy, that's trivial..."

"Not so trivial, young lady," says the captain from behind me. "Most people on Earth don't even know what L2 is." She looks at me, approvingly. "By the way, it's official now. You don't have to go in Cryo."

A start hopping up and down with joy.

"Great!"

The captain smiles. She's black, very kind, probably quite old. They say that she's the one who discovered Zeta, already three decades ago. She never talks about that. I imagine that she doesn't want to remember what happened with the first colony, apparently it was really tough.

"Yes, but it will cost you. You know this ship does not admit passengers. I have convinced Control that, since you're astrobiologist, you can help us with the astrophysics instruments, and take care of the secondary IT system."

My eyes go wide open. That's far more than I could ever imagine. Some real practice before starting at Thuis...

"That would be great, Laura."

She takes a cloth insignia from her pocket, and places it on my clothes. It's the same insignia that all crew members carry.

"Captain for you, auxiliary astronaut Martin. You are now part of the crew."

I stand at attention, as I have seen that dad does.

"Yes, captain!"

I could have sworn that she laughed, but probably it's just my imagination because she's turning towards my father.

"XO, the shuttle is at one hundred clicks. Take over the transfer of the colonists; I'll be on the bridge."

My father salutes. I take note of how he does it; from now on, I will have to do that also.

"Yes, ma'am." He looks in my direction. "Go to the engine room, auxiliary Martin. Report to the chief engineer. I want you to start familiarizing yourself with the astrophysics equipment."

I repeat his salute, as serious as I can. It's not daddy who's talking, it's the executive officer.

"Yes, sir."

He responds seriously to my salute and I leave. But I have the impression that those two are crying with laughter.

I take one of the electric carts to go to the engine room. Of course I could walk, but it would take quite a while. And after all, am I not now a crew member? I can't be wasting time taking a walk, and the ship is really huge.

Sparks is busy, disassembling a machine that I recognize as a spectrum analyzer. In reality his name is Reinhardt, but everybody calls him Sparks. He lifts his head when I enter.

"Hi, Tanit!" he greets me. "Taking a stroll?"

"Not really, sir," I respond formally. "I am your new assistant."

He places the screwdriver on the desk and pries at me.

"You better explain me that."

I show him the insignia that the captain has adhered to my clothes and repeat dad's orders. He scratches his head, thoughtfully.

"Well, I won't deny that I could use some help. And though you're only ten, you manage pretty well. Do you dare finishing the repair?"

I look at the spectrum analyzer. To be honest, I've never disassembled one, though I know how they work. But I was always pretty good messing around with electronic stuff; I have been helping my parents to repair things since I knew how to hold an electric screwdriver. Which, by the way, I had also repaired.

"I will need the manuals, sir. But yes, I can do it."

"I'll smack you on your head if you call me again sir, Tanit. You know that we're not very formal on this ship. Wait a moment while I log you onto the system so that you can get access as a crew member, the manuals are not in the standard library." He busies himself a few moments with the lateral console. "Done. Give a scream if you need help, I'll be with the flux condenser."

"Yes, s..." I see how he lifts his hand and I correct myself quickly. "Sure, Sparks."

"I'll call you Sparkie," he laughs, and he leaves me with the damaged analyzer.

I log on to the console with my fingerprints. The menu has changed, there are some new options that I did not see the last time I logged onto the system. I'm not crazy enough to use them, as I could cause some good ravage on the ship. It may be that I am officially a crew member, but that does not mean that I am qualified to do anything important. Of course, the system probably will not allow me to do it anyway.

But the library is something different. There is a totally new panel, which allows accessing the ship's navigation records, the manifest... I see that the ship's mass is changing progressively, and I enter to have a look. Of course, they're loading the colonists. One hundred seventy two so far. While I'm looking, the number increases. One hundred seventy three. I return to the menu of the library and I search for the ship's technical section, auxiliary equipment. There's the spectrum analyzer. I open the manual, skim through it and start working.

It takes me half an hour to finish the disassembly and another two hours to find out what is wrong with it. The repair involves a lot of work, and takes me another hour. However, the assembly lasts only fifteen minutes. I carry out the functional tests, and it seems to be all right. As indicated by the manual, I record the repair that I have done in the ship's logbook and sign it with my thumb.

"It was about time!" I breathe.

"You certainly took your time," says the voice of my father.

I turn around. He and Sparks are comfortably seated on two chairs.

"How long have you been there?"

"Like half an hour. You're like your mother, when she's engaged in her work she doesn't notice anything. Sparks, would you mind having a look at that analyzer, to see what out little genius has done?"

"Sure."

The chief engineer stands up and executes again the functional tests. Then he plugs the device into one of the ship's connectors and performs a test with a random signal. Finally, he checks the record that I've made of the repair. He nods, apparently pleased.

"Not bad. With a lot of effort we could make a real crew member out of her. In ten years or so. She has still a lot to learn."

"Sparks!" I protest.

Then he starts laughing.

"Just pulling your leg, Tanit. You've done a good job. Go have dinner with your father and then go to bed. I'm expecting you at 08:00. You're hired."

And this is how my first job begins, and not less than on a starship.

Though most people are surprised to hear it, a starship requires a quite small crew. In reality, the *Moon shadow* —that's how our ship is called— only needs fourteen crew members, fifteen if you count me. The ship's size is impressive, slightly more than two thousand feet, but it doesn't need a huge crew, almost everything is cargo and the systems are automated to an unbelievable level.

There are only three officers, the captain, my dad and Sparks, who is the chief engineer. Then there are two astronavigators, two propulsion and systems engineers, the cook, the communications guy, the head of cryogenic systems and his assistant, the two people in charge of the hydroponic gardens and a sailor who does all the heavy duty stuff. Well, and me.

Though everybody salutes the captain, soon I realize that Sparks is right: they are not very formal here; they almost look like a family. And all of them seem to believe that they can make fun of me. Only after correcting them several times when they think they can trick me, they start to treat me more seriously. I might be a girl, but I have finished my studies at the university and I wasn't exactly born yesterday. There are plenty of things about which I am more knowledgeable than most of them.

That does not mean that I know about everything, and to my great surprise they place me on a tour of all the jobs while we leave the elliptic of the solar system so as to position ourselves for the stellar jump. Dad explains to me that those are the rules: On a starship everybody must know about everything, in case something happens and one of the crew members cannot perform his tasks —there must be always somebody who can replace him.

One of the system engineers is new, and he's also been familiarized with the other positions, but they do it at different moments in time, so we never meet for a same lesson. It makes sense: The know-how of all job positions is thus covered twice as quickly. If he is familiarizing himself with one position and I with a different one, then we cover two positions between both of us. It is for that reason that I am very surprised when after two days the ship's loudspeaker calls for both of us at the same time.

"Crew member Johanssen, auxiliary crew member Martin, report to the bridge."

I finish the cryogenic system check that I am carrying out, lock the system and enter the verification data into the terminal. The very first thing that they have taught me is that, unless the order indicates an emergency, all systems must be left in a secure state before doing anything else. The head of cryogenics nods with pleasure when I log out of the terminal.

"Excellent, Tanit. For a moment I was worried that you would run away, leaving this poor colonist melting..."

I start laughing. There are not many possibilities that the colonist can leave his icy coffin, all systems are OK, as indicated by the main green light and a small one that blinks at his heart rate.

"Even your cat wouldn't do that, Massimo."

The Italian roars with laughter. He's very proud of his cat, an animal with black long hair, called Bagheera. He once told me that the name comes from a story written a few centuries ago, where a black panther was called like that. I don't know what a panther is, and Bagheera is the first cat that I've seen in my life. It started smelling me the first time we met, turned around me and decided I was harmless. The sentiment was certainly not mutual, and Massimo had to insist that I caressed it and then would brush her hair. It's a somewhat weird beast, but I believe it likes me. I think. I don't have that much experience with animals.

"Bagheera has a lot of common sense. Go to the bridge, they must be waiting for you."

"Wait." I point out, two full seconds before an alarm sounds. "Yellow light!"

He lifts his head, checking out the coffin where the green light has gone out.

"That's B-349. It has a defective valve that fails intermittently. I'll take care of it. To the bridge!"

I obey, while he picks up his tools. As always, the electric cart is waiting for me. It only takes me three minutes to get to the bridge. The captain turns her head from her seat when I enter.

"Massimo says you detected the failure in B-349 before the monitor did."

I shrug. The captain knows absolutely everything that occurs aboard, I don't have a clue how she does it.

"More or less at the same time, captain. I saw the yellow light."

She nods.

"In any case, good job. Well, Jorg, Tanit, it is a tradition on this ship that the new crew members are on the bridge the first time they enter the trans-lux mode. You two ready?"

Johanssen and I nod. I feel a lump in my throat. We are going to abandon our travel through normal space, and we are going to make the jump to the stars. It's my first interstellar travel, the first time that I will be traveling faster than light.

In reality the ship will not be traveling faster than light. But since I have studied Astrobiology, I also had to study astrophysics, and I know how it works. You cannot exceed the speed of light, but there is a trick that allows you to travel faster than it: Bend space.

The principle is really quite simple. We are like an ant that needs to travel from one end of a piece of paper to the other. But instead of doing the whole trip, first we bend the sheet of paper a few times, and only then we make the trip. Instead of traveling fifteen inches, we travel only half an inch. For the stellar travel, instead of traveling fifty light-years, we simply travel a few million miles. It's not exactly a short trip, but it is millions of times shorter that the trip to the stars. Then we unfold the paper, sorry, the space, and we are at our destination.

Of course it is not as simple as it sounds. The energies we use are enormous, but even greater are the space-time forces that we manipulate. Our ship would be destroyed in millionths of a second due to the space distortion if it were not because we travel in a kind of bubble of normal space within the folded space. We move inside this bubble and, as we move and the bubble with us, in reality we are moving through the folded space at unbelievable speeds.

Our relative speed does not even come close to the speed of light, as there are quite a few inconveniences in doing that. For starters, time tends to stop when you approach the speed of light. Not for us, but it does for the rest of the universe. A trip at near-light speed that would seem to take us months would actually last centuries for those remaining on Earth. Nobody wants that kind of time displacement. So we go fast, but not so much as to reach real relativistic speeds. Perhaps our four-month trip will be in reality six months for the rest of humanity, but the difference is acceptable. Daddy always recalls that he was a lot older than mom when he married her, but due to his interstellar travel they are now of the same age. It seems strange, but that's how relativity works. The time that dad spent aboard a starship passed much slower than that of mom. Dad left for a trip that would last only six months for him, without mom being pregnant, and when he returned I was already born. Mom told me that the face he put when he found out was remarkable; for dad this was the fastest pregnancy in human history.

Another thing that must be kept in mind is that there is a limit to the speed that you can have before starting to bend space. If this limit is exceeded, strange things happen for which science has not yet an answer. There must be some kind of interference between the speed of light and the folding of space, because the ships disappear and never appear again. If you travel at a speed greater than half the speed of light and try to bend space, the ship will probably disintegrate into its atoms. An ecological death, I suppose, but not very desirable.

"XO, activate systems. Astro, confirm coordinates."

Daddy starts working with a panel, while the astronavigator checks our positional data. One of the propulsion engineers is reporting data from a panel that I do not understand; the captain starts giving orders, and the three of them commence to move controls and adjust values in the terminals.

"Trans-lux!"

For a brief instant the lights sputter while the *Moon shadow* engines start folding space. Some panels go on, while others seem to shut off. But apart from that, nothing seems to have happened.

"It didn't work?" Johanssen asks naively.

Then I point to the main screen. The stars have disappeared; it seems to be flickering. It's an anticlimax, but we're in trans-lux mode.

"I think it has worked."

The captain turns toward us. It seems as if she's sniggering due to some unknown joke, but her voice is pretty serious.

"Of course it worked, mister Johanssen. You can return to your posts."

"Aye, captain."

We leave the bridge, but we don't walk more than two steps. A bucket of water falls on us as soon as we exit, leaving us soaked. I look around, still unable to react. The whole crew is there, roaring with laughter. Behind me, on the bridge, they are guffawing.

Then Sparks approaches us, handing us a piece of paper. We pick it up, still bewildered, while the rest of the crew continues laughing. I look at mine: It's a certificate that says that Tanit Martin has received today her stellar baptism. Baptism! I am soaked!

Later, after we have dried, they explain it to us. It's a tradition that everybody who enters trans-lux must be baptized; all of them have gone through this, even dad and the captain. Now we are real stellar crew members.

But after three months we are totally fed up with being crew members aboard a starship. The ship works automatically in trans-lux mode; there is nothing to do, apart from checking that all systems continue to work normally. I have gone through the basic training for all crew positions, and I have returned with Sparks at the engine room. There is not much to do, except repairing broken machinery. I always thought it was very exciting to be on a starship, but in reality it's pretty boring. Luckily dad has agreed with the captain that we will spend our free time together, or else this trip would have been the most boring period that I've ever had. I understand why starship crews are always well equipped with books, films and video games. If they weren't, they would jump into space out of pure boredom.

On the other side, they do have their hobbies. The one from Massimo is obviously his cat. He teaches it all kinds of tricks. Funny as it is for an astrobiologist, I have almost never seen live animals:

There are very few of those on Mars. Thus, I don't know whether teaching them is easy or difficult, but daddy tells me it's not easy at all. He has his own hobby, which is building model ships. Not space ships, ships like the ones that in the past traveled over the seas on Earth. Floating on water, no matter how odd that sounds. Obviously there is nothing like that on Mars, but dad was born on Earth, and the Dutch were apparently great seafarers in the past. Dad told me that his grandfather once took him for a trip on a small boat. It sounds very dangerous, but dad said that it was very exciting.

Sparks plays with very old video games that he has managed to replay by writing simulators. These are not immersion games, like the ones that we have today; no, as strange as it may sound, these games are flat, they are not even tridimensional. It's very funny to see games without depth, though I must recognize that some of these are pretty charming. Like that one where you have to throw birds against some funny constructions where weird round animals hide. I have no clue what those beasts are. Sparks swears that the birds on Earth are like that and do those things, but I know that he either has no clue what birds are or he's trying to make fun of me. I am an astrobiologist: I might have never seen one alive, but I know exactly what a bird is and how it behaves.

Other games are historical and they do a lot of very strange things that I don't understand at all, and some of them seem to be based on a future that does not look at all like today. His favorite game is one called *Mass Effect*; the game is full of aliens, though everybody knows that aliens don't exist. He seems a small kid.

After trying a lot of things, I finally settle on creating light sculptures with discarded optic fiber. You can make marvelous light effects if you know a little bit about optics and are somewhat handy; very soon the whole crew has asked me for one of my creations. Actually, I am finishing a fancy sculpture for the captain when the call comes.

"Auxiliary crew member Martin, report to the canteen."

I leave the optic fiber splicer on the work desk and sigh. I suppose they want me to help collecting the garbage. That's the problem with being the youngest crew member, everybody wants to get rid of the dirty tasks and give them to me, supposedly because I am less qualified. In reality, my academic records must be in the top three of this ship, and not necessarily in the third position. But there's nothing I can do about it.

I look around, but I can't see Sparks. He probably went to check again the flux condenser. Well, I imagine that he has heard that they called me over the P.A. system.

I take the transport cart with a serious lack of enthusiasm. Now, letting me travel through the whole ship to let me pick up the trash from the canteen... because it won't be anything else, Samantha does not allow anybody to enter her kitchen. Even the captain has the access forbidden.

Finally, I get to the station on deck thirty and I get off. Then I return the transport cart to the engine room. Those are the rules: there must be always a transport cart at each station.

I pass through the rest area and to my surprise there is nobody. Usually most of those that are not on duty stay there, playing cards, chatting, reading or playing one of the video games with somebody else. Suddenly I feel hopeful. Perhaps the captain wants to tell us something, she usually rounds up the crew in the canteen to do exactly that. With some luck I will not have to collect the trash.

Yes, it must be that, because there is nobody in the corridors. I speed up my steps, until I reach the canteen. The door opens in front of me, but I hesitate. The room is in absolute darkness. What the heck is happening?

Then the lights go on.

"Surprise!"

I remain open-mouthed. The whole crew is there, and on the central table there is a cake.

"Happy birthday, Tanit!"

It takes some effort to close my mouth. I didn't even remember it was my birthday.

Dad picks me up, laughing, and lifts me above his head. He has been doing that forever, but for the first time it looks as if it takes him some effort to do it. He tosses me up once, after which he gets me back to the floor and kisses me. Then everybody surrounds me, with the men patting me on my shoulder, the women kissing me.

"Eleven years already! She's almost a woman!" comments Sparks. Apparently he had sneaked away from the engine room while I was not looking. "Henk, soon you'll have to worry about the guys going after her! I don't envy you!"

Daddy laughs.

"No problem at all. You know she has learned martial arts. Tanit knows how to take care of herself. She broke a guy's arm when he tried to be fancy."

The others also laugh, but Sparks shakes his head, apparently with grief.

"No, no, I wasn't worried *about* them; I was worried *for* them... A little genius that also knows martial arts. And she just looks like a pretty face. Poor guys! They better run for cover when she's the one to go hunting!"

Now we all laugh. Sparks loves to poke fun at me, but I know there is no malice in him.

Finally they seat me before the cake. There are no candles on a spaceship; they consume too much oxygen, not to speak about the risk of fire. But Sparks has made some electronic candles that almost look like the real stuff. He explains that they have an air flow sensor that will put them off.

"But only if you blow really hard. So you better do your best..."

I'm ready to puff out my cheeks. But I never get to blow, because suddenly a thundering bang resounds throughout the ship. All jump to their feet.

"You heard that?"

"What the fuck was that?"

I see that my father and the captain are looking at each other.

"It sounds as if something has hit the ship's hull."

"Captain, we're in trans-lux mode. It's impossible that we make contact with anything physical."

Another tremendous knock clangs around us.

"Emergency stations! XO, to the bridge!"

While the captain still speaks, dad grabs me and tears me from the chair. Just behind us there is one of the shelters. He throws me inside and pushes the emergency button. The door closes before my face.

"Tanit, stay there!" he shouts.

I recover my balance and run to the door, looking through the window. What happens next, I will recall for the rest of my life: The ship's hull is being ripped open as if it were made out of paper by something that looks like a giant claw. And everything that there is in the canteen is dragged away by the air escaping to the outside. Desks, chairs, furniture... and all people. The last one to disappear though the huge breach is Sparks. For a second I see that his eyes have exploded due to the vacuum.

I feel such dizziness that I have to sit down. All my friends... sucked into space. Dead. One minute ago, they were laughing with me. And now... Suddenly I realize something terrible, even far worse than that.

"Daddy!"

I jump to the door, looking through the window. Nothing. Nothing at all. Looking desperately around, I see the opening button and press it with fury.

"Emergency mode," reports the impersonal voice of the computer. "It is not allowed to open doors to the vacuum by personnel without a spacesuit."

Then I see the red light: There is no air on the other side of the door.

"Daddy..." I mumble, stupefied, letting me slide to the floor.

It can't be. No, it can't be. The captain ordered him to go to the bridge. He must have run for it immediately after placing me in the emergency shelter. He must be on the bridge. Yes, that's it; he's on the bridge, planning my rescue. He can't be dead. Not my daddy.

The intercom. I jump to my feet and rush to the intercom, at one side of the refuge. I push the button.

"Please, dad!" I shout. "Daddy! Please answer!"

I wait for long minutes, calling while I feel a terrible pain tearing through my chest, but nobody responds to my pleas.

"Daddy..." I sob, collapsing onto the floor. "Dad, it can't be... It can't be! Please answer! You can't be dead!"

I don't know how much time I have spent like this, sobbing, with tears blinding my eyes, but it must have been hours because suddenly the computer voice calls me.

"Crew member Tanit Martin. Use the oxygen bottles to breathe. The air conditioning system is blocked due to damage to the ship."

As soon as I hear the voice, I raise my head. For a moment I think somebody has survived, for an instant I hope that daddy might have survived. But no, it's the ship's soft voice, which I know very well. Oxygen? Then I realize that I am starting to have difficulties to breathe. I am in an emergency shelter of less than fifty square feet. And I am running out of air. It won't take much before I will asphyxiate.

"You're a Martin, Tanit," I recall my father saying. "A survivor. You will pass the colonization tests, I am sure. You will survive, Tanit.

To anything that might happen. And we will live together on Thuis. Our new home. I am very proud of you."

He told me that after mom left for Thuis. When I decided that I would study Astrobiology at the university, so as to be able to get back with mom. He always encouraged me. He always supported me. He always put his trust in me.

"I will, daddy," I sob. "I will survive. I will get to Thuis, with mom. And you will be proud, I promise."

Swiping my tears with the back of my hand, I try to get up. But it's not easy at all, the air is more rarified than I imagined. I can hardly breathe. It takes a lot of effort to get up; to lift myself until I can grab the emergency oxygen bottle becomes a real torture. But finally I manage to put on the mask. The system recognizes that there is a person on the other side, and the oxygen starts flowing.

After a few minutes I start reacting; I realize that I have been on the verge of losing consciousness. But the near-pure oxygen entering my lungs lifts me up, though it's not only the oxygen. I know that there are stimulants and anxiolytics in the bottles so as to ensure that the people using them are in full shape in case of an emergency. Adrenaline runs through my veins, and suddenly I am no longer afraid.

I look around. This is a minuscule cubicle, only illuminated by the emergency lights. And outside... I glimpse through the window in the door. Nothing. The canteen no longer exists. Through what was once the ship's hull I see the blinking of the space folds. We continue in trans-lux. Whatever has damaged the ship has not prevented that we continue traveling towards Thuis.

I lean with my back to the door. What will I do now? If somebody from the crew has survived, he cannot have reached the bridge, for he would have heard my calls through the intercom. Just in case, I try again. But there is only silence.

Fifty square feet. I look at the oxygen bottle indicator. I have perhaps two hours. Then I will asphyxiate. But with all the drugs that there must be in the bottle I hardly feel preoccupied, I notice it with a clinical coldness that surprises even me.

Luckily, I remember the mandatory survival classes that we had during the colonization course. All starships have emergency shelters for the crew, in case of decompression. This is one of them. But these refuges must also have a spacesuit and rescue capsules.

Instants later I am opening the rear panel. Yes, there is the emergency spacesuit and three balloons to be used for the transport of wounded, children and other people that don't have a spacesuit. Obviously, I will have to use the suit.

But a quarter of an hour later it is evident that I will not be able to do it. The central part is rigid, because that's where the spacesuit closes. Unfortunately, when I sit down on the central part, my feet don't touch the floor. And the worst of all: My head does not even reach the helmet. This suit is intended for an adult, not for an eleven-year old. I cry of rage and despair when I finally understand it. My hands can't reach the gloves either, and the suit is too rigid to roll the arms up, so I won't be even able to put on the helmet.

It's evident that I am going to die, but that thought doesn't scare me due to all the drugs that the air bottle contains. At least I won't die terrified. But I'll asphyxiate slowly as soon as the oxygen bottle is empty.

I sit down on the floor. Why should I wait for two hours? Well, perhaps one and a half hours. It makes no sense to extend my agony. The best thing is to open that door once and for all, and be sucked into the vacuum. It will be very quick, and I'll be back with my father.

"You will survive, Tanit," says the voice of my father, and it's so real that I lift my head as if he were at my side. But no, there is nobody.

"No, daddy," I whisper, standing up. "You know I can't survive."

Then, furiously, I hit the opening switch, knowing that in seconds I will die.

Nothing happens. Well, in reality something *does* happen. The computer protests.

"Emergency mode," it states again stubbornly. "It is not allowed to open doors to the vacuum by personnel without a spacesuit."

"Stupid machine!" I scream. "Let me die! Don't you see that I can't get into the suit? That I will suffocate?"

It seems to hesitate. But then it returns with its preprogrammed singsong.

"It is not allowed to open doors to the vacuum by personnel without a spacesuit."

"Idiot!" I mumble when, after breathing again from the bottle, the concentration of anti-anxiety drugs in my body increases. "You don't even know..."

Then I start thinking about it. How does that shitty computer know that I am not in a spacesuit? Well, it has sensors in the shelter. It detects that there is somebody here. And the insignia on my clothes tells it who it is. Though it's not probable it can triangulate where I am, I don't think there are thermal sensors in this place.

Let's experiment. I know my insignia has an identifying sensor. What if I place it inside the suit? No, it does not work. I pull the spacesuit to the door, and I stay close to it, so that if there is a thermal sensor my heat will seem to be inside the suit. Nope, it still refuses to open the door.

Perhaps the suit must be closed and operating? It's possible. I go to the rear panel and pick up the helmet. It has gotten snagged by one of the rescue balloon moorings, and I start releasing it. But suddenly I stop and stare at it.

The rescue capsule is a very primitive version of a spacesuit. In reality it is little more than a bag full of air, with some ropes to attach it to a spacesuit or a towing device. It's supposed to be used for a quick transfer of a person to a rescue vehicle. It has absolutely no protection, nor propulsion, not even a breathing system. It's just an air balloon, thought for people that cannot put on a spacesuit, such as children or wounded. And I am able to get inside.

"You might have found something, Tanit," I tell myself, leaving the helmet carefully on the ground.

Let's see. The capsule will provide me with air for some ten minutes. Well, it's not much, but I still have the bottle hanging over my shoulder. Let's suppose I get inside. Could I open the shelter's door?

Immediately I find out that the answer is yes. Even if the balloon inflates, it's sufficiently flexible so as be able to hit the switch. Then I will be able to get out and go to... where to?

I look again through the window in the door. The canteen has been razed, but I'd say that there are no obstacles, the very few chairs and tables that remain are at one side, close to the destroyed hull through which the space folds flicker. The floor looks stable. I will not be able to walk, but I imagine I will be able to roll over it. Let's hope there is nothing that can perforate the balloon, or I will not live to tell it.

The door through which I entered seems to be blocked; a panel has fallen down in front of it. There is no way I can remove that panel from inside the balloon. Perhaps if I was in a spacesuit I could push it aside, but I won't be able to move in a suit. To be more precise, I won't even be able to put it on.

But the other door is open. I know it provides access to a corridor. If I could close it once I'm inside... All the ship doors are airtight, just in case that the hull should be breached. This would protect the crew members in case of an accident. Unfortunately, nobody ever imagined that the whole crew could be precisely at the location where the breach would occur.

Let's go. I am going to enter the balloon when I realize that I still have the problem about how to open the door. Well, I'll have to test out the original idea to close and start up the spacesuit. But perhaps this time I won't be committing suicide.

I place the helmet onto the suit and close all clips. Then I activate it. If everything is OK, the computer will think I'm in it. Suddenly I realize that, when opening the door, all the air will escape. And it will drag into space everything that there is inside the shelter.

Can I tie the balloon? Yes, probably yes, it has a rope for towing purposes. But how do untie it afterwards? The last thing I need is to be stuck inside the capsule and not being able to move it because I have tied it down. I test the stiffness of the balloon. There's no way I will be able to untie a knot through it, and much less once it's inflated.

I lose a precious quarter of an hour before I come up with a solution. I take the rear panel and I place it across the door. This will prevent that my balloon goes through the door. I will then hit it, making it fall towards the inside, so as to be able to pass.

Though made out of aluminum, the panel weighs a lot, and I am panting by the time I finish. It slips, so I secure it by placing the spacesuit beneath it. It crosses the door, so it will retain me. Fine, I can enter the rescue capsule, seal the closure and push the inflation button. One moment later I'm inside a bubble, five feet across. It's barely high enough for me to stand up.

Then I realize that I cannot reach the opening switch because the balloon is a sphere. I have to lean forward, but I can't touch it because of the angle I have to make. My arm is not long enough. It takes me another five minutes before I have an idea, take off one of my shoes and use it to extend my arm. My time is running out.

The door opens, and I am violently jostled when the air escapes and I hit the panel protecting the door. I fall on my ass, and watch horrified how the panel is getting loose.

"No!" I scream involuntarily when it falls and is projected towards the outside due to the air pressure escaping from the rescue chamber. Then my balloon is squeezed against the door. I try to hold on to the door frame, but it's impossible, there is too much pressure. I pop out towards the outside.

There must be a God that protects little girls, because I hit the opposite wall. Luckily it is a part of the hull that is still attached to the rest of the ship, and I bounce back inside as if I was a ball. The air that is still flowing out pushes me aside and I move sideways, rolling lazily towards the outside. As soon as I realize that, I throw myself to the floor, preventing that the balloon continues to roll. The capsule wiggles, but it stops. I am only ten feet away from outer space.

I notice that I am panting. The air inside my bubble is rarefied, and I place again the oxygen mask over my mouth. I have to breathe heavily a few times before I dare to look around.

The canteen is torn apart, as I already knew. But now I'm seeing remains on the floor. I'll have to be careful, I don't know how strong the rescue capsule is, and whether it will survive a cutting edge.

Carefully I stand up and start moving, making the balloon roll over the floor. I am lucky that the propulsion is still active so that there is gravity; if I had to do this in null-gravity, then I would have to abandon all hope. It takes me ten minutes to reach the door of the corridor, since I have to avoid all the rubble that has not been thrown into space.

But finally I am inside the corridor. Now what? OK, there is the switch to close the door. I have again the same problem as before, but far worse: the surface tension of the balloon in the vacuum makes it so rigid that I cannot bring the capsule surface closer than four inches to the wall. This is a sphere, and the sphere radius is well below the damn switch.

Can I jump? No, it does not work. I can't push upwards when my feet are retaining the lower part of the balloon. I squint. Could I perhaps...? Well, if I don't puncture the globe, it could work.

It works. My training in martial arts, even though not very feminine, has served me well. A high kick achieves that I was not able to do by pushing: the balloon is deformed sufficiently to press the button. The door closes.

I roll towards the other side of the corridor, and encounter the same problem. But this time I won't have to repeat my ninja trick, the computer has detected my presence.

"Pressure equalized."

I hear the voice. As I know that sound does not travel through the void, there must be air in the corridor. I poke the balloon wall with a finger. It looks as if the diameter is smaller, and it is far more flexible than just a few minutes ago. There is air in the corridor. Carefully, I open the closure of the rescue capsule.

Yes. There is air. When I closed the door, the computer has filled the corridor with air. I am now in the habitable section of the ship. I drop the oxygen bottle, finish getting out of the balloon, and run to the bridge. The lights are off, but the emergency lights are working.

"Daddy!" I scream as soon as I enter.

But there is nobody. I look around in the semidarkness.

"Dad?"

There is an open console, and I log on. After all, I am a crew member, am I not? I switch on the ship's intercom.

"All crew members, report immediately to the bridge!"

But half an hour later, to my anguish, there is still nobody. The effect of the anxiolytics of the oxygen bottle is wearing out, and I feel that I am starting to panic.

"Is there anybody?" I yell through the intercom. "Please answer!"

Then I remember that there is another way to find out whether somebody has survived.

"Computer, identify the crew members aboard the ship, as well as their position."

The machine responds immediately.

"Auxiliary crew member Tanit Martin, bridge."

I wait for a few seconds, but it does not continue.

"Who else? Provide the full list."

"Auxiliary crew member Tanit Martin, bridge. There are no more crew members."

Then I fall on my knees, sobbing. I am alone. Totally alone.

Suddenly the memory hits me like a punch. The colonists! There are three thousand colonists in hibernation! There must be someone who knows about spaceships.

"Computer, identify space engineers between the colonists."

I must admit this piece of junk is efficient, it responds immediately.

"Engineer Vladimir Svoboda, cryogenic compartment A34. Engineer Tanvi Bahtnagar, compartment H176."

I recall that Massimo showed me the reanimation controls. One moment later I am running towards station thirty, to pick up a transport cart. It looks like an eternity how long it takes before I reach cargo hold seven, where the colonists are.

But as soon as I enter, I notice that something is wrong. The green lights that greeted me on my last visit are no longer there, nor do they blink to indicate the slow heart beats. No, the whole cargo hold is dark, with long rows of red lights. Bewildered, I stare at them. I know what that means. The energy went out. All the energy, including the one that kept them alive. I am now traveling at a speed greater than light on a starship full of corpses.

Slowly I return to my steps, incapable of supporting any more blows. I drop onto the seat of the transport cart, without touching the controls. What will I do now? What can I do?

"Meow?"

I stare, incredulous. It's Massimo's cat. It has survived. It wasn't in the canteen and it has survived.

"Bagheera?"

It leaps onto the cart, and smells me out. This seems to be satisfactory, because it sits down on the seat at my side.

"Meow!" it seems to answer.

I scratch it behind the ear, where Massimo told me, and it starts to purr with satisfaction. Who could be a cat, and not feel what I am feeling!

"Computer" I murmur. "Confirm status of colonists."

For one moment I have the impression that it has hesitated, as it takes two incredibly long seconds before it answers.

"Status undefined. The primary energy system is not operable; it is not possible to determine the status."

"Activate secondary energy system."

"That command requires authorization by an officer."

"I am alone!" I explode. "There are no more officers!"

"As per article twenty-seven c, section four, second paragraph of the Navigation Code, you must take over the command if there are no higher officers."

I stare into emptiness. So I am now the captain? I suppose I am, as I am the only living person aboard this starship.

"How do I do that?"

"Declare that you take command. Your declaration will be recorded in the ship's logbook."

I swallow hard.

"Taking command of the ship." I look at the cat, while pushing the start button. "And you have just become my crew."

"Command transferred," announces the computer while the cart jumps forwards. "Crew member Tanit Martin has taken command of the ship."

"Then switch on the secondary energy system!"

The lights go on immediately. But my eyes see nothing while the cart advances through the service tunnel.

When I wake up, I don't even know how I reached my cabin. I have slept very badly; my dreams have been a huge nightmare, where I saw over and over the face without eyes of Sparks disappearing into space. I look at the ceiling. What will I do now? I am alone, completely alone. Then I glimpse the movement out of the corner of my eyes. Bagheera is lying on one side of my bed, eying me.

"Meow?" it asks.

I sit down and put my feet on the floor.

"I wish I knew the answer," I respond, gloomy. "But meow yourself."

Suddenly I notice how hungry I am. I don't know how much time has passed since everything happened, but I am famished. And by the way that the cat is licking its mouth, I suppose it is also hungry.

Within all the bad things that have occurred, the kitchen has survived; the door to the canteen was locked and the computer has blocked it. The cold is horrible; I assume that it's because there is open space at the other side of the door. Quickly picking up some cookies and the food for the cat, I then run outside; next time I'll enter well wrapped in clothes, assuming I can find some winter garments. Otherwise I'll have to survive with the products of the hydroponic gardens, unless I want to risk freezing to death.

So I return to the bridge. In reality I don't know why, but it seems the correct place to be. I suppose that if I want to return with mom, I'll have to control the ship. I am now the captain. Eating the cookies on the bridge, I look around, with Bagheera enjoying whatever it is eating. Some small balls that have a very disgusting look.

While I continue eating, I inspect the ship's control panels. There's no problem in understanding some of them, but there are others that

I will not understand in a million years despite the training that I have undergone. When I activate the external cameras, the continuous flickering confirms that we're still in trans-lux. This confuses me for a moment. Then I remember that you need a huge amount of energy to deploy space again. Unless I do something, I'll stay in this strange state my whole life. On Earth they call it hyperspace, even if the term is totally incorrect.

I search for the navigation manuals, and start studying them. It's complicated, they assume knowledge about many things that I have never studied, and I have to search for supplementary information in the library. But if the information is there, I will learn how to handle the ship. What the heck! Am I not supposed to be a genius? I started my Astrobiology studies with eight years, and I have finished in a little over two years. Even mom needed five years. It can't be that complicated to be able to manage a starship.

But it is. It takes me two weeks to review the main documentation, and by the time I finish I already doubt my capacity. Yet I know sufficient to be aware that the ship has been extremely damaged. I don't have a clue about whether I'll be able to leave the trans-lux state, but if I succeed it will be impossible to enter it again. In case that I get the coordinates wrong, I will be light-years away from Thuis and I will never see mom again.

The problem takes all my time. I eat and sleep, but the rest of the time is dedicated exclusively to see how I can get to Thuis. I hardly take the time to comb Bagheera, or scratch its belly when it calls for my attention, so focused am I in my study. Probably it's better like this, so as not to think about what has happened. I feel the pain in my breast, and my dreams are full of nightmares, but concentrating my mind on the study allows me to forget my horrible memories. But finally I lean back in my seat, and sigh deeply. The cat looks at me, surprised.

"Meow?"

"That's what I say. Meow. We're in the shitter, you know?"

Then it yawns, and placidly goes to sleep. Our situation doesn't seem to preoccupy it a lot. Well, it preoccupies me. I don't know how we'll get out of this mess.

Almost all trans-lux flight instruments are destroyed. I don't know why, but almost all were on the port side, where something monstrous has ripped open the hull. There are twenty decks with the hull damaged, open to space. It's a miracle that anything works at all.

There is no spacesuit of my size, but in the workshop I manage to tailor one for me by removing segments from the legs and arms, as well as part of the central ring. Even so, there is too much suit for me everywhere; it's horribly uncomfortable, but at least I can use it. After making sure that the suit is airtight, I start inspecting the part of the ship that is under vacuum, and start the repairs.

But after two days, it's evident that I will not solve anything; the damage is far too big. I return to the bridge and study again the manuals. This ship will never work again as expected, it's necessary to use the emergency systems.

I get back to the engine room; it's pretty weird that Sparks is not around. The flux injector has tripped, and I attempt to repair it for three days. Finally, I bypass the speed limit circuits and use the parts as spares for the injector. That is pretty reckless, but by now everything is pure temerity.

I attempt to write a program to calculate my position. At least I know how to program, that is also part of the Astrobiology studies, but my knowledge of trans-lux mechanics is not sufficiently good to calculate the correct position. Finally, I do an eyeball-approach. Given that I am aware of the exact time that it would take us to reach Thuis, I'll leave trans-lux at that moment in time. It won't be very precise, but I think I can hit the target with an error of less than one light-year. It might then take me as much as two years to get to the planet, but at least I won't be lost. I'll be able to get back to mom.

I don't think about daddy. It's too painful. I don't want to think, I bury myself in work. But sometimes, when I try that the sleep closes my eyelids, I feel the burning tears. Bagheera then comes to lie at my side, and sometimes it places its paw on my arm, as if it wanted to comfort me. It's a very weird cat. But at those times I would become mad without her.

Less than one week remains to leave trans-lux when I realize that the secondary power system will not have sufficient energy to perform this function. I check the computer, and to my surprise this reports back that we *do* have sufficient reaction mass. I frown. We have lost all port tanks; it's impossible that we have sufficient mass.

It's when I start investigating that I realize what has happened. The computer has injected all the colonist corpses into the organic converter and has recycled everything it could. That is, now I am drinking water extracted from dead people. And the plants in the hydroponic garden also get nutrients from the colonists, so I assume that I have been also eating them. I grimace with disgust, but I suppose there is nothing I can do about that. Everything that could not be recycled has been sent to the reaction mass converter.

With the help of the computer I make some calculations, my knowledge about electricity and electronics is insufficient to do it by myself. Shit! I will have to overload the circuits: the secondary power system is not intended for that kind of energies. The most likely thing that will occur is that we are blown to pieces, or simply disintegrate when we exit trans-lux. But I don't have many options. Either I take the risk, or I will continue flying like this for all eternity.

I wait. The waiting becomes eternal. I brush the cat until it gets tired of it, hisses at me and tries to bite me. Playing some computer games doesn't distract me: they actually bore me even more. I try to read, but suddenly I realize that I am reading the same page over and over. Then I go to sleep, but sleep doesn't come.

After five days I'm so nervous that I could try to climb up the walls and walk on the ceiling. Even the cat has grown tired of me and has left for some other place in the ship; honestly, I can't blame it. But suddenly there are only hours until the expected moment, and then only minutes.

My finger is on the button that will make me leave the space-fold, while I stare at the screen, looking how the seconds are counted down until the correct moment. The computer must be broken, it's not normal that the seconds take so long to pass. I notice that I am sweating. Within one minute I'll be back with mom or I will be one more piece of space trash. If it's the latter, I hope it's quick. A shiver goes down my spine when I remember how Sparks' eyes burst because of the vacuum. I press the button.

The console seems to explode; I am projected backwards while sparks jump through the whole bridge. All lights blink, there is a noise like a giant squeak, I feel that my guts are stirred as if somebody had wrung out my stomach... and suddenly everything has finished. The lights burn normally, and I see a lot of symbols on panels that I thought were broken because they had never shown anything. I get up carefully from the floor, massaging my aching limbs, and look astonished to the screen. To my great joy, it displays a sun. I've made it. I've left trans-lux.

"Meow?"

Bagheera has appeared at my side. She seems annoyed, but I pick her up in my arms and kiss her, getting my mouth full of hair. I don't care; I am laughing and crying at the same time with relief. Soon I'll be back with mom. Sure, it might still take me a couple of weeks or months traveling through normal space, but at least I am back.

"Meow!"

Bagheera bites my hand. She must be really pissed off. But even that cannot spoil my euphoria.

"Silly cat! We have arrived!"

It's obvious she doesn't care, because she churns in my arms and I am forced to let her go. Well, it's only an animal and obviously does not understand that we are saved.

I sit at the communications console. Thuis must have an emitter, I suppose. Unfortunately, I neither know its frequency nor the calling protocol. Well, I'll let the computer search for it.

It takes the machine three hours to find something. Three hours! They must be using a really weird frequency. Then I notice the received signal. What the hell is this? A holographic video signal? Yes, but a very strange one. It doesn't use the standard dimensions. Neither does it look digital. If that were not enough, it is double, in two parallel frequencies, and the signals don't match.

The dimensions are much easier to identify than I expected —they use prime numbers, so the signal factorization is trivial. The coding is hexadecimal, but it's something that I've never seen before. I need to write a computer program to decode the image. Or the images, because it looks as if there are two of them. But finally I finish, and the computer projects the result on the main screen. I fall literally on my ass. It's not that the images are sideways, as it seems that I placed the dimensions in the wrong order. No, it's not that. I thought I was picking up a television program. But apparently what I have done is intercepting a communication between two spaceships. One is piloted by something that looks like an octopus; the other is some kind of insect. There are more of them at the back.

I get up and rush to cut the communication, thunderstruck. Aliens? There are no aliens. We have never met aliens, and we have explored a radius of almost sixty light-years around Earth. It's impossible that these are aliens. But if they use spaceships, it's obvious that these... things are intelligent. I feel that my throat is dry and I feel sick with a sudden apprehension. Where am I supposed to be?

Then I remember that we're again in normal space. Even if I don't know where we are, the ship's navigation computer can calculate it, triangulating our position on the basis of the known quasars.

"Computer, identify our position in the current solar system."

It takes quite a while, and, in the meantime, I almost bite my nails off. The computer needs to scan the whole firmament, so as to identify the quasars and establish our stellar position using them as a reference. Then it inspects the solar system, detecting and analyzing the gravity wells. But after a really long, long time if happily jingles, informing me that it now knows where we are.

The outline of the solar system appears in front of me. Eight planets. The one from Thuis has only six. I feel a lump in my throat. It looks as if I'm not in the correct solar system.

"Zoom out. Display in the context of nearby systems."

The computer displays the stellar map and marks our position with a slowly blinking yellow dot. I look attentively. I do not recognize any of the stars that are displayed. This certainly does not look like the Dorada constellation, which I know by heart. So I further zoom out the map, to enlarge my visual field. Nothing. I frown and continue zooming out, enlarging the scale, until the whole Milky Way fills the image. Then I stare at the yellow dot, suddenly conscious of where I am. I search for the gas and dust concentration that we call the Orion arm, within the spiral arm of Sagittarius, halfway between the border and the center of the Milky Way. I know that the sun is there, at almost twenty-eight thousand light-years from the galactic center. I compare the distance, using my fingers. And I remain staring at the map, aghast. Something went horribly wrong. I have strayed a lot from where I was supposed to be. A stranger orbit than dad could have ever imagined.

I am fifteen thousand light-years away from home.

First contact

I'm staring at the galactic map, still horrified about what I have just discovered. It's not possible. No, there must be a mistake. This ship does not have the capacity to travel this far, nor as fast, nor can it have changed course in trans-lux. Our trip should have lasted six months and then we would arrive at Thuis, forty-nine light-years away from Earth. It's impossible that after that time I'm now fifteen thousand light-years from my home, in a totally different direction.

"Computer..." My throat is dry, and I have to swallow before being able to continue speaking. "Computer. Verify the current position. It's impossible that we are at the indicated location."

"The position is correct, captain."

"Verify it!" I scream, finally losing my nerves. "Twice!"

I try to calm down, while it scans again the firmament, detecting the quasars that will allow us to triangulate our location within the Milky Way. I look at my hands: They are trembling. It can't be. I have lost my father, I have lost the whole crew when the ship hit something while in trans-lux, though supposedly it is impossible to hit anything while in that state. If that were not enough, I have intercepted an extraterrestrial emission, though we have never encountered aliens in known space since mankind left Earth. It can't be that I have strayed from my course, that I won't see mom again. And I'll never see her again if I am fifteen thousand light-years away from home.

"Position confirmed, captain."

I look at the hologram. The intermittent dot has not moved. The Orion arm, where the solar system is located, is far, far away. I'm almost at the start of the Scutum-Centaurus arm, very close to the galactic center.

"It's impossible...," I wail. "Impossible."

It's unfair! I am alone, more alone than a human being has ever been. With a damaged ship. With eleven years. They say that I'm a genius, but at this moment I'm just a frightened little girl. My father is dead and I will never see my mother again.

"Meow?"

It's Massimo's cat, Bagheera, which is looking at me with its head tilted. The only other living being on this ship, apart from me. Apparently it's no longer pissed off with me. I take her in my arms and I hug her, while I sob. It's the only thing left from my home.

Bagheera is a cat with a very strong character. Usually it does not permit anyone to hold her. But his time it remains still, as if it understands that I need her, that I have to hug her because I have lost everything.

"Meow!" it states when my sobbing calms down.

"Yes, Bagheera," I respond, leaving it on the floor and wiping my tears. "Meow. We are alone, you know? We won't be able to get back. Not unless we find out how we have arrived here."

It yawns and starts licking a paw. It doesn't seem to be very preoccupied about our problem.

"Computer," I ask, wiping my snot with the sleeve because I don't have a hankie. "How did we get here?"

It takes the machine at least three seconds to respond.

"Insufficient data, captain," it reports. "Based on the elapsed time, we should have left the trans-lux mode at Gliese 163. There is no logic explanation of our current position."

I snort. No need for a computer to tell me that. I know that already! Based on our estimated speed, I made the calculations to leave the trans-lux mode close to Thuis. It doesn't make sense that I'm three hundred times farther than what I am supposed to be. I make a brief calculation. Assuming that the ship works and goes at its normal speed, it will take me some hundred and fifty years to return to the solar system. I won't live that long. But something has made me jump to this location in less than six months. Weeks, if it was when the accident occurred. What did we hit in trans-lux mode? What happened? If I can find out, then I'll be able to go back.

"Damage report."

The main screen goes on and I see the damage to the ship. Some of those I already knew, such as that during the mysterious collision we have lost the whole port side, along twenty decks, as well as the primary energy system. But when exiting the trans-lux mode I have also burned half the secondary energy circuit, as well as the space folding engines. There is no way that I will be able to enter the trans-lux mode. It's no longer a hundred fifty years to return. We are talking about returning through normal space. Some twenty five thousand years of travel, if I am lucky. There is no chance at all that I'll be able to repair the ship. I could not do it after the accident. And the new damage is even worse. I feel how despair is gaining the upper hand on me again.

Then I straighten in my chair. One moment! I can't repair the ship. But perhaps there is somebody else who can. Who perhaps can improve the ship sufficiently so as to get me home.

With a sudden hope I switch on the telecommunication system. I intercepted an exchange between two starships. Well, I suppose these were starships and not simple spaceships. But one of the pilots was a kind of octopus and the other was an insect. I suppose they came from different worlds. And if the two species talked with each other, I can then assume that they are not hostile. Well, at least they must be sufficiently civilized so as not to kill each other. Perhaps they can help me to return home.

I order the computer to search again for the holographic transmission that I captured. But the transmission has disappeared, the computer can't find anything. Then I order it to search all frequencies and, in the meantime, I let it reproduce the emission that I intercepted. Luckily, all communications are recorded automatically in the ship's logbook, I didn't think about telling the computer to store it into its memory.

The images appear again, and I command the computer to roll the holographic image over two axes. When I identified the dimensions, I apparently specified them in the wrong order, and the image is sideways. After a brief calculation, I finally can see the initial hologram and I stop the movement in order to have a close look on the two beings that appear on the tridimensional display.

Humanity left for outer space a little bit over two hundred years ago. It took us more than a century to develop interstellar travel after we extended throughout the solar system. We have only colonized two extra-solar planets. But we have explored the space around us, in a globe of almost sixty light-years. And we never detected aliens. I am the first human being that is truly seeing extraterrestrials, even though there are some crackpots on Earth that think that ETs have been visiting us for millennia. On Mars we are not that crazy. In reality, most people on Mars defend that aliens simply don't exist. I grimace. Well, those people seem to be wrong. They exist. Of course, I have found them fifteen thousand light-years from home.

Let's inspect first the one on the right. It's a kind of octopus, I would say. A stocky body, with three eyes and a weird beak that is vaguely similar to that of the terrestrial octopus. Tentacles with suction cups. I am not sure how many tentacles it has, but I'd guess it has six. If the color is accurate —which I won't dare assuring, as I had to make a few guesses about the color coding of the transmission— then it must be light blue. It looks like an invertebrate to me, and a maritime one at that, but it does not seem to be in a liquid environment. I can't calculate its size, as I lack reliable references. The machinery surrounding it could be anything between four and twenty feet high, I simply can't say. The alien can therefore be something smaller than my five feet to something that could eat me with one bite and ask for more. I shudder at the thought.

The other alien seems to be an insect. At least it shows most of the characteristics of the insects. Head, thorax and abdomen. It has an obvious exoskeleton, very thin legs, composite eyes that are disproportionately big and antennas. It has a greenish color. Behind it, there are others, and I perceive that they have eight legs with a kind of double pincers instead of hands on the front legs. Again, I have no references to estimate the dimensions, but it is evident that it must be much bigger that the insects on our worlds. The biggest insect we know, on colony Zeta, measures sixteen inches, but that must be too small to have a brain that is capable of thinking intelligently. I look at the legs, trying to estimate how much weight they could carry. It doesn't seem to be very much. Assuming that it comes from a low-gravity planet —like Mars, or even less—, it can't weigh too much. I guess it must be between four and seven feet.

Suddenly I feel very satisfied with myself. I am thinking again like a professional. Like the astrobiologist that I am, the youngest in history. My professors at the university would have been proud of me. Mom, being the greatest expert on alien life in the solar system, would have been also proud, I'm sure.

I wince. Mom. I have been trying not to think about her. She's probably starting to get worried, since our ship should have arrived already at Thuis, where she is waiting for dad and me. She won't be really preoccupied; after all, the ship might have had a delay of days or even weeks. But soon she'll start wondering about what is happening. She won't suspect that daddy is dead and that I'm farther away than any human being in history.

I look again at the octopus and the insect. Let's hope that they can help me to repair this ship. That they can add a propulsion system capable of making the jump of thousands of light-years that separate me from my mother, since I don't have a clue how I got here. That they help me to get home.

I replay the record again. It's short, it only lasts two minutes. So I replay it again. Then I realize that I will have a really huge problem. They are exchanging sounds, but these have no meaning for me. I don't speak their language.

"Meow?"

Looking sideways, I spot that Bagheera is sitting close to me and that it is looking at me as if it was waiting for something. It is licking its mouth, and I realize that it is hungry. To be honest, so am I.

"Meow," I answer. "I wish it was that easy to understand the aliens, Bagheera."

It licks its mouth again and I leave for the kitchen to get its food as well as something to eat for myself. Contacting with the aliens is going to take a lot of time.

Or perhaps not. I have just started eating when the computer indicates that there is an object in transit in the solar system. By its thermal signature I can tell that is not a meteorite. If that were not enough, it is decelerating. I drop the plate out of surprise, but I couldn't care less.

"Establish communication," I command the com-puter.

I am biting my nails off for long minutes while the machine tries to establish contact with the remote ship. No way, it does not answer. Then a terrible suspicion corrodes me, and I run to the communications console. A look at the parameters of our call confirms my fears. We are using the communication protocol and frequencies that we utilize in human space. In other words, here it is as if we did not exist. I feverishly establish a new communication protocol using the parameters of the call we intercepted. I call it 'ET protocol'.

"Establish communication with ET protocol," I order, and after approximately one minute the connection hologram is displayed. It's again the octopus that I already knew. It seems to be looking me directly into my face.

For a few moments we stare at each other. Then the ET speaks.
"Es hanua to yeenk se vuit?"

I don't have a clue about whether it is greeting me or mentioning my ancestors, or both at the same time. During the colonist training that I performed on Mars they gave us a brief course about how to deal with aliens, in the improbable case that we would ever meet one. The course basically consisted in not doing any kind of hostile gesture, try to exchange gifts —pretty difficult to do by radio— and call somebody more qualified for the negotiations. It's a pity that anybody more qualified than me —except Bagheera— is some fifteen thousand light-years away.

What the heck do I answer? Suddenly I realize that I don't have the slightest idea of what to do. I suppose that first we will need to learn each other's language.

"Hello." I try to smile. "I'm Tanit. It's a pleasure to meet you. How are you?"

I barely said it when I realize how stupid it sounds. Am I not supposed to have the intellectual quotient of a genius? Well, I'm talking like a little girl. But what can you say during a first contact with an alien species, especially when you don't have a clue about what they are saying?

About a minute has passed, and the ET has not spoken a word. It has turned, as if it was doing something. Is it ignoring me? Then I hear my own voice, as a faraway echo. The octopus turns towards me, looking at me again.

"Herrit na sev yuu werahs?"

I blink, confused. I have not understood anything. But now I know there is a delay in the transmission of at least thirty seconds in each direction. I check the sensor indicating the position of the alien starship. It's about six million miles away. This means that, due to the speed of light, everything I say will take about half a minute to reach the alien ship. One minute to get a response. Let's see if I can come up with something coherent by the time it answers me.

"I am sorry, I don't understand you." I think furiously. How can we start communicating? Perhaps with math? They have always said that mathematics is the basis of everything. I place my hands on the light panel of the terminal, and start creating a symbolic program with my hands. I'll start with one. "One." I launch the program and dots start to appear as I speak. "Two, three, four..."

Nothing happens for one minute, and the octopus seems to be doing something with his console. I hear the echo of my voice on his ship and the image suddenly disappears.

"What has happened?" I ask, alarmed. "Computer, why has the transmission been interrupted?"

"Communication canceled by the external terminal," reports the computer, coldly. "Receiving data entry."

It takes me a moment to assimilate it. The octopus has interrupted the call. But it is sending data. I look at the Comms terminal. Something is coming in, initially very slow, then faster and faster. What the hell is this being sending me?

The transmission seems to last forever, it takes more than two hours to complete. But when it finishes, we have received several terabytes of data. I have no clue what it is, but it seems important. I try to connect again with the alien starship, but there is no response. Whatever the alien wants to tell me, it's buried in the message that he has sent me.

It's evident that it's not binary. But it isn't that complicated, within a few minutes I decipher that it's hexadecimal. It doesn't take me long to find out that the first thing is a zero, then a one, then another one, then two, three, five, eight...

A Fibonacci series! I knew it; math is the basis of everything. I start looking at the code, but I soon realize that I'm being pretty stupid. There is an awful amount of information here. It will take me years to analyze it. But the on-board computer does not have my limitations, and can digest all this in a few hours. I start working with the light interface of the terminal. Luckily, the Astrobio-logy studies had a pretty strong programming workload. And as I wanted to join mom, that was precisely the career that I studied. I am the youngest astrobiologist in history, though probably not the youngest program-mer. Even so, my programming know-how is very good; I could program my ship to shake hands with that octopus if I wanted it to. A robotic hand, that is.

It takes me four hours to prepare the program. A little bit of data mining, some artificial intelligence, a few genetic algorithms... Luckily, the ship has computer code libraries for almost anything. Finally, I launch the process and breathe heavily.

"Let's see how long it takes you, sweetie," I tell the computer.

"Not computable", responds that stupid machine. It's really annoying that they do not admit real artificial intelligence in critical systems, such as a starship. But they say it's for safety reasons. The HAL[1] syndrome, they call it. I never really understood what they mean by that. Because an intelligent computer would now come in handy.

I pick up the plate that I dropped from the floor. That naughty Bagheera has seized on the opportunity to eat my dinner. Well, in any case I was not going to eat it after cleaning the floor with it, so I imagine that it's not that important. The cat is licking its mouth and purring, so it had to be good.

Obviously I return to the kitchen for more. Bagheera looks at me, expectantly, but it has eaten already too much and I am hungry. By the time I am finished, the computer has not even reached one percent of the work, so I decide to go to sleep. I brush Bagheera's hair, and then I get into my bed. The cat lies down at my feet. I should throw it out, but apart from me, it's the only living being on this ship, and I need some company. Soon I fall into a restless sleep, where the nightmares of the terrible accident shake me, making me cry out of fear. I don't know how many weeks have passed since that happened, but I still see the burst eyes of Sparks while he was sucked into space. At least I did not see my father die.

I wake up soaked in sweat. The cat is placidly sleeping at my feet, and I exploit that to have a shower. When I return, it demands that I brush it with a very characteristic meow that I already recognize. It's easier to understand a pussy than an alien, and that even despite the fact that I never had any pets.

After getting dressed and having breakfast I return to the bridge, but the computer has not yet finished. Even so, I have a look into what it has deciphered up to now. It's what you would expect. Mathematical formulas of increasing complexity. There is a moment where even I get lost, even though I am supposed to be one of the most brilliant minds in the solar system. This math is too much for me, I don't think that the human beings have reached that level yet.

But the scheme changes from a certain moment on. It's no longer math. I frown, trying to capture the strange outline of what is being represented. It takes me a long while before I get it. It's... I jump onto my feet as soon as I realize that what I'm seeing is a language course. Not the kind of crap that we use in our solar system. No, it's something

---

[1]   Author's note: See *2001, A Space Odyssey* by Arthur C. Clarke.

far more sophisticated. It's based on mathematics, it associates sounds to concepts, concepts to words, words to an elegantly simple grammar.

Immediately I realize that the octopus could not prepare this in the brief minutes that we tried to talk with each other. It's... brilliant. That alien noticed that I could not understand it, and it sent me the formula to be able to do it. A kind of universal language that allows different species to speak with each other. All starships must have this course prepared in case of an encounter with a new race. They simply send it and the newcomer —assuming it can understand what it is about— will learn how to talk with them. And if he does not understand it, then I suppose that such species must not be sufficiently advanced, and it's not worth communicating with them anyhow.

Suddenly I recognize that I will also have a big problem in speaking it. This is not something that you can learn by repetition, like we usually do in our solar system with normal languages. The grammar looks very simple, but the language itself is quite difficult, in the same way that with basic math you can define extremely complex problems.

It takes me two days to think about a solution. The computer has finished generating the course, and by then I am furiously working on the problem, adapting the hypnotic reader from the library for this purpose. The reader is supposed to help you remember whatever you are studying, but it needs a visual stimulus for this purpose. Usually it's a text, but this time it is not. Finally I manage to convert the alien course into a mixture of sounds and images. Most of the images have in reality no meaning at all; they are simply a visual stimulus to fix the concepts under hypnosis. So as to be sure, I also convert the words into their phonetic representation, and I overlay them to the images. It's complicated, as the course does not use a proper alphabet, but I finally manage to do it. Under the disapproving look of Bagheera I place the hypnotic helmet on my head and start studying.

They call it Common. It's a kind of universal language that is at the same time extremely simple and incredibly complex. Something that probably any living being could pronounce, though the pitch can change significantly from one species to another. As poetic as the space trash surrounding Earth. More technical than the flux injector manual. And yet so simple that even I can understand it. A language so practical that if you want to indicate an emotion you have to state it explicitly, given that the intonation does not mean anything.

"Anger," I tell finally Bagheera in Common. "This language is a biological waste."

The cat tilts its head and looks at me, obviously puzzled by the strange sounds.

"Meow?" it asks.

"Summarizing, it's pure shit," I explain, removing the helmet to take a break. "I think it would be easier to talk with you than with those aliens."

We have lunch, and then I return to my studies. It takes me a whole week to do the full course, but thanks to the hypnotic reader the whole course has been recorded in my brain at a subconscious level. I know that I will not forget it. Apart from the hypnosis, this language is so logical and structured that once you have understood the underlying math, it's almost impossible not to be able to speak it. Though I don't manage to grasp some of the more advanced concepts. It seems that there are several civilization levels around here, and the human beings are not sufficiently advanced to understand certain things. It does not matter; I know perfectly what I need to ask that they do with my ship.

I verify my new knowledge with the record of the first conversation that I intercepted. It's something trivial, they are negotiating the exchange of some merchandise by the time they arrive at a location called *Meeting Point*. Well, I assume that it's a physical location, because the insect uses a grammatical construct that implies that *Meeting Point* is a name. The method of payment are Erneigg crystals (or something that sounds like that), in exchange for Rool stars, using an exchange rate of four hundred seventy two thousandths to one. Which, honestly, does not tell me a damn thing.

Then I check the record of my conversation with the octopus. The alien asks me to identify myself, and that I declare my intentions. And I answer with a stupidity. Then it asks whether I do not speak Common. When I speak again in my own language, it apparently decides that I do not speak it, and cuts the communication. At least it was kind enough to send me the dictionary. For a first contact with an alien race, this was less than glorious. I think that at home they would reconsider that I am a genius, and send me back to kindergarten.

Leaning back in my seat, I start thinking. Well, the next step is pretty evident, isn't it? I already know how to speak with them. Now I need to establish contact. I order the computer to search for ships in the solar system, but right now there does not seem to be a lot of transit, because it does not detect any movement. Ordering it to initiate a permanent search, I start looking at the records of the three ships that I have detected so far, checking their trajectories.

I stare at the vectors for one moment. They do not seem to go anywhere in particular. Then I realize that they are following elliptic trajectories, which is logical if they take advantage of the gravity of the sun and local planets to save fuel.

My Astrobiology studies obviously covered the basics of astronavigation, but I also followed an accelerated course when I boarded this starship and was accepted as an auxiliary crew member. Those are the rules: every crew member must know about everything, so as to be able to replace another crew member in case of any mishap. Of course they never thought that I might be the only survivor out of a crew of fifteen. In any case, I know enough to be able to calculate an orbit, and the difficult part is made by the computer. It's insultingly easy to extrapolate the origin and destination data for the three ships.

Well, in reality, there are only two of them. The ship of the octopus with which I had contacted is the same one as the one of the octopus of the first conversation that I intercepted. It simply was in a different orbital position, but the trajectories overlap. By the way, that allows me to calculate its speed. Slightly more than half the speed of light.

Assuming that both ships will meet, as they were talking about getting together, the meeting point would be... I frown. There is nothing at that location. Absolutely nothing. I use the ship's computer to confirm it. Nothing at all. Are they going to meet in the middle of space? And where is the insect's ship?

I check the trajectories. OK, the ship of the insect must be now at the other side of the sun. Then I realize something: Perhaps they are going to meet in some place that is orbiting the sun.

This is only slightly more difficult to calculate, but I know the position and the approximate time of the encounter, assuming a constant deceleration. I only need to find something in orbit that could be close to that position at the moment of the encounter. Keeping in mind celestial laws, the exercise is really much simpler than it might appear. And when I tell the computer where to look, it confirms that there is a small gravity well in that orbit. Something very small, so small that the computer cannot give me the mass; it can only detect the gravitational perturbation and a small dot in front of the sun. It must be what the two aliens called *Meeting Point*.

I feel a sudden excitement with this small victory. Well, I know where they are going. Now I also have to go there.

But that is slightly more difficult than I had thought. I have to restore the speed limit circuit that I had used as spare for the trans-lux engines to its original position; the normal engines don't work at all without it. It's also necessary to repair at least part of the secondary energy circuit, or I won't have sufficient power. Luckily, all manuals are in the library, I have (almost) all necessary spares and I have all the time in the world. After eight days of work I return to the bridge, and cross my fingers when I tell the computer to switch on the engines.

Hooray! It works! Unfortunately, I immediately understand that we are starting to accelerate in the wrong direction. I break a nail entering hurriedly the coordinates of the encounter.

While the ship starts turning, I realize that I messed up again. It won't be of any use that I get to that point if *Meeting Point* has changed its location when I arrive there. And it *will* have changed because it is orbiting the sun and I will arrive a lot later than the two aliens. Astronavigation is slightly more complicated that it seems. It takes me half an hour to adjust my heading.

Then I bore myself to death for two weeks, while my orbit converges slowly with whatever this *Meeting Point* might be. I am not exactly in the best position to make the orbits converge, and I don't want to force the engines, which are not exactly in a very good shape. Therefore I use the time to repair as much as I can of the secondary energy system, and I disassemble the peripheral trans-lux equipment since I do not dare to enter the engine chamber without a radiation suit. But there is none of my size. I repair what I can, but it's obvious that I'm trying more to spend time than to really fix the system. This repair really exceeds by far what I can do.

The alarm from the bridge startles me while I am sleeping. What the heck is happening?

I get to the bridge in pajamas, still panting from the sprint. Object in transit! And its orbit is converging with mine. Why had I not seen it before?

A glance at the holographic screen provides me with the explanation: I was only looking for objects in the elliptic of the solar system, and this ship was above the elliptic. However, once it got close enough, the computer decided that it was about time to alert me. It's very close, around one and a half million miles away. Seven light-seconds. And approaching.

"Computer," I command. "Establish communication with ET protocol."

I can't avoid biting my nails while I wait. Mom always quarreled with me when I did so, but I can't help it. You simply don't contact aliens every day.

The Comms signal goes on. But there is no image.

"Is there anybody there?" I ask in Common. "I don't receive any visual signal."

"Regret," a weird voice says over the loudspeakers after fifteen seconds. "Our communication system is broken. Identification is required."

Well, at least we can understand each other. It seems that my efforts have brought some results. I inhale deeply. The first contact with aliens. In reality, it's the second one, but we better draw a shaggy veil over the first one, as we say on Mars. Or a stupid veil, as Massimo said, playing with the original Spanish word. I try to imagine some grandiose phrase for history, but Common is not particularly well suited for grandiose phrases. And I can't think about any either.

"I am Tanit, of the human race. Who are you?"

Shit! That wasn't exactly grandiose. Not even passable. Probably it was even quite stupid. Well, there's nothing I can do about it. I wait impatiently the fifteen seconds that it takes them to answer.

"I'm Yyve, from the Rokuz race. Declare your intentions."

I lick my dry lips. Let's hope they can help me.

"My ship is damaged. I need somebody to help me to repair it."

This time it takes far longer than fifteen seconds before they answer. Finally, the loudspeaker creaks again.

"We observe important cracks along the whole hull of the ship. It's not possible to repair the ship except in a shipyard. Identify internal damage."

"Primary energy system inoperative. Secondary energy system and maneuvering engines damaged, but operative. Life support system intact. Interstellar jump system not repairable by me."

Again, it takes a while before they respond. About thirty seconds.

"Identify number of crew members."

"One."

This time, the silence lasts more than one minute.

"Confirm that you said one."

"Affirmative. One."

They must be thinking about it, because, again, they take their time before answering.

"A crew of one can handle a ship of this size?"

I grimace.

"We had an accident in trans-lux. The whole crew was sucked into space. Only I have survived. And I'm only a girl."

"Gal?"

I realize that I've used a human word. Let's see how I explain that in Common.

"A non-mature female. I need help to repair my ship. I am fifteen thousand light-years from home and I want to get back."

The silence lasts this time so long that for a moment I fear that they have cut the communication, even though the Comms panel indicates that there is a carrier signal. Then the radio squawks again.

"We will dock to your ship. Open and mark an airlock. Identify the ship's atmosphere and gravity."

OK. I'm lucky; they're going to help me. I open the outer door of the front personnel airlock on the starboard side, and let the lock positioning lights blink while I detail the composition of my atmosphere.

"Atmospheric composition, by volume: 78% nitrogen, 21% oxygen, 1% argon, traces of other gases in very small amounts. The atmospheric pressure is 96% of the standardized universal pressure. Gravity..." I hesitate one moment, making the conversion to the Common units in my head. "0.92 standard gravity."

This time they respond immediately, after fifteen seconds.

"Atmosphere and gravity acceptable, they do not require protection on our side. Keep the course, while we dock the ships. Do not maneuver."

I activate the cameras along the hull, but there is nothing to see; it takes almost half an hour before a dot appears on one of the cameras, and I only spot it because the collision alarm is triggered. I have to switch it off and tell the computer to ignore the object that is heading towards us. It's not usual at all that two moving ships dock with each other, at least in human space. And yes, I make sure that the cameras record everything. After all, it's the first contact with an alien species.

It must be recorded for future generations. If I am able to get back, this will the most famous event in the history of mankind.

The aliens must have a lot of practice with this type of maneuver, because they equal my heading and speed so elegantly that it almost looks like as if they're just playing. Their ship is certainly more maneuverable than the *Moon Shadow*. Then they start approaching until our ships almost touch each other.

I watch the show, truly amazed. The alien ship is much smaller than mine, some two hundred sixty feet long by about one hundred twenty wide. It's plump, asymmetric, with multiple structures around it that I cannot identify, except a series of devices that look like antennas. They seem to have reaction propulsion engines, but both by the shape and the way that the nozzles light up, it seems that they are not of the same kind as those of my ship.

The alien ship finally stops more or less at my airlock. Well, when I say it stops it is a way of speaking, as I'm traveling at three hundredths of light speed, about a hundred thousand miles per hour. They equal their speed to mine, so it looks as if they have stopped at my side. Then a kind of gangway deploys from their ship, and starts approaching my airlock.

I puff heavily and get up. Show time. I'm scared to death, but I don't have many options. Not if I want to get back home. I have to meet these aliens and hope for the best. I pray that they are not hostile, because I won't survive if they are. There are no weapons of any kind on my ship, and even if there were, I would not be able to use them.

Though... Before leaving the bridge I turn, and give the computer a command: If I don't give a counter-order, in twenty-four hours it must block all terminals and all the doors. Then it must change course, launching itself against the sun. If they finally end up being hostile, at least they will not have my ship, and if they kill me, with some luck I'll take some of my murderers with me. Let's hope we don't come to that.

I run through the corridors towards the airlock that I have opened and I wait. The delay becomes endless while I stare at the red light above the airlock door. Something is happening to my legs, suddenly they seem like jelly; I have to lean against the wall or I will fall down. I wince when the airlock light becomes green. There is pressure on the other side of the door.

After ordering the computer to start recording everything that happens around me, I then open the airlock door. There is a long semitransparent corridor that extends to the other ship. Two shapes are slowly advancing through it in my direction.

I have to swallow hard when I see them. They are... ugly. Incredibly ugly. Even disgusting. A strange mixture of penguin and bat. They have very long feet, with long yellow hoofs. Short legs, hardly twice as long as their feet. The cardboard-like body is of a very unpleasant brown; they have a vestige of wings that indicate that their species could fly in a remote past, but which nowadays will not be able to sustain them. The faces with two small eyes close to a creased beak seem to indicate that they must have evolved from a scavenger species. And they stink. A pestilent odor that fills the whole corridor. They wear a kind of dark gray sleeveless uniform.

My studies as an astrobiologist are what allow me to calm down and try to look at them with a clinical eye while they approach. Obviously I cannot judge them by human aesthetics. But I must also admit that I don't like them at all. My first contact should have been with a race that could have been beautiful by human standards. Instead, I get... that.

I breathe in deeply, trying to calm down. Big blunder. Immediately I start coughing. Whatever this species is, they must segregate some kind of repelling chemical agent. Probably it's an evolutionary defense system, though I can't imagine in what type of environment these beings have evolved. I can't even classify the gender to which they belong, though I am wondering whether they are birds or mammals.

"We recommend not to approach us too much," says one of them in Common, with a squeaking voice. "Some species encounter physical disorders when close to us."

Disorders? I feel like vomiting because of these beasts. OK, so they're not beasts. They are intelligent beings. But it takes me a lot of effort to see them as such. I swallow hard. Whether I like it or not, I'll have to endure. They are my only hope to return with my mother.

"I see you." Common has hardly any complementary phrase, if at all, but the word used for 'I see you' is the closest to 'welcome' that there is. "Feeling pleasure to have you on my ship."

They stare at me. I suppose that I've said something weird, or perhaps these aliens don't know what being polite is. Finally, the one on the right talks again. His squeaking voice attacks my nerves, but I guess I'll have to bear with it.

"We are Rokuz. I am Yyve and he is Proet."

It's pretty evident that they have no clue about what good manners are. Well, when on Earth, do as the Earthlings, don't you? At least that's what they say on the other side of the galaxy.

"I am human. I'm Tanit."

They continue to stare at me. I am starting to get nervous. Well, more than I am already.

"You said you were Gal?"

Shit. Let's see how I explain that. I'll better pass.

"Yes. Can you help me to repair my ship?"

They chatter a few moments between them in their own language. By how pitched some of the sounds are, I suspect that part of the conversation is in ultrasounds. Not that it matters a lot; I'm incapable of understanding whatever they are talking with each other. Then they look at me again.

"Let's see the engines."

I take them to the transport cart, to go to the engine room. I exploit the opportunity to seize an oxygen mask from the wall, so as not to breathe the toxic ambient surrounding them. Not that I intend to explain it, but they make no comment; I suppose that they must be already accustomed to the fact that other species have problems near them. The anxiolytics that are mixed with the emergency oxygen calm down the distress I feel in the presence of these two nightmarish beings accompanying me.

Obviously they cannot sit down in the cart because they do not have knees; they end up standing on the seats. Luckily, the transport cart has no roof. Even so, I'm relieved when we get to the machine room and we can get out; I am too conscious of the two who are traveling behind me.

I first give them a tour of the conventional space propulsion, but they don't seem very interested. But when we get to the trans-lux engine area, even I can perceive their interest, no matter how alien they may be.

"It seems a very rudimentary design," they comment. "You say that you come from a distance of fifteen thousand light-years? It does not seem that this design is capable of traveling those distances."

I shrug. Now, that's not exactly new.

"It wasn't designed for those distances. But something occurred while we were in trans-lux. We hit something. I lost the crew. When I was able to exit trans-lux, I was here."

They chatter again between them.

"It is impossible to hit anything in trans-lux mode."

I snort, though they probably have no clue about what snorting is.

"That's what we also thought. But you've seen the hull of my ship. Something ripped it open across twenty decks. And I ended up here. I don't know what happened. Can you modify the engine so that I can return?"

They look at me for at least one minute before they answer.

"There is no engine that can travel fifteen thousand light-years. It has never existed. It is impossible to travel that distance."

I feel that my world is falling apart. This was my only hope of returning home.

"But I did," I stammer, on the verge of crying. "It's possible! I did it! I don't know how, but I did it!"

They chirp to each other; it's a very unpleasant sound.

"We can investigate that happened and try to reproduce it," they finally snap. "But we need instrumentation. We suggest going to *Meeting Point* and investigating there."

I nod, trying to compose myself. After all, I intended to go there. And perhaps my new friends can help me to find out how I could travel across half the galaxy in a matter of weeks.

"Very well. Can you tell me what *Meeting Point* is?"

They explain it to me while we return. We're in a quite inhabited zone of the galaxy; there must be at least a hundred species in a radius of sixty light-years. And this solar system is in the middle of the main commercial routes. It does not have any habitable planets, but some millennia ago somebody built a space station so as to facilitate commerce. They are not very sure about who it was; that detail got somehow lost in the fog of history. What really matters is that *Meeting Point* has been for many centuries a very important commercial center.

It also seems to be a pretty dangerous place. There is no piracy in this solar system as every pirate ship would be destroyed by the defensive systems spread throughout the system so as to protect commerce. But the only law in effect in the station seems to be the Rules of Commerce, which is the only agreement that all species have reached. Anything that the Rules of Commerce do not cover —and they do not seem to cover much— is possible. What some species call contraband is free commerce for others. What some call stealing has no meaning whatsoever for species that don't have a sense of property at all. Murder for some species is simply a duel, if not an outright merit. The things that some species consider illegal are a virtue for others. Suddenly I wonder whether it's a good idea to go there. But my new friends explain me that it is impossible to try to find out what happened to my ship without the space station's resources.

I give them a brief tour of my ship and we end up on the bridge, where I show them the position of the Earth on the galactic chart. By how they chirp to each other, I know that they are excited. It's not surprising, if they can't travel either at the speed I did! This calms me down a bit. These Rokuz are as interested as I am to resolve the mystery of how I got here. It will allow me to get back, but they will also find out how to travel throughout the whole galaxy. We all win.

Switching off the hologram, I realize that they are paying attention to how I give commands to the computer. They raise some questions about how they can help me to control my ship, but I explain that the computer performs the important work, and that they will not be able to control anything as they do not speak my language. They chirp a little more between them in their own language and then they tell me that they are going to return to their own ship; they will radio me the instructions about how to get to and dock at *Meeting Point*. We'll see each other there, to find out how I can return.

Half an hour later I am alone again, but with really high spirits. For starters, I no longer have to endure their irritating smell. They might be nice, but they really stink. Second, I finally have some hope. It's not much of a hope, but at least I have some.

It takes me another two weeks to reach *Meeting Point*, and by then I have detected another eight ships in transit. The Rokuz have been giving me detailed instructions about how I must approach, how I must contact the station and what the correct docking protocol is. But I make darn sure that the computer has understood it. Apparently, here they do not allow for mistakes; if the maneuver is not correct and they consider you a danger for the station, they shoot at you without previous warning.

Luckily, they have a tractor system for the ship for the last miles. As soon as I receive the message from the station, I switch off the engines and let them tug the *Moon Shadow* to the designated docking location. The station is immense; despite its two thousand feet my ship looks tiny compared with this monster. It's so big that it has a gravity well of its own. It's at least six or seven miles in diameter, I can't even imagine how they could build it.

"We'll meet at the exit of your airlock."

The Rokuz have been docking in parallel. Given that their ship is much smaller, the docking maneuver has been quicker. I am happy to have some friends here. They are ugly as hell, and they stink, but at least they are trying to help me. Not that I know whether the other ETs will be so kind to me.

I check whether the ship is docked by means of the external cameras. Yes, there are some kind of brackets placed around the hull that keep the ship in position. Because of their size I have the impression that they have been designed to hold ships even much bigger than mine. There is also a type of tunnel that has unfolded towards the front airlock, attaching itself to the hull.

Placing all systems in orbital mode, I lock the access to the terminals after ordering the computer to open the external door of the airlock. Then I walk to the lock. To be honest, this time I don't run. I am somewhat apprehensive. The Rokuz were already pretty weird. But here I will meet other species, possibly even stranger. What is it that I will see here?

Upon reaching the airlock, I verify that there is an atmosphere at the other side. Yup. The pressure is slightly higher than mine; my eardrums are going to hurt. Instead, there is somewhat more oxygen, 23% in volume. Other parameters do not differ too much from those of my own atmosphere, except that there is slightly less nitrogen and the argon percentage is twice what we humans understand as normal. Well, I can breathe it, which is what really matters.

I open the lock and I feel the caress of the air flowing, as pressures start to balance. Rapidly entering into the lock, I close the door behind me. In reality, I should not have had both doors open at the same time, but I did not have much choice in that respect. The outer door had to stay open so as to verify that there was pressure in the airlock and so as to check the type of atmosphere. You can't measure that outside the ship. A starship is not supposed to ever enter an atmosphere, so it does not need that type of sensors.

Another alien is waiting for me at the end of the corridor. Pretty weird. It has four legs, with a central body, a head with two great eyes and two abnormally long arms finishing in four-finger hands. The skin looks like silk, with a somewhat weird gray color. It must be about seven feet tall and does not carry any clothes, except a sort of bag hanging on one side. A kind of handbag, I assume. If he has sexual organs, they are not in plain view.

"I see you," it greets me. "Place your extremity on the sensor to confirm responsibility for the ship."

I stare at him, with no clue of what he exactly wants. Then he makes a gesture of placing his hand against a black panel beside the door, more or less at the height of my head. I place the hand on the panel, and feel a kind of tickling inside. Something very strange. Then, to my great surprise, I hear a voice in Spanish:

"Docking confirmed. You are granted access to the station."

How in hell do they speak Spanish around here? I turn towards the alien, but to my amazement it is filtering itself through the wall. No, it certainly wasn't him who talked with me. This looks like magic.

Any sufficiently advanced technology is indistinguishable from magic.

I recall suddenly that quote from a classic writer whose name I do not remember[1], and feel much better. It's not magic; it's an advanced technology that I cannot understand yet. Probably they have induced that message directly into my brain; after all, on Mars we speak Spanish. And regarding that going through the wall...

I advance, and try to touch the wall. But my hand simply goes through it, as if did not exist. It's either an illusion or a material that can become solid or permeable as required. Impulsively, I advance and after feeling a light resistance —something like hitting some sort of dense air— I am suddenly inside the station.

Well, I am in a hall. The walls have a strange glare; I can't say of what material they're made of. A yellow lighting illuminates everything, but I can't say where it comes from. I'd swear that it's the complete ceiling that provides the light, because it seems slightly brighter than the rest of the walls. There are gaps in the walls that seem entrances to several corridors. On one side there is a hologram, about eight feet high. It's showing a scene of what seems to be a city. Several aliens of different shapes are looking at it.

---

[1] Arthur C. Clarke

I can't see anything more, because the Rokuz approach me immediately. Now they are six, but I am unable to say which of them were the ones that visited my ship.

"We come to make you a proposal," squeaks one of them. "We want to buy your ship."

I remain open-mouthed. Sell them my ship? But why should I do that? It's my only hope to go home!

"What?" I splutter. "Buy my ship?"

It extends its hand with something; I take it instinctively and look at it. It's some kind of crystals, greenish, very bright.

"Deal closed."

I raise my head, surprised.

"What? No! There is no deal! I didn't agree to anything!"

They don't answer. They simply pass at my side and go through the wall where I entered. But when I try to follow them, I hit the wall; the door is suddenly solid. I hit it with my fists, suddenly terrified.

"Open!" I scream. "There is no deal! I don't want to sell my ship!"

I look around. The aliens that were watching the hologram have turned around and are looking at me. I realize that one of them is the quadruped that made me touch the panel on the wall. I run towards them, desperately. They can't do this to me! These aliens have to help me!

But they're not willing to do so. They hear my explanations, my appeals, but finally they simply point to the crystals that I am still holding in my hand.

"You accepted the payment. The Rules of Commerce state that if you accepted the payment, then the deal is valid."

I look at the crystals in my hand. I don't know how much they are worth, but even if they were ten times the value of my ship I would still not sell it. It's the only thing I have, my only hope to return with mom.

"But I did not want to sell my ship!"

They start to depart. The quadruped looks at me one more time before answering and leave.

"You accepted the payment, even though it is much less than the value of your ship. You should have negótiated better."

They all walk away, except one, which remains at a distance, while I remain aghast. What have I done? They have cheated me! I thought that the Rokuz wanted to help me, and they simply wanted to steal my ship. But as they could not pilot it, they waited until I arrived here, so as to take it from me using a legal trick. I feel the tears running over my cheeks. What am I going to do now?

Then a claw closes itself forcefully over my wrist, forcing me to open the fist that holds the crystals. One moment later, it has taken them from me. By the time I turn, I only see the back of a kind of lizard running towards a cavity in the wall.

"Thief!" I scream. "Give that back to me!"

I run behind the reptile that has robbed me. It's essential that I recover those crystals; I might still be able to undo the deal, but without the crystals that will be impossible. I must wipe my eyes; I have them veiled due to my tears of fury and despair.

The ET enters the opening in the wall. To my surprise, it starts rising until it disappears from view. When I get there I see that it's a kind of tube, like an elevator shaft. I peek inside. The alien is already about twenty-six feet above me, and going up. Yes, this is a lift, though not of the kind with which I am familiar.

I hesitate for a moment. This shaft is very deep, and there does not seem to be a lifting mechanism. But I am so desperate that I have no choice but to use it. Well, the thief is going up, isn't he? I should also go up. I inhale deeply and jump inside.

One instant later I am screaming in terror while I fall into the void. I am dropping! I am going to die! And I just wanted to go up!

After barely thinking it, my falling speed slows down, until I eventually stop in midair. Then I start slowly going up. It's as if the elevator has read my mind.

That must be it, because there is no kind of controls. I look up, searching desperately for the thief that has stolen my crystals. But there is no longer anybody in the shaft. It escaped.

I have no clue how I got out of the lift. Probably I walked to the outside when I passed through the entrance to one of the floors. But suddenly I am in a corridor, sitting on the ground, leaning against a wall while I stare into nothingness, trying to think. What am I going to do now? How am I going to get back? I feel that the despair overwhelms me; I raise my knees, put my head on my arms, and I weep inconsolably. What am I going to do? What can I do?

I don't know how long I have been like this, but it must have been hours, feeling how my stomach roars. And I am very thirsty. Wiping my tears I stand up. I'll have to do something, or I'll die of hunger and thirst.

The corridor ends in the open air. Well, it looks like open air because it is a gigantic hall, more than three hundred feet high, at least four hundred feet wide and about one mile long. On the floor there are strange structures, a small lake, and gardens. A lake! At least I'll be able to drink there.

There are ramps to descend, which is my luck as right now I don't have the will to use the lift again. But it's a long walk, as I have to descend at least fifteen stories.

Aliens are everywhere. Tall, short, thin, thick... there are insects, mammals, reptiles... and some that I would be unable to classify using human definitions. Hundreds of them, of dozens of species. Some walk or crawl, others seem to be talking between them. One jumps from one of the terraces into the void, deploys its wings and glides towards the other end of the hall. I stop for one moment at the balustrade and watch the scene. No human being has ever seen anything like what I am watching now. Something incredible. Something for which the scientists in my home world would pay anything. And I instead would pay anything to be back with my mother.

I try to stay as far away as possible from the aliens while I walk down the ramps, but ultimately I have no option but to mix with the crowd; there are too many of them to keep the distance. It's very strange and I am looking around with quite some apprehension, given all those strange life forms that surround me. But the ETs simply ignore me; for them, I am simply another species, and also much smaller than most of them. They must think that I'm pretty harmless, which is obviously true.

The worst of all are the scents. Some aliens smell quite well, but of course there is pretty much anything around, and the strongest odors are usually the most unpleasant ones. My nose can hardly process the strange mix of smells that surround me, from subtle scents similar to roses with cinnamon to strong stenches with evident ammonium content. Aromas that are unlike anything that I have ever experienced. Well, unlike any human being has ever experienced.

But when I reach the lake it becomes evident that I will not be able to quench my thirst. The water is murky. There are plants —similar to algae— and by the way the liquid moves, it must contain something like fish, or similar. I don't dare drinking it; probably it is dangerous.

Time to think. Probably the best is to go to the authorities. After all, I am still a girl. I suppose it's better to be tutored by an alien than to die of hunger and thirst.

I hesitate one moment, looking at the incessant flow of aliens. After my experience with the Rokuz, I don't trust any of them. Finally, I take a decision and I delicately stop a vaguely humanoid being that is one head shorter than I am. I simply don't dare to talk with the taller ones.

"I see you. Regret for stopping you."

It watches me with three eyes with perpendicular eyelids. Really strange eyes.

"Alarm. I don't identify you."

I retain it softly when it tries to leave. So I have scared it. I have to swallow to undo the lump in my throat. I am far more scared than it might be.

"Alarm not necessary. I will not hurt you. I only need some information."

Probably this calms him down, because it blinks twice with the three eyes, but no longer attempts to leave.

"I will share available information."

It takes me quite a while to explain the alien what I want, but when it walks away, I remain even more confused and shaken than I already was. There is no such thing as the authorities here. Actually, there is an authority which manages the station, takes care of its equipment and maintenance and charges for the services, but in reality it's like a company, not a government. What we call social services doesn't even exist; the alien didn't understand at all what I was talking about. If somebody gets sick, either the members of his species take care of him, he pays for a session in an autodoctor or he dies, and they throw his corpse into the mass converter providing energy to the station. The few kids that are around are safeguarded by their parents or at least their respective races. And if not, they have to survive by themselves. Or they die. Nobody cares.

I take a deep breath. It's pretty obvious that I'll have to take care of myself, because nobody else will do it for me. Either I smarten up quickly, or I will die in the middle of general indifference.

Curiously, that thought calms me down. Very well. I'll show these bug-eyed monsters what a human girl can do. I will survive. I'll recover my ship and I'll mock those Rokuz bastards in their stinking faces. I got here against all probabilities, didn't I? Well, these insensitive monsters are going to see something. After all, I am a genius; I'll think of something.

But first things first. Water and food. I look around. If I am really desperate, I can try drinking in the lake. Perhaps even try to fish whatever lives inside it. But only as a last resource. It's pretty likely that it could poison me. Let's look first for some other options.

I try to stop some of the aliens walking past me, but they are all bigger than I am and simply ignore me, so eventually I stop one that only reaches my chest by the simple method of stepping in front of him —or her, who knows— and not letting it pass.

"I see you," I greet it in Common. "I am not hostile. But I need some information from you."

It looks around nervously. It's like a kind of squirrel, and perhaps that's why it looks nervous to me. Or perhaps, knowing how things work around here, it does not believe that I am not going to hurt it.

"Detail the information you require," it finally says with a shrieking voice.

I get a little bit closer. The squirrel cringes; I assume that it is out of fear. It smells nice, much better than most of the aliens that I have seen passing by since I arrived here. Actually, I like its smell as well as its appearance. Contrary to the Rokuz, this seems an amicable species.

"Where can I get food and water?"

It turns around and points to a lateral corridor. It explains to me that there is an automatic kitchen in the middle of the corridor that will prepare anything I want. I insist a little bit and it describes me the kitchen, a kind of blue square machine with the logo of the station. Then it points to one side to show me the logo of the station. I look, but by the time I turn back, the squirrel has disappeared. Probably it was as fearful about me as I am about all the aliens that surround me.

I continue walking down the corridor, dodging a real herd of a kind of ostriches with arms coming in my direction. Then I pass beside four stocky aliens in what seem to be spacesuits; it looks as if not everybody in this space station can breathe this air. I assume that I am lucky, after all. If this atmosphere was not breathable, then probably I would be already dead, as I would have run out of air by now in my spacesuit.

Finally, I get to the kitchen. It's pretty easy to identify it, as some aliens are extracting a recipient with something steamy from a gap in the machine. I pay attention to how they do it. One of the ETs places a hand on a black panel like the one there was on the quay, and the food or drink comes out through the cavity. It looks pretty easy.

Only it isn't. When the aliens leave, I place my hand on the panel. And absolutely nothing happens. I frown. I was expecting that some kind of controls would appear to make the selection, but there is nothing like that. How can I order something to eat or to drink?

Then the machine surprises me, telling me in Spanish that I am not classified. I blink, puzzled, and try again. Nothing. I think about how thirsty I am and that stupid machine tells me the same thing. It probably induces the message directly into my brain. I remember what happened in the elevator. The machines here apparently can read your mind.

Finally, I reach the conclusion that I'm not going to achieve anything, so I'll have to ask again. This time I stop an ET who is some eight inches taller than me. It looks like a mixture of a cat and a bird, but by now I no longer pay attention to those things.

"Surprise," it states in Common, with an unexpected low tone of voice. "I don't identify you. We do not have shared arrangements."

This language is sometimes very stupid, as it has to be adaptable to many different civilizations, but at least it is understandable. He is surprised that an alien species is trying to make contact with him. Or her, as I have no clue about its sex, assuming it has one. I think furiously before answering. A statement like 'Sorry' does not exist in Common, the language is far too direct and does not seem to support polite phrases. It is also very likely that most alien species don't even understand what being polite means. I have bullied the other aliens with my height, but this one is taller than me and must weigh at least twice as much as I do. Let's try not to annoy him.

"Regret for occupying your time," I state, trying to be polite in a language that has not been thought to express that kind of things. "But I cannot identify anybody in this station, so I must request information to unidentified beings."

He stares at me with an expression that I am unable to interpret.

"Providing information implies establishing a commitment to reciprocal exchange."

I suppose he is stating that if I request information then I must give him also information, because if he wants me to pay him then I'm going to be in serious trouble.

"If I have information of your interest, of course I will provide it to you."

He continues staring at me. Then it makes a strange bobbling turn with its head.

"Commitment accepted. What kind of information do you need?"

I point to the automatic kitchen.

"Can you tell me why the machine states that I am not classified?"

He finally gets it after I repeat the action with the machine.

"You have to go to one of the banks of the station; they have to record your mental pattern so as to allow for payments," he explains. "You can exchange payment methods or request an initial credit that you must return before leaving the station. There is a bank in that direction."

He points to one of the corridors and I bow, showing my respect.

"Eeeh…" Shit! I don't have a clue how you say 'Thank you' in Common. Assuming that you can say it. "In debt with you," I finally declare.

"Debt can be settled with other information," he clarifies. "I need to know the whereabouts of another member of my species with identifier Neger."

I blink. I never saw anything like him.

"Regret. I have never seen another member of your species. But if I see him, I will inform you immediately."

It makes again that strange bobbling turn with the head. It must be some kind of acknowledgement.

"I will be on this deck. Ask for Ramher."

He continues his way, and I watch as he leaves. A bird's head on a quadruped body with fur is something really, really weird. Well, if I see that Neger guy then I suppose that it won't be a problem to come and tell it to him. After all, this cat-bird has helped me.

Walking through the corridor that he has pointed to, I end up in a kind of round hall where there are some rooms full of strange objects; I imagine these are the shops or something like that. But I'm unable to identify the bank. Finally, I approach one of the shops, trying to find out what they sell. Then a billboard appears before my eyes —in Spanish! — telling me all the marvelous characteristics of the weapons they have, capable of killing a Gregg with one single shot, whatever that might be.

I blink in surprise, and the billboard disappears. It must be something that is projected directly into my mind; I don't think they speak Spanish here. However, I must admit that it's pretty effective as publicity.

Standing in front of the second shop, I see myself bleeding all over the place. It looks as if I am very seriously wounded. My image then takes a small device and scans the whole body with it. One instant later, it is no longer bleeding and smiles at me. Then my image talks to me, also in Spanish.

"Nothing like our portable autodoctor for your battle injuries!"

Wow! The advertising agencies on Mars are simply amateurs when compared to these ETs. But of course, on Mars we do not know yet how to project images into a mind, and even less images adapted to an alien brain. I approach a third shop.

It's when I get to the fourth one when I find out that it's a bank, because I have the impression that I am entering a bank on Mars, though with an employee that has three feet and three arms. It looks like a six-foot high stool with arms. It has a single eye looking at me, but due to a reflection on the wall I realize that it probably has two other eyes on the other side of the body.

Obviously, I enter the bank. Usually I would have assumed that it was just another shop, because it has some chests on the ground, full of... things. It must be something very valuable, because above each chest there is a kind of small cannon targeting me carefully and following every single movement I make. I look at the chests. It's a kind of bright mineral. It actually looks a bit like diamonds, except for the little detail that the color is changing continuously.

"I see you," greets me the stool in Common. "Do you want to do business with us?" It extends one arm towards the chest I'm looking at. "As you can see, the Krill is of the best quality. We also have Enen and Yestal."

I look at the mineral. To be honest, I don't have the slightest clue about what that is, whether you can eat it, use it as an ornament or it has industrial applications. And I would not be able to distinguish the quality of that Krill even if I had a ton of it. Regarding Enen and Yestal, I can't even guess what he's talking about. It can be anything from precious metals to alien guano.

"I come to register my brain pattern," I explain. "So as to be able to buy things."

"Or course," he answers. "You are new in *Meeting Point*?"

I don't bother explaining that I am a girl. Probably he doesn't care a damn. And no way that I am going to tell him my age. Because if he realizes that I am a minor, then probably he will simply kick me out.

"I arrived a few micro-cycles ago."

He points to a corner, and I stand in a blue circle painted on the floor, while he starts making funny gestures in the air. Almost certainly he is operating a computer, but I cannot see the interface; probably it is only visible to him. I assume it is projected into his mind. In the meantime, he does not stop talking.

"If you are new, we need to create a credit account. You can use any payment method; we accept currencies from all species."

Ooops! I don't have any money. Well, I do have some loose coins in one of my pockets, but I am perfectly aware that I am not going to convince him with that. Probably the coins here must be like the seashells some aborigines used on ancient Earth. As exotic and useless as those.

"I have been told that I can ask for an initial credit."

"That is correct. Without a guarantee you can receive an amount that is equal to your corporal mass at market price."

I blink, puzzled.

"Can you explain that to me?"

The clarification is bone-chilling, and I shudder at hearing it. What it means is that if I try to leave the station without returning the loan, they will simply kill me and sell my corpse on the market for the carnivores that live on this station. Though the automatic kitchens can prepare food that is almost indistinguishable from the real thing, some species prefer the real bloody meat. And they are willing to pay for it. They don't mind if it's another intelligent being. Actually, they don't even mind if he's alive when they start devouring him.

"Obviously our company does not allow for that," he clarifies. "We supply the meat while it is still warm, but the debtor is dead when we sell him. We also verify that he's not toxic for the buyer. We have a reputation to maintain."

"Very praiseworthy," I mutter, quite startled.

"Correct. Of course, you have nothing to fear as long as you return the credit with six percent interest per standard cycle. You accept the initial credit under these conditions?"

I think furiously. I don't know how I'll return that credit, but without it I will not last even two days, without food or water. I am risking my life, but if I don't accept the credit I won't survive either. Luckily, I won't have to return the credit until I want to leave the station. Until then, I'll be safe.

"Affirmative."

"Place your extremity on the panel to confirm the transaction."

I place the hand on the panel he indicates me, and I feel a kind of weak cramp. One instant later, I know that my account has been increased by six hundred standard accounting units, also known as credits. I don't have a clue about whether that is a lot or not, but it's not very reassuring to know that somebody can eat me for that price.

"Pleasurable to transact with you."

"Yes, very pleasurable," I mumble as I leave the bank.

I inhale deeply once I am outside. I recall that at home, when people speculated about extraterrestrial life, they all assumed that the ETs would be superior, both technologically and intellectually. That they would have higher ethical values than we do. Well, they were correct about the technology. But for the rest... Eat alive other intelligent beings without anybody making a fuss about that? What a gang!

Then I see another cat-bird. I know it's not the same because this one has a kind of stain around one of the eyes. Following an impulse, I approach it. After all, the other cat-bird has helped me.

"You are Neger?"

It turns towards me. It's somewhat taller than the other one.

"Affirmative. I don't identify you. You bring me a message?"

"Something like that. Your friend Ramher is looking for you." I point. "That way."

To my surprise, it runs off in the direction that I have pointed to. Probably it was missing his friend a lot. I follow it slowly; after all, the automatic kitchen is in that direction.

I have almost reached the place where I met Ramher when I find that the corridor is blocked by a barrier of aliens looking at something. Luckily, some of them are very tall, and by ducking I can see between their legs. And I remain stupefied.

Both cat-birds must have fought, because one of them is lying on the floor, all bloody, while the other one is licking its wounds with a long tongue coming out of its beak. Nobody seems to care much, the wall of onlookers is starting to dissolve once the spectacle has finished. I grab one of the aliens by its shoulder when it starts to turn so as to leave.

"Don't we have to alert..." I think furiously. Common does not seem to have a word for 'police'. "The guardians of the law?"

It takes my hand from its shoulder with two delicate pincers, as if it was something dirty.

"The only law on the station is the Rules of Commerce," it explains. "And this does not say anything about duels. If they want to fight, that is their problem."

It leaves me in the lurch. To be honest, everybody starts to leave, until I'm alone with the dead cat-bird. It's the one with the stain around the eye. Neger. It seems that those two were not friends after all.

Suddenly a machine appears from one side, with some clamps that grab the corpse and drag it to the side of the corridor. A panel opens, and the robot dumps the cat-bird unceremoniously into the hole. Then it labors around the location of the fight, cleaning up the spilled blood. After hardly two minutes there is no longer any sign of the incident and the machine returns to the inside of the corridor's wall.

I feel like as if butterflies are churning in my stomach. Talking about the intellectual and ethical alien superiority! I approach the automatic kitchen, but I am no longer hungry. I place my hand on the machine; now I get a message in Spanish stating the amount of credit that I have and requesting my order. Though I have no clue about how to do it, the machine must detect my thirst, because it spews out a bowl of water. Now that's lucky; not only does it calm my thirst, but it also relaxes the sensation that I want to vomit.

Sitting down in a corner of the corridor, I try to think, holding the half-empty recipient between my knees. What am I going to do now? I don't have the slightest idea about how to recover my ship, assuming that it is even possible. If that were not enough, I can't abandon the station either, not if I don't want to be killed and become the main course of an alien carnivore.

OK. Survival comes first. That means first food and drink, or at least money to pay for it. I have some money, but keeping in mind that I have been charged half a credit for the water, this will not last long. That means that I will need to find work. It's obvious that there are no freebies here, and the fact that I am a minor is absolutely irrelevant for the aliens.

What kind of work? The problem is that even though I am a genius, the technological level of the human race seems to be well below what seems to be the average here. No matter how intelligent I might be, right now I am like a savage that has been placed in the middle of a modern city. I hardly know how to move throughout the station. It's impossible to work in anything sophisticated. I might be able to learn, but initially I'll have to do with non-qualified work. And also jobs that don't imply a lot of physical effort, as neither my age nor my constitution allow for them.

I drink the rest of the water, leave the bowl on the floor and stand up. But I have an urgent need to go to the restroom. A very urgent need. I can't simply do it here in the corridor. It's evident that they must have toilets here somewhere, but I neither know how they look like nor how to identify them.

So I stop another alien. This one is at least biped and more or less my size. It takes me some effort to explain what I am looking for. Finally I tell him plainly that I need to release some biological waste and he points immediately towards one side of the corridor.

"Next corridor to the right."

When I get into that corridor, I notice it ends in a totally empty white hall. For an instant I think that I am in the wrong place, but then I see on one side of the hall a kind of gazelle without horns on four feet, relieving itself. I am still in doubt when some ETs of different species enter, go to different sides and also start releasing their poop. It's curious how many different ways they have of doing it, and how they open their clothes to do it, assuming they have clothes in the first place. Some don't. One, who is wearing something that looks like a spacesuit, simply releases a hose from its suit and drops the content on the floor. Probably all the waste that has been accumulating in the spacesuit.

I suppose I should be shocked by the spectacle, but to be honest, it's as shocking as a herd of cows dropping their excrements. I simply can't see them like human beings. Obviously, the human privacy rules for this kind of things don't apply here.

Then I notice that the room is extremely clean, even though dozens of aliens have pooped here. It even doesn't smell bad; to be honest, it doesn't smell at all. I note that the excrements pass immediately through the apparently solid floor. Another technology that I don't understand. Pretty weird.

Well, it's obvious that I won't have any privacy here, but I imagine that for them I am also just another cow. I sigh, and after unfastening my clothes I squat down.

I wince when some electrostatic tickle caresses my ass. I am tempted to touch it, but then I notice that on the ET that is in front of me the rests of poop are detaching themselves from his shitty hole and flying towards the floor. They have here a very sophisticated way of cleaning your ass. Better than how we do it on Mars, which is very rudimentary when compared to this.

When I leave the restroom, I realize that this kind of system makes a lot of sense. There must be at least one hundred species in this station, all different, and it is impossible to have a different toilet for each of them, so they have a common system. It's not even separated by sexes, but I suppose that here it would be very difficult to make that distinction. And that's assuming that all species have only two sexes, which is something that I couldn't swear.

Once relieved, I decide to go to the shops that were next to the bank. If I need to find a job, I suppose that being a shop assistant must not be excessively complicated. That should be something that I can do. It does not require a lot of technological know-how nor excessive strength. But obviously it will not be exactly well paid. And God knows what the working conditions are around here. As I have never worked in my life —except for a few months on a starship, as auxiliary crew member—, I don't have any clue either about the working conditions in human space.

But there is no luck. None of the shops need help. However, one of the aliens tells me that there are many shops two floors below. So, scared stiff, I enter an elevator, thinking furiously that I only want to go down two floors

It works. Instead of falling outright, like last time, I not only drop slowly, but also stop when I reach the second floor below me. It's really awesome that these machines react to your thoughts, once you get accustomed to it.

There must almost one mile of shops in the wide corridor that I have reached. It's pretty sure that one of them needs help. Unfortunately, after almost three hours I have achieved… nothing. The shops are highly automated, and apparently one assistant is more than enough. In some cases, they don't even need that, everything is computer controlled and the assistant is a tridimensional virtual entity. It seems that my idea is apparently not that smart.

Then a group of aliens surrounds me. There are six of them, similar to... yes, to the Weirdies in the Zeta colony. Chubby, but with long legs, they look a little bit like Champaign corks on toothpicks. They have very thin arms and some very disquieting red eyes.

"I see you," greets one of them. He notices that I'm looking around, seeking how to escape, and he adds quickly: "We do not have hostile intentions."

"Then don't surround me," I reply. "I am uncomfortable having somebody behind me."

"Regret. We do not intend to scare you." He chirps something, and those that are behind me move to the side of those in front of me, which certainly reassures me quite a lot. "We are Ching. My name is..."

He pronounces a name that sounds like spitting. Then he introduces his companions, with names that are even more unpronounceable.

"I am human," then I introduce myself. "My name is Tanit."

"We have heard that you are looking for a job."

"Yes, I..." I manage to rethink what I intend to say on time: I don't want them to know how desperate I am to get hold of some money. "I arrived recently at this station. I'd like to stay here for some time, but I have limited funds, so I will have to shorten my stay unless I find a job."

"Would you be interested in one hundred Erodon pearls?"

I look at him with my best poker face, though he probably can't read my expressions.

"How much is that in credits?"

The Ching seems to hesitate.

"About two hundred sixty credits."

Well. That isn't bad at all. It's almost half what I am worth in weight as meat on the market. Then it continues talking and leaves me open-mouthed.

"Each pearl."

Now that leaves me a little suspicious. What he is offering me is a lot of money. So that means that it is either dangerous or illegal. I don't hesitate, and spill it right out. The Ching raises the hands, as if horrified about the idea.

"Of course not!"

He takes me to one side and explains me that they are merchants. They have a warehouse in the upper floors, but the door access control is broken. However, it will take the equivalent of almost three days to repair the access, and the warehouse has a lot of perishable products. By the time that they open the door, the losses will be tens of thousands of Erodon pearls. They could perforate the door, but that will cost them even more than what they are willing to pay me, apart from the fact that they could then not protect the rest of the merchandise.

I look at the alien, frowning. OK, so that might be true. But that does not explain why they need me, or why they're willing to pay so much. He releases a kind of whistle when I ask.

"The door has an emergency release mechanism inside. Just in case somebody gets trapped inside. We want you to enter and open it."

"Why me?"

"Look around. How many beings do you see of your size?"

I look. To be honest, there are very few aliens of my height. And the few that are as tall as I am are also far more corpulent than me, as I happen to be quite slim.

"There is a duct. It's very narrow. You could enter through it. If we pay so much, it's because you could get stuck and you would have to wait for a long time until we could rescue you. There is a certain risk, I admit it."

So there is some danger. That explains why they are ready to pay so much. I take a deep breath. With a hundred pearls I will be able to return the loan that can bring me onto an alien plate, assuming they use plates around here. And I'll have money to live for some time, while I look for work. The risk seems to be worth it.

"Very well."

"Then let's go; every nanocycle is costing us money."

They accompany me to the elevator, chatting excitedly in their language between them. They must be really preoccupied about the deterioration of their merchandise. One descends quicker than the rest, and is waiting for us in a corridor by the time we arrive downstairs. It makes us a sign and we join him.

There is like a small room some sixty-five feet in the corridor. With a huge door.

"Here it is."

I look around.

"And where do I need to enter?"

We walk a few feet to the right, and the ET points towards a grid above me.

"It's very simple," the alien explains. "You simply enter through the air duct and open us the door. We regain access, pay you and then you can leave."

I stare at him, suspicious. After my adventure with the Rokuz and seeing how they treat each other, I do not trust any of these aliens. And I have a strange feeling, as if something were amiss.

"Is there any other exit from the air duct?"

The Ching seems to hesitate.

"No."

By the way he answers, I suddenly am sure that these beings are hiding something from me. Apart of the risk of getting stuck, perhaps the air duct has some hidden danger. There is something weird here, and I don't like it at all. But I don't have much choice. Not if I don't want to die of hunger and thirst. Because the little money that I have will not last for long. Apart from the fact that if I do not return it, I will end up in an alien stomach.

"I want the double. And you will pay me before I enter the duct."

I could swear that I have pissed him off, by how he changes color and its voice becomes higher in pitch.

"No way!"

I shrug.

"Then there is no deal. You might forget to pay me after I open. And if there are no other exits from the duct, why is that important? I won't be able to go anywhere else."

They start talking excitedly to each other. I can see that for some reason they don't seem to consider it a good idea. That worries me even more. I don't know what is happening, but I like less and less what they are asking me to do. Suddenly, one of them turns towards me.

"We will pay you one and a half times what we have offered you. Not more."

I am tempted to accept. But I have a strange feeling in my stomach. Something is wrong here. I'm feeling the urge to leave. Even if I lose a good deal.

"Three times as much. And if you try to haggle again, it will be four times. So decide now, I don't have the whole day."

Again, they start chirping to each other. By how they look at me from time to time, it is pretty evident that they are quite pissed off with me. I decide that I'll run away as soon as I open the door; these weird beings are quite capable of taking away from me whatever they pay me.

Finally, the one appearing to be the chief imposes order. He whistles an acute tone which sounds like 'Shut up!' and turns towards me, grabbing the bag that hangs from its belt.

"Three hundred Erodon pearls," he mumbles, obviously annoyed. "You males are hard negotiators."

I shrug, not sure how he came to the conclusion than I am male. But I won't bother explaining that I am a girl.

"If I don't defend my own interests, nobody will."

The Ching groans some kind of assent and starts counting the pearls onto my hand, one by one, so that I can count them too. As my hand is too small, I place them in my pockets every time that he finishes counting fifty. He tries to take advantage of that, and tries to stop the count when I pocket the pearls for the fifth time.

"Still fifty missing," I remind him.

The ET does not answer, but hands me over the remaining fifty pearls. I pouch them and then seal carefully my pockets; I would not like to lose this money while I crawl through the tunnel.

Then the boss says something, and they surround me. I suppose that it is to make sure that I do not flee with what they have paid me. But to my surprise they suddenly turn their backs on me, looking all outwards while their chief opens the air duct panel. Then, between him and another alien they grab me by the waist and lift me, helping me to enter the duct. Moments later I am inside. It's pretty narrow, I can hardly move. I can't even get on hands and knees. It does not help either that it is triangular; I can't reach the ceiling.

I am barely totally inside when one of the aliens replaces the panel. Turning my head, I see that they're fixing it from the outside. I can no longer turn back; there's no way out here anymore.

So I start to advance. It's dark, but luckily I still wear the clothes I had on my ship, and my belt has a few gadgets that are essential for a starship crew member. I press it briefly, and it starts emitting light.

As I am on my belly it does not exactly provide a lot of light, but the reflection from my back allows me to see where I'm heading to.

Advancing through the narrow duct, after some sixteen feet or so I find a fork in the duct. Shit. Wasn't there supposed to be just one exit? Which direction should I take? I feel that there is an air current coming in from the right. Perhaps there is a fan there, which could be dangerous. On the other side, the door that they told me to open should be on the left, so I better take the left duct.

I must crawl another forty feet before I reach a grating. It's not easy at all to move through the duct, I estimate that it has taken me half an hour to get here. I push the grid, but it does not move. I shove with all my force, to no avail. Well. That is unexpected. And I am not strong enough to tear it from its place.

I blindly search in my belt, as I don't have even space to see what I am doing. During the trip that ended so dreadfully, I assisted in the machine room. After the accident I also had to do a lot of repairs. I repaired a lot of equipment, and for convenience I carried around some small tools in the belt pockets. Including... yes, there it is. A mini-blowtorch and drill for small parts.

On inspection, the grating proves to be triangular, like the duct. It looks as it has only three attaching points. I apply the blowtorch to one of them and press the perforating button.

It takes me a good fright and I almost get burned. The panel seems to explode and bursts in a thousand burning pieces. I don't know what kind of material this is, but it does not resist the blowtorch very well. I clean my face of dirt and particles; I have been pretty lucky that nothing has gotten into my eyes, but I closed them instinctively. However, by the smell it seems that I have burned part of my hair.

Leaning out of the gap in the wall, I inspect the room. It is dark, but I unfasten my belt and look around using its light. It looks like a warehouse. Big boxes and machinery that I am unable to identify. Then I look down.

I am seven feet high and I can't turn in the duct. I'll have to jump, and I risk breaking my neck, as I will have to jump head first. Below there is nothing that can soften my fall, only a box that by the looks of it might actually be harder than the floor.

After thinking about it for a few seconds, I drop the belt to the floor, so as to have some light. Then I realize that I still hold the blowtorch in my hand; but I cannot put it away. Hoping that it does not break, I also drop it. With a lot of effort I turn around, until I am on my back inside the duct. I lift my hands and slowly start pushing my body outwards, holding to the border of the duct.

I manage to get out my butt, and I have not yet fallen down. But that is because I am holding myself by pushing one of the legs against the ceiling of the duct. I take out the other leg, but it's pretty evident that my acrobatics are nearly finished. I am losing my grip on the edge and the leg in the duct is starting to slip out. Breathing in deeply, I try to get it out.

Immediately I lose my grip and fall down. My extended leg rebounds against the box below and I drop backwards. Then I slam against the floor so hard that I remain there, hurt and gasping heavily. Wailing, I stay on the floor for over a minute, trying to recover. Then I stand up slowly, massaging my aching back, trying to ignore the protests of my body. At least I did not kill myself.

I pick up my belt and after a short search I find also the blowtorch beside a big chest. It's on standing up and seeing the content of the chest that I realize how I have been cheated.

This is not a warehouse. It's a safe or something like that. I've seen these materials in the bank. These are precious minerals; they are probably worth a lot of money. That's why the aliens were willing to pay me whatever I asked. I wasn't helping them to open their own warehouse; I was helping them to rob it.

The impression overwhelms me, and I have to sit down. What will I do now? I am now a criminal. I don't know what they do here with the criminals, but it's unlikely to be much good. And here they don't even know that I am a minor. Or they don't care. For all those ET, I'm an adult. And they'll punish me as such.

I look at the hole in the wall through which I entered. Could I get again inside? Get out by where I got in? I climb on the box that there is below, and try it out. No, no way. It doesn't work. I can lift myself to the entrance of the tunnel, but I can't enter, there is nothing I can hold to.

Getting down again, I sit on the box, thinking furiously. How could I have been so innocent? How could I let them fool me like that? I was so anxious that I believed anything. And if previously I was desperate, now it's much worse. Before this, I just wanted to survive. Now I'll be a fugitive, chased by all police forces of this space station.

Assuming that they don't simply execute the criminals, I might spend years in jail. Or worse.

I inspect the room. No, there is no exit except the door. And the Chings are waiting outside for me. Not only will they take away what they have paid me; it's also likely that they will kill me, as I know that they have tried to rob here. They won't want any witnesses, and I have already seen that life is not worth much around here. How is it possible that I have gotten into this mess?

I breathe in and out, trying to calm down. OK. I'm really in the shitter. Now I have to get out of this mess. I must think about a way to escape.

Let's see. The only exit is the door. Where the Chings will be. Will they shoot me as soon as I open the door? I don't think they will do that if their weapons make noise, though I have no clue about whether that is so. Probably they'll try to grab me, get me back inside and cut my throat once the door is closed again. They might even invite me to stay; knowing how stupid I am, they will probably think that I don't suspect anything. Of course they don't know that I am now sure that they're going to kill me.

Could I use a weapon against them? No, I don't have any weapons and I am so small that if I grab something to hit them, they will just laugh. It's impossible that I can hurt them. I am not strong enough.

The blowtorch? No, it hardly reaches six inches. Perhaps I can hurt one, but not more. I could short-circuit the blowtorch battery, letting it explode, thus making a bomb. But I have no delay fuse, and if I hold it in my hands when it explodes, I'll be the first victim. It's not a big solace that I'll kill them too.

I get up, puffing. Well, I'll have to use the oldest trick in the world. In my solar system, I mean. With some luck, they won't know it on this side of the galaxy.

Once decided, I stand beside the door and breathe in, trying to give me some encouragement. Then I smile, though probably they don't know what a smile is in the first place. I push the contact that opens the door.

Obviously, they were waiting for me. They are all lurking there.

"What took you so long?" mumbles the boss, entering quickly.

"Well, it was pretty difficult," I respond happily. "Come in, come in. Your merchandise is waiting."

They enter all together. But there is one who stops in the door frame, as I feared that they would do. So as to prevent me from escaping. Their chief inspects briefly the interior and then turns towards me, extending his arm to grab me. I pretend not to notice it and point outwards, feigning surprise.

"Who are those?"

The oldest trick in my solar system is a total novelty here, as all turn to look. I take my opportunity and scurry away below the legs of the one at the door. Then I start running.

The wall explodes beside me. To be precise, just behind me. I stumble and duck my head. Those bastards are shooting at me! I run as fast as I can. Another two shots fail; I hear them scream behind me. Then I turn a corner and hit something.

"What's happening?"

There is a huge alien in front of me. As big as a rhinoceros standing up, and not too different from one. I see that it wears the insignia of the station. Perhaps it's a crew member, but by its looks, it must be a guard. I point hurriedly backwards.

"There are some Chings robbing a warehouse! I saw them, and they tried to kill me!"

It roars something into an intercom and takes from its back the biggest weapon that I have ever seen. It looks like a monstrous cannon. The corridor thunders with its steps when it charges in the direction I came from. Instants later, I start hearing explosions. Given that everybody is busy now, I make damn sure that I disappear from the scene.

I use an elevator to descend four floors, walk for a long time, then descend five more levels. After that, I walk for about half an hour until I am sure that I am staying clear of this event. Then I descend another two floors and look for a bank. I don't want to carry three hundred pearls with me; I risk being robbed, as it's pretty evident that law and order is not something that is in high regard here. But, just in case, I keep fifty when I deposit the rest into my account. Who knows, I might have to flee again, then perhaps needing some cash.

By the time I finish, the balance of my account is very satisfactory, even though I'm quite sure that the bank is applying me a very disadvantageous exchange rate. But now I have almost sixty-three thousand credit units. This will allow me to survive for quite some time, while I find a job. I take the opportunity to cancel the initial credit with the associated interest; obviously I don't want to risk being devoured if at a certain moment I want to leave the station, or just because the bank wants its money back. After everything that I have experienced so far, I don't trust any of these ETs.

Then I descend two more levels and seek accommodation. To my knowledge, there are no hotels here, but when I ask one of the aliens, it points me to an area of rental bedrooms. I place my hand on the door of one which has the vacancy sign. Immediately I see that my own image informs me how much my credit account has been charged and the door opens. It is exactly what I was looking for. A small room, not too expensive, with an automatic kitchen and drink dispenser. I'm unable to identify half of the furniture, but there is an elevated platform that looks like a bed and three cubes that I suppose are chairs or perhaps a table. I imagine that it won't be a problem to sit on those. On one side there is a device that I have already seen in the corridors: a kind of holoprojector. In the corner there is a white square which, by its aspect, looks as if it is the toilet.

It takes me a while to find out how the kitchen works, but it proves to be quite easy. You only need to think what you want, and the machine will prepare it for you after charging your account. It spews out some brown slush-looking nosh; apparently I'm not exactly good with imaging food. I nip it carefully; it tastes weird, but it does not seem poisonous, so I eat it with disgust. Actually, I don't have much choice, as I'm very hungry. At least the water tastes like water, colorless, odorless and insipid. It allows me to swallow whatever I am eating.

While I eat, I manage to switch on the holoprojector with the news. It isn't difficult: I simply think that it is on. That the machinery can read your mind is really awesome, because otherwise I don't know how I'd handle some alien controls.

I don't know whether this device has some kind of entertainment program. In any case, even if it has one, probably I won't understand it anyhow, so my interest in that kind of program is nil. But the machine has perceived in my mind what I want to know, and shows me the news item that I am looking for. I don't have a clue whether they are transmitting this in real time or it's something that they broadcasted some time ago and the device repeats because it's what I am interested in. In any case, they are reporting a robbery attempt to a warehouse. A security agent was killed, as well as four of the robbers.

The two remaining ones have been dumped unceremoniously into a mass converter. All the bandits are dead. The case is closed, though nobody understands how they could enter or why they opened an air duct that was obviously far too small for them to be able to escape.

I switch the holoprojector off and breathe out, relieved. I am sorry about the guard, but now that the Chings are dead, no one should know my role in all this business. Apart from the guard, nobody saw me, and I am very far from the crime scene. However, I'll stay hidden in this room for a couple of days, until everything calms down. Just in case. Perhaps my first illegal act was very lucrative, but after seeing how they treat the criminals here, I think it's better to stay on the correct side of the law.

I lay down on what seems to be a bed. It's really huge for me, though pretty hard, but as soon as I think that, it softens and adjusts itself to my body. The lights go off and I close my eyes. Tomorrow will be another day. I'll find a way to recover my ship. To return with mom. I don't know how I'll do it, but I plan to survive. It does not matter that I'm on a space station occupied by thousands of aliens. On Earth they'd say that finding them is the greatest event in the history of mankind. But honestly, I don't care a rat's ass. With that thought I fall asleep, far, very far away from my home.

The Krogan's nest

Even though it is fifteen thousand light-years from home, the bar is surprisingly familiar, very similar to the photos that grandpa showed me of the one he had on Earth, before emigrating to Mars. It is paneled with something that looks like wood (which it isn't, I checked), tables of the same material, benches instead of chairs, and a bar around which the customers not sitting at the tables crowd. But the patrons of this extravagant place don't look like anything that my granddad might have ever seen in his bar.

I suppose that if I had met them only one month ago, they would have been the main characters of my nightmares. Well, to be honest, they *were* the main characters for a couple of days, until I got used to them. There are insects, mammals, centipedes, reptiles, some mollusks and at least a dozen of species that I am unable to classify, despite my doctorate in exobiology. There is even one or two that I could swear that are plants, and one looks as if it is a mineral. An incredible variety of aliens, when just weeks ago I was convinced that aliens did not exist.

Almost all of them are much bigger than I am, though that is not so strange. With eleven years, I am just four feet and eleven inches tall. In the gloom of this bar, only illuminated by the changing lights of the counter, they're even more bizarre than outside, in the rest of this space station. It's the mother of all space stations, the size of a small moon. *Meeting Point,* it is called, for it is located at the center of one of the biggest trade routes on this side of the galaxy.

"Two Lamia juices for table seven. Try not to trip over, the juice is corrosive."

The bar owner descends the drinks to the lower shelf, as I don't reach the counter. I take the bowls with care and place them on a tray, which locks them in place. The boss is already taking care of the following order, grabbing another bottle while shaking a cocktail with two of his six arms. It's really weird that with the extremely advanced technology that they have here, a bar works almost like one on Mars or on Earth. And that includes that they have a waitress to serve the drinks. That is, me.

I approach the counter, and this recognizes me as a staff member; it seems to melt, opening a gap through which I can pass. That's another thing I can't get accustomed to. Why can't they have a simple door? Evading the customers, I approach table seven.

Oh, oh... I know that species. A few days ago I got badly burned simply by brushing past them. It's better not to touch them. I make a small detour around table eight, so as to approach from the side of the table that they don't occupy; the three feet of these weirdies are as dangerous as the rest of their body. I place the drinks on top of the table, obviously on my toes, so as to see what I am doing.

"Two Lamia juices," I say in Common. "Request. Perform payment."

I pay attention and verify that they have placed their hands —well, in reality a three-fingered extremity— on the table, so as to confirm the payment. If a customer leaves without paying, Hermia will deduce it from my salary, and I don't earn that much as being able to afford it.

To be honest, I earn very little, not much more than what I need to pay for the lodging where to rest after some exhausting thirteen hour work shifts. The benefits include that I can eat as much as I want, though it did cost me a serious looseness to identify the food that I can eat. I am also allowed to drink whatever I want, provided I don't get drunk. My boss does not understand that I only drink water, but he does not comprehend either that I'm a little girl. As far as I know, there are no kids in this station; for him and all other ETs, I'm an adult. Of the Gal species, or something like that. I told him I was a girl, and the misunderstanding got too complicated to explain. Not that it matters much; after all, I'm the only human being in this part of the galaxy.

"Gal!" they call from one table away. "We want Nes't with rodent dressing!"

I look towards the table, to the aliens that have called me. Shit! Those are the Rokuz that stole my ship. Yes, it was damaged after the accident that killed my father and brought me here, but at least it was the closest thing I had from Earth. The only thing tying me to my home. And these cardboard pigs took it away from me by means of a legal trick.

"Immediately," I mumble while returning to the counter, wishing I could find the equivalent of rat poison as the perfect sauce for their Nes't. Though that food must be something quite similar, by the looks of it. I did not dare tasting it.

"Nes't with rodent dressing for six, table eleven," I report to the kitchen through my intercom while I filter myself again through the counter.

"Affirmative," reports the synthetic voice of the auto-chef. "Two nanocycles."

I step on what looks like a skateboard behind the counter, and the plank immediately lifts me until my breast is at the same height as the upper side of the counter. In reality, it's a kind of stair, but because of its shape it reminds me of a skateboard. It took me a while to learn how to control it with my mind, but now I move it instinctively. Collecting empty bowls from the counter, I start placing them in what I suppose is the equivalent of a dishwasher. At least I don't have to clean the dishes. And, when it finishes, the glasses move by themselves to the shelves. I don't have a clue how they do it; to me, they look like ordinary glass. But I won't complain, since that saves me a lot of work.

"Tranel poison," states suddenly my boss, leaving a recipient the size of a bucket in front of me. "Table twenty-four."

I stare at the huge bowl. My manager told me this is the strongest drink that there is in the bar. And there is a customer that is going to drink a whole bucket?

"But who is going to drink this?"

He gestures towards the end of the room, where a hulk is seated beside the most solid table we have. The beast does not seem exactly reassuring. It's huge, some ten feet, and it looks as if it is armored. I'd say it's a reptile. It reminds me a little bit of the dinosaurs that we studied at school. But there is no doubt that it is biped. It has paws with four claws.

"It's a Krogan," informs me Hermia. "Careful with him. You better don't displease him."

Krogan? I recall that prehistoric game that Sparks was always playing. *Mass effect*, I believe it was called. It had an alien species that was called like this, not all too different from the beast I am watching. Did the game designers see this animal? Did they dream of it?

Telepathy? If so, I must be very careful. Those aliens in the game were fearsome, and this one looks very much like it.

"Come on, Gal!" The Arnian is getting irritated, which is not good news. "I don't pay you to admire the clients! Move you short legs!"

I sigh, grab the bucket and let my skateboard descend. Filtering myself again through the counter, I almost hit a patron that is approaching. Luckily, he's a quadruped and pretty tall, so in the semidarkness I manage to sneak away between his legs without anybody noticing. Hermia would not appreciate it that I hit a client; possibly he would fire me, and I need the job to survive.

I am panting by the time that I reach table twenty-four. I must be carrying about three gallons of liquid, and I only weigh ninety-nine pounds. So in reality, I'm carrying more than one fourth of my weight. It takes me a lot of effort to lift it and place it on the table.

"Tranel poison," I report. "Request. Perform payment."

He must be very thirsty, because that monster ignores me totally. Grabbing the bowl, he starts drinking. I stare at him, suddenly terrified. That particular drink is expensive. If they deduce that amount from my salary, tonight I will have to sleep in the station's corridors, at the mercy of any assailant. I have been here only for two weeks, but I know those things happen. There was more than one corpse in the corridors. Though I have some money stashed away, I already suffered sufficient hunger and thirst so as not to spend my money on lodging instead of food.

"Perform the payment!" I scream, grabbing his arm.

The beast is so strong that the fact that I hang myself from his arm does not prevent him to continue drinking. But then he seems to notice my presence. He snarls, leaves the drink on the table and stands up. It's a huge mountain rising over me.

"What do you want, you lousy little insect?" he bellows.

One week ago, I would have run away, scared to death. But by now I have gotten used to all kinds of aliens. And it scares me even more to spend one night in the corridors. Law and order do not seem to be the rule here.

"You have to pay before drinking," I press him.

The beast shoves me aside, derisively. I imagine that for him it's just a little push, but he's so strong and I am so small at his side that he actually throws me back, knocking me down. Half of the bar starts laughing, but I'm furious when I get up. Actually, I am so furious that

I jump forward, and with my best martial arts jump I kick him between both legs, putting all my force behind it. It's well known that men have a very sensitive spot there. So do many aliens. I hope this beast has it too.

The tremendous bellow shakes me. Yes, I must have hurt him. And now he's furious. He drops on four feet, opens the mouth and releases a long roar that almost leaves me deaf. But I can't move, my fury has been replaced by a sudden fear and I am paralyzed while watching the huge cavern of sharp teeth at only inches from my face.

Then he straightens, and his paws close around me, holding my arms, lifting me as if I was weightless, bringing me to his mouth. Suddenly I know what he is going to do: He is going to bite my head off. Or perhaps he is going to cut me in half; his mouth is big enough for that. But it is obvious that I am going to die.

I don't know why I do it. I am scared to death, but I know that my pleas are not going to appease this monster. As I know that I am going to die, I will not give it the satisfaction to hear me beg. I can't move, with him holding me, so I also roar, as loud as I can, while those big teeth approach my head.

To my amazement, the movement stops. The Krogan lifts me, until my eyes are at the same height as his. He tilts his head. I have the feeling that somehow I have surprised him. Then I show him my teeth, and roar again. Beside the bellow he gave, it must be like the mewing of a kitten.

He tilts the head again, this time to the other side. While he looks at me, I bare again my teeth, so that he can see that I don't fear him. The alien tilts again his head. Then he straightens and leans backwards. He then starts emitting some dry sounds, while his body shakes without control.

"Ke, ke, ke, ke..."

It looks like as if he's coughing. He leaves me carefully on the floor and releases me. Then he leans back, sitting on the floor and hits the knee with the right paw. With the other one he hits a table, which totally collapses, suddenly converted into splinters. And in the meantime, he continues coughing.

"Ke, ke, ke, ke..."

I look around. The bar is totally empty; it pretty looks as if everybody left in a hurry. A furious Krogan must be sufficiently dangerous so that all customers have decided to get the hell out of the bar. I look towards the exit. Will I reach it on time if I start running, now that it looks as if he has a seizure? No, there is not a chance. But I'll have to risk it.

He must have read my mind, because suddenly a seven inch claw is placed against my throat, his face approaching mine. I show him my teeth again, though I am scared shitless. Then he starts coughing again.

"You are very funny, little one," he snaps at me in Common, and I realize that this coughing is his way of laughing. "But you have honor. I like it. Few species have honor. I'll invite you for a drink before our duel."

"Duel?" I ask weakly, trying to control the shake of my voice.

"You have defied me," he explains. "We have to fight." Suddenly he emits a low growl, and his eyes become small slits. "Assuming you have honor."

Suddenly I get it. A roaring in the face is a challenge for the Krogans. He was going to kill me as casually as one swats a fly, but when I defied him I rose to his level. But if I refuse to fight, I will be a fly once more. A fly that he will swat without any further thought.

"I will kill you for doubting my honor!" I shout, trying to muster the little courage that I do not have. "I will crush you! I will rip you apart!"

He starts laughing again. I assume it must be very funny when a dwarf half your height challenges you, but it's not funny from my point of view. Because I am the dwarf.

"Ke, ke, ke, ke... I like you, little one. You will fight with honor, and it will be an honor to kill you. Come, let's have a drink."

He takes me by the arm and brings me to the counter. Unfortunately, it's well over my head. The Krogan tilts his head when he notices the problem, but then he picks me up carefully and sits me on the counter. He reaches behind the counter and takes a bottle, or something similar. And two glasses. Bucket sized.

"I can't drink there," I protest. "It's too big for me."

It stares at me and tilts the head again. It must be a gesture of surprise or curiosity. Then he shakes his head, half a nod, half denial.

"I understand. The drink must be proportional. I would have an illegitimate advantage if I gave you a disproportionate amount. There is no honor in that."

The monster reaches again towards the back side of the counter and picks up another glass. This one is much smaller, about half a pint. He then takes the bottle and fills both glasses. As I have been doing since I work here, I wonder how the hell it is possible that so much liquid can come out of a bottle that appears to hold only half a gallon at the most. I don't understand the alien technology.

The Krogan then presents me his fist.

"I am Groar," he introduces himself. "From the K'Raugh clan. Thus you will know the name of your victor before you die."

Closing my fist, I hit his with mine. Some species seem to greet each other this way.

"I am Tanit," I respond, decided not to let him intimidate me. "From the human clan. Fight well, and I will remember you after you die."

He laughs again. Handing me my glass, he takes his and raises it in a salute.

"To a bloody fight!"

"And may the best win!" I toast, knowing that I will not even last the first round.

He brings the bucket to his lips and starts drinking. I look at the blue half-fluorescent liquid and hesitate. What if it is poisonous? Then I sigh. In any case I won't last more than a few minutes; even if I try to flee, this brute will be able to grab me and tear me apart. Perhaps it's better if this is poison and I let him win his fight by abandonment.

I bring the glass to my lips and sip it. Now, that isn't bad. No, it's not bad at all. I see that the other is finishing his bucket, and I also empty my glass with a long drink.

"Aaaah!" says Groar, leaving the huge bowl on the counter. "A real drink for warriors! Not what they drink here, which is like Rocana pee. Another drink?"

I nod. While we drink, I'll stay alive.

"Of course."

He looks again at me, head tilted. I have the feeling that somehow I have impressed him.

"I like that," he praises, while refilling the glasses. "Never saw anybody who was not a Krogan drinking more than one glass of Tranel poison without falling down like a block. I like you, little one. I'll regret it when you're dead."

Nobody has resisted more than one drink? I thought this would be alcohol, or something similar, but it feels like a soft drink. Perhaps my metabolism is so different that it doesn't have any effect on me.

Suddenly I get inspired. It's a mad idea, but it could save me. What if I can get him drunk? There is no way that I can reach the door without him grabbing me first; however, if this potion makes him drunk and does not affect me, perhaps I can leave him KO and escape. Let's at least try it.

"Don't regret it," I boast, taking my glass. "Because it's you who will die today, I intend to continue living for many cycles. But I will also regret your death. I'm starting to like you too. So I'll make sure you suffer as little as possible when I kill you."

He roars with laughter.

"Let's toast to that."

We drink again, but halfway he lowers the bucket that he uses as a glass.

"I'll let you choose the weapon," he offers generously.

I have never used a weapon in my life, but how do I explain that? This brute is a kind of warrior, and probably he can't conceive that somebody does not want to kill somebody else.

"I don't have any weapons. You'll have to loan me one."

Again he tilts his head, obviously surprised.

"How is it possible that a warrior walks around unarmed?"

I leave my glass on the table, ready to sprint off if he decides that I am again a fly that he must squat.

"I am not a warrior. I am a girl.

"A Gal?"

"Girl," I correct him. Then I realize that I've used a human word. "A young female."

He tilts the head to the left. Then to the right. He narrows his eyes.

"A female?"

"Yes."

The beast grunts something. It looks as if he's not happy.

"There is not so much honor in fighting a female. Are you gravid?"

Gravid? Ah, he means pregnant. I shake my head.

"No. I'm not old enough for that."

Again he makes that strange movement halfway between assent and denial.

"That's good. It's not honorable to kill a pregnant female."

Shit. I really messed up. If I had said that I was pregnant, perhaps he would have pardoned me. Despite being a brute, apparently there are things that he does not consider ethical. Then he tilts again his head, much more that the other times.

"You say that you are not old enough to be pregnant?"

I shrug.

"I am only eleven years old." I make a quick calculation. "Five cycles."

He stares at me.

"And how much is that exactly? At what age do your females have their cubs?

"Eh..." I feel that I am blushing. "Usually they marry from eighteen years onwards. Eight cycles."

The big brute stares at me for so long that I start getting nervous. Then he grunts something and approaches his face, grinding his teeth. It's a very unpleasant and disturbing sound.

"You are a puppy!"

What the hell do I answer to that? He doesn't seem to like puppies. For one moment things seemed to go well, but this is getting worse by the minute. I show him my bare teeth and growl, a deep and sustained growl. It's the only thing I can think of.

"I am old enough to fight with you and kill you."

He snarls at me. But his snarl is far more dangerous than mine.

"There is no honor in killing a cub. But you have attacked me. And then you have defied me."

Well, he's at least talking and does not seem as decided to kill me. It even looks as if he is looking for an excuse not to do it. Perhaps I might live for another day.

"You pushed me. My honor does not allow me to be pushed around. You were the one who defied me."

He tilts his head again. It must be a typical gesture of his species. Then he snarls at me. I snarl back. If I have understood it correctly, he's now probing to see whether we can be friends. I really hope so.

"I like you," he grunts. "But a challenge cannot be undone without blood. I will have to kill you, even if there is no honor in it. Unless..." That big fellow starts pondering for a few instants. "Do you have a male of your own?"

What the...? Perhaps he wants to fight with my supposed husband. I feel that I am as red as a tomato. He notices my color and tilts again his head with interest.

"No."

The dinosaur stares at me, approaching his eyes until they're only inches away from mine. I respond to his stare, trying not to blink, without knowing what he pretends. To my surprise, he has blue eyes, with yellow pupils. Really strange eyes. Then he places his right paw on my shoulder, takes my left arm and places it on what would be his right shoulder if he had those.

"Tanit," he orders. "Repeat what I say."

The beast pronounces some growls, and I repeat them as faithfully as I can. He speaks some more words in his language and I also repeat them, probably with a horrible accent. From the corner of my eye I see that the aliens are again entering the bar, with caution, but I continue saying whatever Groar is dictating me. Then he releases me and takes some kind of necklace from his neck, hanging it around mine. He has to give it four laps, so big is it for me.

"Now," he explains in Common, "you belong to the K'Raugh clan. I'll be your male, and you are my female. We no longer have to fight."

The patrons of the bar shout something, but I am shocked as soon as I understand what has just happened. I am eleven years old. But I have just married an alien that is ten feet tall. And I thought I was in trouble!

"Waiter!" bellows Groar. "Drinks for everybody! My female and I invite! But no Rocana pee! If somebody wants to drink, he must drink like a warrior!"

My boss comes back and hurries to serve the drinks. I take my glass and drink it in one go. They refill it while my husband finishes the bucket that he's drinking. He is starting to wobble; probably he's already half drunk.

I don't feel very well either. Actually, I'm feeling very light and slightly dizzy. This blue potion that we are drinking is not as harmless as I thought and is starting to affect me. And if that were not enough, I am married to a huge monster. Feeling that everything starts turning around me, suddenly everything becomes dark.

I awake in half-light, with a horrible headache. I am stark naked, resting on my back on a kind of bed that feels like fur. Something at my side breathes heavily, something that smells like a mixture of cinnamon and sweat. Then I remember what has happened and I sit down as quickly as I can, crawling back until my rear hits something. At my side lays that Krogan, Groar. He looks even huger than when he was standing, perhaps because he was bending at that time. Now he's staring at me.

"We have not copulated," he informs me.

Copulated? I stumble with that word. Then I get it. He's saying that we have not had sex. As if I wanted to make love with him! I am eleven years old; I am certainly not old enough to have sex with a man, much less with a Krogan. What the heck, I did not even have my first menstrual cycle yet! I swallow hard. Perhaps I did not know it, but I've married this monster. I suppose that gives him the right to... well, to copulate with me. Even if I am terrified. Because I'm sure it's going to hurt. It's going to hurt a lot.

"Are... are you going to do it now?" I ask with a shaky voice.

He moves the blanket covering him, and I see what in a man would be a penis. Yes, I know what a penis is, and what you use it for. But this one is really huge, like half my arm. I have to swallow at this terrible vision. If he tries to fuck me with that, he'll rip me apart.

"You see? I would kill you if I did," he answers. "You are not big enough, you're just a cub. But you're my female. We will do it when you have the adequate age for your species. When you're eighteen years. I can wait."

I feel a tremendous relief. At least he's not going to rape me. That is, for now. Unfortunately, I'm married to him. I wonder if they know here what a divorce is.

Groar then sits on the bed, subsequently standing up. He's towering over me. Staring. Then he snarls at me.

"Get up!"

I do as he orders, unsure of what he pretends. And suddenly I am rolling over the floor, trying to recover from a playful jab he has given me. He laughs, with that laugh that sounds like a cough.

"Ke, ke, ke, ke... And you wanted to fight with me? You will have to learn a lot, little Gal. But a Krogan female is not a harmless toy. And you're now a K'Raugh."

He tries to hit me again, and I scurry away under his arm, running towards the door. I'll escape, even if I have to do it naked. But the door is closed. I turn around. Groar is slowly advancing in my direction. He tries to grab me. I slip away again, but this time I escape between his legs. I've had martial arts as part of my training on Mars, and I know perfectly well what to do. Lifting my head when I'm below him, I use it to hit his testicles, which are each bigger than my two fists together. He roars of pain and then grabs me by the neck before I can escape again. Now I'm sure that all is lost. It's obvious that he's going to kill me this time.

To my great surprise, he releases me and bends forward, until his eyes are at my height. He opens the mouth in what almost looks like a smile. Though in such a monster it is really terrifying.

"Ke, ke, ke, ke... Better, Gal. When you do not have the strength, you have to use your agility. And you must hit the most vulnerable places. But you have still a lot to learn. Let's go to the weapons room."

I blink, amazed, while he opens the door to another room. He does not seem to be annoyed, it almost looks as if he appreciates that I managed to hurt him. Krogans are really weird. Carefully, I enter the room.

It's a kind of gym, with a lot of weapons on the sides. He points to something similar to a bench, making me sit down. Then he takes a staff from the wall and stands in the middle of the room. One instant later, dozens of beasts throw themselves at him. It takes him less a minute to dispatch them, either by breaking their necks or perforating them outright with his staff. He isn't even sweating, assuming this monster can sweat. Neither does he pant. This, for a Krogan, must not be even a warm-up.

"Now you," he orders, throwing the staff at me. "Something easy."

So he wasn't attacking me. Just the opposite, he is trying to train me so that I can defend myself. I take the staff, hesitating, and go to the center of the room. The dead beasts get up and return to their original positions. I suppose they must be some kind of robots. Then they attack me.

I don't even last a minute. I've slashed two of the robots, but then the others have brought me down. Several of them have bitten me, some very painful bites. And one of them has its teeth around my throat. I thought that the harsh colonist training that I had on Mars before starting my journey would have prepared me for such a situation, but apparently it wasn't sufficiently exacting. If these animals were real, I would be dead.

Groar does not laugh, which is something that I really appreciate. But by the way the warrior growls, he seems disappointed.

"We will have to work very hard, little Gal. Even if you're just a cub, you need to be able to defend yourself. You're now a Krogan."

There is nobody better that a Krogan in both defense and attack. Krogans are professional warriors; they are the result of millennia of evolution under desperate circumstances where any other species would have simply disappeared. But as masters, they are ruthless. I have no option, I must learn how to fight; I simply can't refuse when an alien ten feet tall and over four feet wide demands it and I'm locked up with him. When he only gives me food if I meet his mandatory program. We train every single day, all the time. It is true that I am not very strong, but I am very quick, and Groar teaches me to take advantage of my agility. He teaches me combat techniques, he shows me the weak points of the different species and known beasts, and he makes me repeat it over and over, until I react instinctively at everything he throws at me. Every day I end up exhausted, aching of the blows or bites that I have not been able to avoid, but the Krogan is undeterred by my protests.

"You won't go out until you're able to defend yourself properly," he warns me. "Even a cub must be able to defend itself. And my female must be able to fight like a K'Raugh. If you die in combat, your enemies must be able to chant about your honor and your power."

Honestly, I don't have the slightest interest in dying in combat. But how do I explain that to a creature whose only purpose in life is to fight with honor and die in an epic fight so that even his enemies recognize his valor?

He does not treat me bad, I must admit that. Initially, he rationed my food until I met the goals that he had established, but after the first days he adapted to my learning skills and I do not starve. Sometimes he hits me, but it's what a Krogan understands as a friendly blow. Soon he finds out that what for someone of his species is a simple patting hurts me quite a lot, so he makes sure to be careful. Apparently he's quite civilized for a Krogan.

Apart from that, it's very strange to be with him. Krogan habits are weird, sometimes outright disgusting. For example, we have to relieve ourselves in front of the other, while he keeps guard, as if somebody would attack us in this closed compound. Or eat back to back, so that nobody can ambush us. And he lies on top of me during the night, so as to protect me with his body. At least he does not rest on me, as he would crush me with his weight if he did. But it's a very uncanny feeling to have him above me, sleeping on his folded elbows and knees. Especially when sometimes his... thing has an erection and lays on my belly. I know that he has promised not to... well, not to copulate with me, but I am very conscious that he could rape me if he wanted to, and that I could not stop him from doing so even though I know that it would kill me.

With time, I learn a lot about the Krogans. They evolved in a high-gravity planet with a really brutal wildlife; they only survived by being even more brutal than the planet where they were born. And when they finally managed to dominate their environment, their struggle for limited resources was even more brutal than when they simply fought to survive. But they developed a sense of honor besides which the old samurai were just simple country bumpkins. A Krogan without honor is inconceivable. They will kill for their honor. They will die for it. Honor is everything for a Krogan.

Only when Groar explains me how their society works do I start to understand why he has married me. The Krogans are organized in clans, each of which is ruled by a matriarch. The Krogan females are their most valuable possession, as they are the only ones that can have the cubs who will grow into the warriors that will protect the clan. A male cannot join a clan; he grows in it. But a female can select her own clan, and the clans fight to obtain valiant and strong females that can beget valuable warriors. The females command; the warriors fight.

That's the reason why Groar took notice of me, why he has not killed me. Because I challenged him; I was even ready to fight with him despite the fact that I did not have the slightest opportunity to win. Thus, I meet all the characteristics that the Krogan admire in their females. The fact that I am human and not Krogan seems to be less important than the qualities he seems to find in me. But though in a clan I would be his superior, for Groar I am still a female cub that cannot decide by itself. He has admitted me into the clan, but I will not be allowed to have an opinion of my own until I am also a warrior. Only then will he obey me. Once I understand that, I strive to finish my training. To become a warrior means to be free.

I lose track of time. There is only this exacting training with a relentless teacher, harsher and harsher, more and more intense. I don't know how much it lasts; I am too tired to even think about that. But

I have spent weeks, perhaps months, locked in Groar's quarters when, on awakening, I see that he has his combat armor on. A Krogan awes already, when in armor he will scare anybody. It's far easier to stop an old battle tank.

"Get up, Gal," he tells me. "You're going to fight. Today is your Ragh-Ar-Khar."

I get up from bed, apprehensive. During the time that I've spent with Groar, I have learned a lot about the Krogans. And I know what the Ragh-Ar-Khar is, the passage of maturity. A test that every single young Krogan must pass before being considered an adult. A combat exam where quite a few die.

My mate —why can't they simply say husband? — points to a pile of clothes in a corner. To my surprise, those are my own clothes, but complemented with an individualized Krogan breastplate. Tailored to my person. Groar must have manufactured this armor during the last weeks while I slept, stealing time from sleep. Or perhaps a Krogan sleeps less than a human.

I dress slowly. It's a very strange feeling to be dressed; I have been naked since Groar locked me up in his quarters, I don't know where he had stored my clothes. The breastplate adjusts well to my body, but provides a strange rigidity that makes my movements slightly forced. If I am going to fight, then I have to keep that in mind. But it weighs less than what I expected; the Krogans have been perfecting their armor for millennia.

Then Groar opens the door. How many days have I dreamed of escaping? Of opening that door and running away? Only when I exit do I realize that I am in the Krogan quarter of *Meeting Point*. If I had escaped, they would have captured or killed me within minutes. And now I cannot escape either. There must be hundreds of Krogan all around me. But then... there is also the Ragh-Ar-Khar, the passage of maturity. I have been so long with a Krogan, training for this, that it is simply unimaginable that I do not participate in the Ragh-Ar-Khar. Furthermore... once I have endured the passage of maturity, I will not have to escape. I will be officially an adult. I will be free.

There is a Krogan leaning on a wall, looking distantly into the crowd of Krogans that is passing on its side. But when he sees me, he hisses, showing me his teeth. I know that gesture, and also how to respond to it. Leaning forward, as if I wanted to jump onto him, I open my arms to grab him; then I bare my teeth and snarl in a clearly defying tone.

He straightens quickly, adopting the combat position. But I see that he is looking at my breastplate, and then inspecting the necklace that I am wearing. He glimpses behind me and I know that Groar is also adopting the combat position. Then the Krogan nods, abandons the combat position and turns his head. I accept the recognition and pass on his side, on my way to the arena.

"Well done, Gal," growls Groar as soon as we turn the corner. For an instant, I feel extremely proud. My husband hardly ever does a compliment. Then I frown. Husband. Now, it's really, really weird that with eleven years I have a husband. It might be true, but how the hell will I get out of this?

The arena is a big abandoned hangar for spaceships. There are Krogans on the walkways, close to the ceiling, encouraging the cubs that are going to pass this exam. Apart from me there are eight, six males and two females, all a lot taller than me. They receive me with strange looks; I can detect that by how they tilt their heads. But they do not pay me attention for long, because three females approach us. I know what they are: The judges of the event. They will decide what we will face, and whether we have or not passed their test.

They say something in the Krogan language, but my knowledge of that idiom is not sufficient to understand it, so Groar translates it for me. It's an invocation to their gods, so that they give us the force to pass the exam. But I know the last sentence of the ritual; Groar does not need to translate it because he has already repeated it to me dozens of times.

"Fight valiantly and overcome or die with honor!"

Then Groar offers me his weapons. Actually, those are not his weapons, they are a smaller version of what he uses normally; I would be incapable of even lifting his dagger or his gun. But what he gives me is something I can handle. A shorter lance than what we use normally for training. A small knife, more adequate for me than the cumbersome thing he uses. A gun with eight explosive bullets made for the size of my hand. My husband has taken a lot of trouble to equip me.

"Listen," he whispers after handing me the weapons. "Your strength is your speed and agility. Don't allow anybody to block you in a position."

"I know," I respond. "To get blocked is to get killed."

He nods. Suddenly, I don't see him as a monster, despite his shape. He seems genuinely preoccupied about me.

"And keep away from the males. Especially at the end."

"Why?" I wonder.

"Just keep away from them."

"Why?" I ask again, but he's already leaving.

I look around. The adults are withdrawing, and the cubs are taking combat positions, scouting quickly around them, searching for the danger that they know is here somewhere. I quickly turn around, taking a mental note of the situation. Yes, I am scared to death, but I am determined to survive. The preparation that the Krogan has subjected me to makes the tough colonist training that I performed on Mars look like a mere picnic. I know that I can face almost anything.

But first I have to get away from the males. I don't know what Groar fears from them, but he seemed preoccupied. I run to the left, towards some abandoned machinery.

The screams from the walkways tell me that the spectacle has started. I hear the heavy thumps behind my back, and run with all my forces. Then, when I know that whatever is pursuing me is going to catch me, I throw myself to one side, turning on the ground, placing the shaft of my lance against the floor and lifting it towards my haunter. It's similar to what on Earth they would call a tiger.

It almost tears the weapon out of my hand, such is the force with which it charges. But it has impaled itself, drilling the lance through the throat into the brain, and when it knocks me down it is already dead. The bad news is that it has fallen on me, imprisoning me, and there is another of those beasts closing up. I hardly have the time to grab the gun from my belt and fire it an explosive bullet in the eye. That's two, I tell me while I fight to get free, looking desperately around.

Just when I manage to wriggle out from below the dead beast, two other animals prey on me. I manage to get rid of one with the gun, and grab the smaller one by the throat, preventing it to tear my jugular apart with its teeth. Its claws strike my breastplate; if I did not wear it, my guts would be spilling out by now. A leg hits my gun, making me drop it. Now I'm supposed to be unarmed, but Groar has taught me well; the fact that I don't have any weapons does not mean any longer that I am helpless. I furiously punch my fingers into its eyes, taking one out. It's disgusting, but very effective. The beast howls of pain and breaks loose, taking to flight. I grab my gun again and get up. Looking around, I pull out my lance from the corpse.

The onlookers above me are applauding or something like that; at least they do make a lot of noise. Others, further away, are pointing to the different combats that are taking place. To the left, far away, two males are fighting back to back against a huge pack of the dogs that have attacked me. Near them there is another one battling with what looks like a giant spider. To my right there is a female, back to the wall, keeping at bay four six-footed carnivores with teeth like knives which are trying to kill her. Three of those animals are on one side, dead.

I don't know why I do it. Lifting my gun, I shoot against one of the beasts that are attacking the female; it falls like thunderstruck, my marksmanship is very good. But one of those monsters turns around and charges against me.

I don't even have time to be scared, my training takes immediately over. The gun is not reliable, not against a target moving so quickly; I drop it. When the animal jumps, I simply slip sideways, plunging my lance into the body, then turning it around, spiking the lance into the throat and turning it until the animal stops moving. I look again at the female. She has finished with the two beasts that attacked her and is looking at me with curiosity, the head tilted. Then she lifts the right arm and throws the lance at me. I jump aside, cursing that daughter of... and then I hear the howl at my back. Apparently I neglected my rear for a moment, and another of those dogs with teeth like daggers has almost ambushed me. But the lance of my new friend stopped it in its tracks.

I look around, while I regain my gun and retrieve her lance, so as to return it. The combats are finishing; there are hardly any beasts alive. And then I see why Groar has warned me against the males. Two of them have appeared behind the female, and knock her down. One sits on top of her, holding her still, while the other starts to remove her breastplate. I recall what Groar told me about the Krogan females. They can choose their own clan. Except if they are defeated in battle and the male takes possession of her.

I hardly remember this when a huge paw grabs one of my arms, making me to drop the gun, then forcing me to turn towards my attacker. Another of the males has captured me, and by how it is unfastening his breastplate it is pretty evident what he is going to do. Groar was going to wait until I am eighteen years old; this one is not going to wait so long. The additional bad news is that the rape will probably also kill me.

Luckily I have been trained by a Krogan who must be a master warrior. My opponent, instead, has not been that lucky or he is so convinced that I am harmless that he takes no precautions; he should have taken note of what happened to the tigers. I draw the knife, and stick it into the paw that is holding me. He screams, suddenly alert, but the lower part of the breastplate is down and he cannot move properly; obviously I know perfectly what his weakest exposed point is. One instant later he is squirming of pain while I run towards the other female, picking my gun from the floor while I do so. These pigs are not going to achieve their purpose, not while I'm armed.

The female is immobilized, her breastplate open, with both purring with delight about what they are going to do. I have arrived there just when the biggest of them bends over her, and I kick him with all my forces from behind, between the legs. He screams, dropping on top of the female, while the other releases her and grabs for his weapons. I point my gun at him even before he is able to get hold of them.

"There is no honor in killing you," I hiss in Common, turning around him so as not to have the other two behind me. "But I'll do it with great pleasure."

Then I bend forward and I roar him in the face as loud as I can. I am challenging him. A challenge to fight until death. He retreats. Then I turn and face the two whose balls I have kicked, who are approaching me. I also roar to them. And they also back down. After all, they are mere cubs who have just passed the Ragh-Ar-Khar. They are not yet ready to fight such a little creature that not only has defeated them, but now also is challenging them to fight until death. One of them points to the tigers that I have killed, and they look wordlessly at each other. Then they bow, place their fists against their chests, and leave.

The female has stood up. When I turn towards her, she's at my side, in combat position, but she's not threatening me. As soon as they released her, she got ready to help me fight those three. Now she relaxes and stares at me. Then she raises her right arm and hits her chest with the fist. Showing her respect.

I hear a cry towards my left and see that three males are on top of the other female. Those pigs! But when I try to move forward a huge paw stops me softly.

"It's too late," the female that I saved informs me. "She now belongs to their clan. Spoils of war. As I would have been if you had not prevented it."

I turn towards her. She's not as big as Groar; she must hardly be seven feet tall. It's obvious: she's a young female, probably the equivalent of sixteen or seventeen Terran years old. But she sure is much taller than I am.

"And you would have allowed them to include them in their clan by force? After they raped you?"

She tilts her head, showing surprise.

"Why not? I would be their spoils of war. Of course I would have bred their cubs. My honor would require it."

I say a dirty word in my own language, as I don't know how to say it in Common. Despite my age, I know what rape is. It's repulsive. One of the worst imaginable criminal acts. That the Krogans consider it a legitimate way of marrying is really revolting. I am glad I kicked the balls of those two shitheads. A pity I didn't do it also with the third one.

The judges arrive, and make us signs to approach them. I see with disgust that the raped female joins her rapists; it's sickening. The three that attacked me try not to approach us too much, and when one of them does, I release a warning growl. He quickly keeps the distance. Then I realize that one of the cubs is missing. We are only eight. One has not passed the Ragh-Ar-Khar.

The judges talk first with the three rapists and the female they abused. They hand them a dagger, say some words, and the four of them leave. To my surprise, the female accompanies them without anybody saying anything about it. It must be true that she considers herself to be part of their clan.

Then the one that tried to rape me gets his license. He takes his dagger, salutes the judges and leaves, tearing a piece of his clothes to make a bandage around the paw that I stabbed. But he remains waiting at a distance, as if he was expecting something. The two others do something similar. Then the judges face the female that I have saved.

"What is your name?" they ask.

"Tara," she responds. "Born in the clan Na'v-Re."

The judges then place a hand on her forehead and sing a strange song. Surprised, I stare at them. They did not do that with the other cubs. The song ends and without any further ceremony they hand over her dagger. I can see that it is heavy, almost one and a half feet of capriciously formed steel. Deadly.

"You're no longer a Na'v-Re," they tell her. "You've earned the right to choose your own clan. Choose wisely. Choose a clan with honor."

Tara then looks at me and I know what she is thinking. She did not earn that liberty herself. I gave her that gift.

She bows to the judges and salutes them, placing the fist against her chest. Then she also leaves, while the judges inspect me. By the way that they're tilting their heads, I know that they're surprised.

"You fought well," states finally one of them in Common. "You fought with honor. You earned the liberty to choose. But you should not have interfered with Tara's fight."

"I had to do it," I respond. "There was no honor in what they were doing. Two males against one single female. Trying to copulate with her against her will. It was not an honorable fight."

They stare at me. I have the feeling that I have impressed them.

"There is honor in you, little one. What is your name?"

"Tanit."

One of them leans forward and takes the necklace from my chest, inspecting it.

"You're a K'Raugh," she states, looking at the pendant. "But not by birth. You already chose your clan."

Well, choosing... I actually did not know what I was doing in the first place. But I can't say that.

"I'm a K'Raugh," I confirm.

"And what nest have you joined?"

Nest? I have no clue what they're talking about. But then I hear Groar's voice behind me, in a tone that I suppose is respectful.

"She has created her own nest, noble ladies. She's my Art'Ana."

Art'Ana? The owner of the nest? Has he just called me by the title that the matriarch receives? I can see that the judges are surprised. They quickly talk with each other, and then the tallest asks me:

"What is the name of your nest, little one?"

I'm so surprised by what's happening that I don't know what to respond. I look at Groar, but he's watching me, expectantly.

"Martin," I finally mutter, because that's my family name.

"Maart'Ing," repeats the judge, like as if tasting the words. "The storm's hammer. A good name for a nest. An honorable name."

The other judges acknowledge that, with that weird gesture that the Krogans have, a mixture of assent and denial. I didn't even know that my family name meant something in their language. Well, at least it means something good for them. Then I realize that they are staring at me again.

"It's not very usual that a nest is created," they tell me. "It requires a lot of courage to start from scratch. And it is unheard that the nest is created by a cub that has not yet passed the Ragh-Ar-Khar and yet obtains the respect of a male to join that nest." The three of them tilt their heads, evaluating me. "Despite your size, you have honor, Tanit. You have valor. And you are not at all common. You will be a great Art'Ana that will bring greatness to her nest. That will beget great warriors."

Now, it would have been better if she'd had left out that latter part. I don't have the slightest intention to have a Krogan cub, assuming it's even possible.

They place all their paws on my forehead and sing something that I do not understand. But in my mind, I have a strange feeling, as if they were talking to me about great battles and heroic feats. I know telepathy is possible, I have a little of that gift myself. But it's not the poor telepathy that I've experienced in the past; it's as if I were contacting with their racial memory, with their history, their dreams. And I know, without any doubt, that I will never be able to abandon my nest. Not after feeling this. To be one with them. To be endowed as the Art'Ana of my own nest.

Suddenly I'm free from my daydreaming. I am in front of the three judges, with a heavy dagger in my hand, and I know it's true. I'm the matriarch of my nest. The owner of everything there is in it. And to my surprise, the three judges bow to me, and touch their chests with their fists, as a token of respect. I'm the only one that they have saluted like this.

"You have impressed them, Art'Ana," says Groar once they have left. "You impressed me. I did well in recruiting your for my clan. In joining your nest."

I turn around to look at him. He's a huge monster, ten feet tall, towering over me. Beside him, I'm insignificant. And yet he's saying that I have impressed him.

"I only fought like you taught me to."

He raises his arm and hits the chest with his fist, showing his respect.

"Anybody can fight. Even the animals. But only a real Krogan can fight with courage and honor, like you did. To intervene when honor is being damaged. Today you brought honor to your clan, Tanit. You've proved that you're really the Art'Ana of our nest."

It's the first time that he has called me by my name, until today he always called me Gal, or cub. I feel dizzy. He no longer looks like the beast that imprisoned me, that taught me how to fight. He now looks like... yes, a Krogan husband addressing the matriarch of his family.

"Am I now really the Art'Ana?"

He nods.

"Yes, you are. Command and I will obey you. I will fight for you. I will die for you."

I stare at him. By now I know sufficiently about Krogans to know that he is not lying —Krogans don't know how to lie. Our roles have changed. It's no longer I who is at his mercy. It's him who is at mine. He will do anything I ask from him. Even kill himself, if I order it. Thus is the Krogan honor.

His warning growl forces me to abandon my reverie. The Krogan that tried to rape me and the two that tried to rape Tara are approaching. I take the combat position, holding firmly the dagger that I still have in my hand. But the three Krogans open their paws, showing me their palms so as to prove that they come unarmed. I look at them, mistrustful. Knowing what they tried to do, I don't trust them at all.

"What do you want?"

"We invite you to join the clan of the Kre're, valiant warrior. There is honor in you, and you deserve to belong to a great clan. With us you can raise powerful warriors that will give honor and glory to our clan."

Shit. A marriage proposal. But what is wrong with these aliens? I'm eleven years old, and they all insist that I start having little Krogans with them.

On my side, I hear how Groar growls. It's a low and prolonged sound. It means that if they continue bothering us there will be a fight. But he's waiting for my answer before starting the hostilities. After all, I'm the Art'Ana of his nest. But what in heaven do I answer? If I'm not careful, there will be a fight. Three against one. Even though Groar is an experimented warrior and the others are novices, the forecast is not good. And I have no illusions about my own combat capability in front of three Krogans, this time I will not catch them unaware. Then I come up with the perfect answer.

"I already belong to the K'Raugh clan. Why should I abandon my clan? There is no honor in that."

They look at each other, but accept the argument. Instants later, they walk away. Groar snarls deridingly.

"Raise powerful warriors with them!" He laughs. "Ke, ke, ke, ke... They are weak, Art'Ana. You defeated them. Obviously you deserve something better."

Yeah. He means himself. What the heck am I going to do with him? Groar is not exactly a fairy tale prince. He isn't even human. But in accordance with Krogan mores, he's my husband.

"Art'Ana? You're the Art'Ana of your nest?"

I turn around at the question. It's that female that I have saved, Tara. She's leaning on her lance, head tilted, looking at me with surprise.

"Yes."

She tilts her head in the other direction. It's obvious that she's very surprised.

"What is the name of your nest?"

"Martin." I recall how the judges pronounced it and repeat it, uttering it like a Krogan. "Maart'Ing."

"An honorable name." She looks at Groar with interest. "Is he a male from your nest?"

I look at him myself. He's watching the female with obvious curiosity. She must be pretty, I imagine. At least she's young.

"The only male."

And one too much, I do not dare to say. Luckily, there is only one, I know that the Krogan nests can have up to a hundred males and another hundred females. That's the least I would need, to be in such a nest.

Tara seems to doubt. Then she carefully places her lance on the floor, in front of me, and removes the rest of the weapons from her body, placing them on top of the lance. To my surprise, she kneels, opens the arms and raises her head, presenting me her throat.

"Art'Ana, I offer you my life. Honor me by accepting me into your nest and allowing me to breed your warriors for the greater glory and honor of your clan."

Shit, shit, shit! But what the heck is wrong with these Krogan? It's the second marriage proposal in five minutes. This time by a female. Al least this one does not want to make me little Krogans, she's ready to have them herself.

I glimpse at Groar, looking for help, but it's obvious that I will not get it.

"It's your decision, Tanit. You're the Art'Ana."

I miss Mars. At least these kinds of things don't happen there. Nobody would propose there marriage to a girl my age. And even less some dinosaur-like monsters that could crush me by simply sitting on top of me. But how is it possible that I am in such a mess? I know that I have an IQ qualifying me as a genius, but for something like this it's not sufficient to be a genius. God Almighty Himself would have trouble sorting this out.

I eye both Krogans. Groar is alternating looks at the female and me. She must be attractive, I suppose, because he's looking more at her than at me. Tara, instead, remains with the head raised, offering me her throat. Suddenly I know that I can only chose between cutting her throat and accepting her offer. Krogans are like that. If I reject her, she'll be dishonored, and she'll prefer to be dead. The heavy dagger in my hand suddenly seems to be wishing for a response.

I should have let them rape her. Then she would be in another clan and I would not be in this shit. But no, I had to save her. What was I thinking about? How is it possible that I've messed up like that?

Looking at the dagger in my hand, I realize that I'm not going to use it. Perhaps a real Krogan would not hesitate in such a case, but even if I now belong to a clan, I'm not a real Krogan. I cannot commit cold-blooded murder. I am not a killer. And Tara saved my life.

I breathe in slowly, trying to calm down, and place the dagger in my belt. Mom always said that the life of an adult was complicated, and I did not believe her. But mom had no clue about how messy life can be outside of the human society. Especially when you're only eleven years old and all aliens are convinced that you're an adult.

Taking the Krogan's left paw, I place it on my right shoulder. Then I place my left at the end of her arm, where her shoulder would be if she had one. She lowers her head, looking me in the eyes. Of course she has understood it, knows that she's not going to die, that I am going to welcome her into my family.

To be honest, I don't recall the words Groar said when he asked me to repeat them. When he married me. My knowledge of the Krogan language is very deficient, and I have not the slightest idea of the ritual that we must follow. But I'm the Art'Ana. If I don't know the ritual, then I'll simply create a new one. What the heck! It's my nest, isn't it?

"Repeat this with me, Tara," I tell her in Common. "I, Tara, join the Martin nest. I will fight for it, die for it. Never shall I dishonor my nest, and I will respect and protect its members with my life. I will have my cubs in the nest, and I will educate them with honor. Thus I swear by my honor. Thus I will do until the day I die."

Well, it's not a Krogan ritual, but it's the closest I can think of. She repeats it seriously, her strange eyes locked onto mine. Breathing in again, I speak then to her:

"I, Tanit, accept you, Tara, into our nest. You will be one of us; we will fight for you, die for you. You will have our respect, you will share our honor. We will father your cubs, and we will help you to convert them into honorable warriors. Thus we swear by our honor. Thus it will be while our nest exists."

I don't know what else to do, so I lean forward and kiss her forehead. Then I step back and salute her, hitting my chest with my fist. To my surprise, she leans forward, as if she is going to kiss my feet. I look at Groar, puzzled, while Tara remains lying on the floor. He makes a motion of lifting, takes his knife from his belt and gestures as if he was going to give it to me.

OK, I got it. I help Tara to stand up. She is expecting it and stands up alone, because I certainly would not be strong enough to help her doing it. I take the dagger they gave me from my belt and offer it to her with both hands. She accepts it and offers me hers. Then she salutes me, and I salute her.

After that, she faces Groar. She bows, and then offers him the dagger that I just gave her. He takes it and exchanges it for his own. They salute each other. The warrior then turns towards me. He bows, offering me my own dagger. I exchange it for the one from Tara and we salute each other. The result is that the only one who has ended up with the same weapon is me. I suppose that it's because I'm the Art'Ana.

Then Groar laughs, bends down and hugs us. He leaves me without breath. An effusive Krogan can unwillingly break your ribs. I hope he has not done that, because they do hurt somewhat.

"We have to celebrate that!" he roars.

Yeah, I imagine we have to celebrate it. I just got married for a second time. With eleven years. At least this time I knew what I was doing. Well, I hope that Groar will pay more attention to Tara than to me from now on. I suppose that she's handsome for a Krogan, though I can't say that I share their concept of beauty. And I can assure that I will not be jealous at all if she monopolizes our common male.

Groar brings us towards the exit, but I stop suddenly when I detect something strange. Everybody is dispersing in different directions. However, there is a group of Krogans huddled together, watching something that is lying on the floor. A body. Suddenly I remember that one of the cubs did not pass the exam.

I doubt for an instant. Actually, I never knew him. But he died trying to become an adult, while I have survived. The polite thing is to go and give my condolences to his family. I barely think it when I am already walking towards them, ignoring the shout of surprise of my new family.

The Krogans turn as soon as I approach. They lean forward, menacing. They don't seem very happy. Perhaps I goofed again. Yup, I did. Krogans don't accept condolences, they consider it an insult.

"You come to despise our clan?" snarls one of them, and all pronounce the growl that precedes the challenge. No, they're not at all happy with my presence. I think furiously, luckily finding the perfect answer. I point to the dead cub.

"I come to honor him. He fought well."

The Krogans look at each other, evidently perplex. Then a female breaks through from behind; she's obviously the matriarch. Now, she's big, almost as tall as the warriors. The Krogan tilts her head while she stares. It's obvious that she does not know what to think of me. But at least they're no longer hostile.

"He was weak. He deserved to die. He did not survive the Ragh-Ar-Khar."

Actually, he was a kid. His size really is impressive to me, but he probably was the equivalent of fifteen or sixteen years old. Krogans are remorseless, but I know that at least his mother will regret his death. They also have feelings.

"He was brave. He fought with honor, died like a warrior. He honored his clan."

Now they're all staring at me. Then all warriors turn to look at the matriarch. Suddenly I realize that she's the mother of the dead cub, but that she cannot recognize him as her son because he did not pass the rite of puberty. Thus are the Krogans. Thus is their honor. She's staring at me, without blinking.

"Nobody will toast to his name."

"The K'Raugh will do it. We honor the brave."

For an endless minute we look at each other. Then she extends her fist.

"I am Ark-At, from the Trek'Naa clan, Art'Ana of the Brak nest."

I hit her fist with mine.

"I am Tanit, from the K'Raugh clan, Art'Ana of the Martin nest. Maart'Ing. What is the name of the warrior we want to honor?"

"He's my son, Brat-At."

They move aside, and I stand in front of the corpse. One of the beasts tore open his throat, and he is covered in blood. But he paid very dearly his passage to the Krogan heaven, assuming there is such a thing. There are at least six dead beasts around him, the last one still impaled in his claws. I know sufficient of the Krogan mores so as to know what to do.

"I greet you, Brak-At. You died the death of a warrior, and died with honor. We will remember your name."

I hit my chest with my right fist and hear how Groat and Tara do the same at my side. Seconds later all Krogan do the same, with a salute like thunder.

Finally, I turn and face the mother of the dead cub. She has tilted her head, with that gesture of curiosity that Krogans have, contemplating me from above. I don't know what she's thinking, but she must be asking herself how somebody of my size could survive while her son did not make it. And she must be very surprised that I went to honor a cub that was not even able to survive the Ragh-Ar-Khar. Then she lifts the fist and hits her chest with it.

"I greet you, Art'Ana of the Maart'Ing nest. You are small, but your honor is great. The K'Raugh are an honorable clan. We Trek'Naa will not forget it."

She barks an order, and the members of her clan lift her son carefully among six of them. They stand in formation and slowly they leave, lifting the corpse high between them. Honoring a fallen warrior.

"You did well," grunts Groar at my side. "He might have been a cub, but he fought with courage."

"I never saw honoring a cub," grumbles Tara. I turn towards her, somewhat annoyed about her reproach, but she's looking at me with her head tilted, clearly thoughtful. "It's not common at all. But a real leader does not do common things either." She stares at me, and then touches her chest with the fist, showing her respect. "It is true, Art'Ana. You are small, but great in honor. Today you've honored doubly your clan. I'm fortunate that you have accepted me into your nest."

And what the heck am I supposed to respond to that? I notice that I'm blushing. I am still a girl, only eleven years old. And here I have two Krogans, capable of killing me with one single claw, who recognize me as their leader and are even praising something that was a really big gaffe and ended up like a flash in the pan.

"Let's go and drink something," I mumble. "I'm thirsty."

Groar leads the way to a bar in the neighborhood. It's dark, as the Krogans like it, and it's crowded. There is no free table, so we sit at the counter. To be precise, I am the one that sits on the counter with the help of Groar; they simply lean against it.

"Tranel poison," orders my male, without asking whether we would like something else. To be honest, I had been thinking about having some water.

While the waiter serves us, I look around. There are at least fifty Krogan in the bar, and all of them are looking at us. Or to be precise, they're looking at me. I suppose it must be quite a spectacle, so small, dealing with two adult Krogan. I bare my teeth, showing that I am not afraid of them, and after noticing my necklace and the dagger in my belt they start again talking with each other. By how they look at me from time to time, I know that I must be the main topic of conversation in this bar.

"I never drank Tranel poison before," states Tara slowly, taking her glass and looking intensely at it.

"Now you're an adult," I say, taking mine. "You survived the Ragh-Ar-Khar. You may now drink the beverage of the warriors." I raise my glass. "To Brak-At, who died fighting!"

"To the valiant who died with honor!" both exclaim; they then drink their glasses in a large gulp from their bucket-sized jars. When they finish, they hurl their jars onto the floor. I empty my glass and do the same. All other Krogans look at us for an instant, and then they finish their drinks and shatter their own jars against the floor. Within an instant the whole bar floor is covered with glass-like pieces. But it's the custom. It's an insult to the memory of a warrior to drink to his honor and then use the glass for something more mundane. In less than a minute we have new jars, fully filled.

"Aaah!" breathes Groar, taking a new gulp. "A drink of the gods! Just what a warrior needs!"

"I didn't know that the Tranel poison was so strong," blurbs Tara, looking at her jar.

Our male roars with laughter.

"Look at Tanit! She swallows it as if it was water! Now, that's drinking like a real Art'Ana!"

Well, the truth is, it does not have the same effect on me as on them. Or perhaps it has retarded effects. But it is true that, comparing what they drink with our respective body masses, I am drinking much more than what they do. Of course, after the fight I am very thirsty.

"You know that it will later knock me down. Like it happened the other time."

He laughs, with his characteristic ke, ke, ke.

"And what is a warrior who cannot drink until falling down? But enough celebration. We have to welcome Tara into our nest."

I suppose that I'm looking pretty stupid. I have no clue what he's talking about. But he obviously cannot read human expressions. I think.

He pays the drinks and turns around, to leave. Tara makes a gesture as if she wanted to help me get down, but I ignore her and jump from the counter onto the floor; it's just five feet. Together we walk towards the exit, and to my surprise not one Krogan even looks at me. They have accepted me; I'm one of them.

I must admit that, on exiting, I am tempted for an instant to flee. But then I have second thoughts. Why should I? Where would I go without a ship? I am alone, fifteen thousand light-years away from my home. I have nobody, except these two. No matter how strange they might be, right now they're my only family. The only ones that will protect me and care for me in a galaxy that is stranger that I could have ever imagined. I sigh. I might have messed up big in the past, but now I have both of them.

We arrive at Groar's apartment, and after palming the entrance to open it, he tells Tara and me to place our hands on the sensor. Now it will open at our contact. I'm no longer a prisoner, or a cub that needs to be protected. After surviving the Ragh-Ar-Khar, for them I'm an adult. Even more, I'm the owner of the nest. The matriarch. I can enter and leave as I please.

Tara is looking around, evaluating her new home. I can't say whether she likes it or not; it takes me a lot of effort to understand the mood of a Krogan, though sometimes I can almost guess that of Groar. Then he approaches and carefully starts to remove my breastplate. He takes away my gun and my knife and places them on my side of the bed. Then he undresses me.

I don't resist. I've been naked in front of him for weeks, and he didn't do me anything. Apparently it's the custom that you need to be naked in the nest. Perhaps it's to show the family that there is nothing to hide.

When he finishes, he starts with Tara. I look curiously as he takes off her breastplate and then the clothes she wears under it. She's slimmer than Groar and has breasts that are almost as big as my head. That surprises me. I thought that the Krogans were reptiles, but by the looks of Tara it's obvious that they are mammals. Her sex is not too different from my own, except that instead of being soft she seems to have scales. Contrary to my fluff, she does not seem to have pubic hair. Well, she certainly does not look at all human. If I had met these two only one year ago, they would have been the main characters of my nightmares. But by now I'm cured of that kind of alien scares.

Groar undresses himself, and makes us a gesture to approach him. We make a circle, holding hands and claws, and both Krogans start singing something in their own language. It's slightly displeasing to my ears, but in some way the melody also resounds in my mind. Then Tara kneels in front of me. Even on her knees, she is taller than me. I look at Groar, looking for a hint about what to do, and he points to the female, then touching his forehead with his paws.

I suppose I must lay my hands on her, or something like that. So I raise my arms and place my hands on Tara's forehead, who has closed her eyes. Then I jump up. Groar is at my back and has placed his huge paws on my forehead. Unfortunately, he has an erection, and I notice how his... thing presses against my back.

Is he going to rape me after all? Despite his promise that we would not copulate until I am eighteen? But then a thought crosses my mind, clear as a crystal.

"No, little Gal, not yet. Your time has yet to come. But the time has come for Tara."

His paws withdraw, being replaced by others, and Groar makes me sit down, then lay on my back, and Tara's paws don't move from my forehead while I do it, nor mine from hers. I feel her thoughts, far and strange, and then comes the pleasure, a savage and brutal pleasure when Groar takes her from behind, making her his, sealing our pact with her. It's a pleasure that floods me, drowns me, and oppresses me until it draws me into the darkness.

I slowly return to life. What has happened? Sex? Not human sex, certainly. Not physical sex, since I never had any intercourse. But it's something that I will never forget.

"She's only a cub. You didn't tell me. We should have never shared the N'aga with her."

Tara's voice seems reproachful. Groar's answer is however very soft.

"She's an adult. She survived the Ragh-Ar-Khar."

"She's a Po'lai. There was never a female Po'lai."

"Now there is one."

Po'lai. I remember that title, Groar told me about it on one occasion. It's a cub that does pass the Ragh-Ar-Khar before reaching sexual maturity. The adult-that-is-not-a-adult. He is subject of pride to the clan, but he is not allowed to have intercourse, not until the matriarch of his nest decides that the moment has come.

"How old is she?"

"If she were Krogan? About five cycles."

Then Tara roars, incensed.

"Five cycles? You made me share our N'aga with a Po'lai that is only five cycles?"

"It was necessary. After all, she's the Art'Ana. She accepted you into our nest. She had to share our union. The Art'Ana *is* our union!"

"An Art'Ana that has only five cycles!"

"She passed the Ragh-Ar-Khar. You accepted her as your Art'Ana. Do you want to fight for her position?"

The Krogan roars again, this time evidently furious.

"You doubt my honor?"

"No."

"She's my Art'Ana. I accepted her. Even if she is only five cycles old. And she has honor. I will not dishonor myself or the K'Raugh clan by fighting with her. But you should not have shared our N'aga with a Po'lai that is only five cycles old!"

I sit down in our pelt bed, still somewhat bewildered. Groar and Tara are face to face, in the combat position, baring their teeth, snarling threatening at each other.

"Enough, you two."

I have understood it. I just had my first sexual experience. Well, in reality it was Tara's experience, which I must have shared telepathically. Something... incredible. But I know that I should not have had it at my age. Not when I've not even started to have my period. Something that I don't want to repeat. That I don't want to experiment again, no matter how pleasant it was. Not until I am much older.

"Art'Ana, I..."

I stop Groar's words with a gesture. When our three minds have touched, I haven't only shared the pleasure, I've also sensed the Krogan soul. Strange, ferocious. I have been Krogan like them. Still are. I know how they feel, and why. And I'm the Art'Ana. I know what it means for them.

Now, I messed up when I accepted to become Groar's female. The fact that I did not know what I was doing does not excuse it. I messed up again when I accepted Tara into our nest. That I did not know that I would have to share this mentally, that I had to share their union, is not an excuse either. The Art'Ana has to decide. She is the owner of the nest, and has literally the power of life and death over the whole family. There are no excuses. It's not a justification to say that I'm only eleven years old and that I got into something that would be too big even for an adult woman. I'm the Art'Ana.

"Tara, you're right," I say softly. "I was not prepared for your N'aga. I'm not old enough for it. I'm not sufficiently adult to experience it." I sigh. "But Groar is also right. As the Art'Ana, I had to share our union." I swallow. "If there was a mistake, it was mine. It was my decision, and there is nothing we can do about it. There is no room for reproach. We are now a nest. The three of us."

They look at each other. There is no longer defiance between them. I almost detect concern.

"You're a Po'lai," observes Tara.

"I'm also the Art'Ana."

"But you cannot copulate with Groar. Not until you have the appropriate age."

As far as I am concerned, I'd skip that part forever. Have sex with a Krogan? I can't even imagine making love with a man once I've grown up. But a Krogan? No, it can't be. There must be a solution. An alternative. But I can't say that. We're supposed to be married. Or something like that. According to their customs, this is like matrimony. That I'm human and they are Krogan does not seem to concern them very much. At least not as much as it concerns me.

"I will grow."

"But we..."

"You can copulate as much as you want. But you will not involve me. Not until the time has come."

"But if the Art'Ana cannot copulate... it is not correct that the other females do it."

I sigh. That's just what I needed. Complete sexual abstinence for them because I am not old enough to have sex. Within a week they'll be on the verge of exploding. Better to let them vent it between themselves. Perhaps they'll completely forget me.

"The females must give cubs to the nest. If the Art'Ana cannot do it, the duty of the other females is to make up for it."

Now take that! I've spoken like a real Krogan. I hope that does not mean that soon I'll have cubs running all around me. But those two are eying each other. I might not know much about Krogans, but I'd swear that those two feel a mutual attraction. When humans look like that at each other, they're longing to get into a same bed. Yes, I might be a girl, but I was not born yesterday.

Tara then sits down at my side, obviously trying to change the subject.

"Where do you come from? I never saw anybody from your species. And if you're really a Po'lai, you couldn't have arrived here by yourself."

I sigh. In fact, I'm not very surprised that she asks, though Groar never showed any interest. Of course, he only wanted to train me; the rest probably was irrelevant for him.

"Actually, I did."

The warrior also sits down, and I tell them my story. How I left from Mars with my father, stopping over at Earth to pick up the colonists, how a terrible accident in trans-lux killed the whole crew, how I had to repair my ship and leave trans-lux.

The two of them stare at me, their heads tilted. I already know that is a sign of surprise. They must be really very impressed.

"And you come from far? Because I have never seen anybody of your species."

"Neither did I," confirms Groar. "And I have visited most worlds in twenty light-cycles around us."

With a thought I command the computer to project an image of the galaxy. At the beginning, it did cost me to control things with my mind, but the apartment systems are very sophisticated and designed to adjust themselves to multiple nervous systems. I point to the Orion arm, where Earth is located. Fifteen thousand light years away from where we are.

"I come from there."

The Krogans look at each other. Even I can detect their incredulity.

"Impossible! There is no ship that can travel those distances!"

I sigh again, dismayed. That's what I feared. The Rokuz had already told me that, but the word of those cheaters that stole my ship is not exactly very reliable. But Krogans don't lie, cannot lie. If Tara and Groar say that such a ship does not exist, then it simply doesn't exist. Well, as far as they know.

"My ship did it. I don't know how, but it did."

They look again at each other. I know that now they're really impressed.

"We must see that ship."

I shrug. Now, that's going to be difficult.

"I'm sorry, but it can't be. Some Rokuz took it from me."

Both pronounce at the same time a low and menacing growl.

"They took your ship?"

I explain it. They don't say I word while I speak, but Groar stands up when I finish.

"Combat breastplates."

"You can't do anything," I protest when both he and Tara start dressing. "The dock-master told me that what they did was legal."

Then they both laugh at the same time.

"Legal? Tanit, put on your breastplate. You have a lot to learn about the Rokuz and Krogans. And how the law works here."

I get dressed and we leave the apartment, armed to the teeth. The warrior explains me what to do and I nod, suddenly full of hope. Those Rokuz might be cheaters, but we're also going to deceit them. Certainly, they're going to be very pissed off. But with two Krogans at my side, I don't care a damn if they get mad at me.

We split when we get to the docks. I continue straight, while Groar and Tara start the encirclement. But right before I arrive to the station where my ship is docked, I stumble upon the Rokuz. I identify them without the shadow of a doubt; they also recognize me.

"You're not serving drinks?" scoffs one of them. "Then bring us Nes't with rodent dressing. We're hungry."

I ignore their jibes. There is a Terran proverb saying that who laughs last laughs best. Soon it will be me who laughs.

"I come to buy my old ship back from you," I rap out.

"And how are you going to pay for it?" asks a voice from one side. I look, and there is the dock-master who helped them to take away my ship.

"With this," I explain, showing them a half-mars coin that I still had in my pocket.

They roar with laughter.

"Do you really think that we're going to exchange the ship for that trash?"

"Of course," I respond happily. "Get it!"

Then, with all my forces, I throw it into their faces. They do exactly what I was expecting them to do: they grab the coin in the air, preventing it to hit them.

"Do you really think that we'll accept that?" they mock me.

Then I laugh.

"You already did. You have taken the offered price. The ship is mine again."

They look at each other, once they realize how I've outsmarted them. Then the one with the coin throws it at me. But I am expecting it: I simply duck and it falls to the floor.

"There is no deal!" they protest. "You fooled us!"

"Back luck. You accepted the payment."

"It is so," confirms the dock-master. "You've sold the ship. It's the same as when the Gal sold it to you."

"We want to cancel the deal!"

"But I don't want to. The deal is firm. Like the other time."

They get together to talk it out between themselves. It's a furious conversation, full of hisses and growls in their language. Then they turn towards me, pulling out their weapons.

"If you die, we can request that your heirs cancel the deal. It's stated in the Rules of Commerce, that a transaction may be canceled if one of the parties dies."

"That sounds perfect," declares Groar behind them. "We'll demand from your heirs that they cancel the initial deal."

The Rokuz turn around, surprised. Both Krogans are with the weapons in their paws, which is a total overkill as their claws would suffice to tear apart a Rokuz with one single blow. Those tricksters turn, ready to flee, but I've also taken out my weapons and am pointing at them with the laser and the gun.

"This is a violation of the Rules of Commerce!" whistles one of the Rokuz towards the dock-master. "It is not allowed to bring mercenaries to a negotiation!"

"Mercenaries?" I ask innocently. "They are not mercenaries. They are my nest." I lift the necklace hanging from my neck, showing it to them. "I am now a Krogan."

The dock-master looks first to one of the groups, then to the other, and after looking again at the Krogans he turns away. Probably he thinks that it's not such a good idea to challenge some Krogans.

"Then everything is in order," he states while leaving hurriedly. "Throw the remains in the waste destructor. I don't like corpses in my docks."

The Rokuz look at each other. I can't read their expressions, but I'm pretty sure that they're quite scared. So I raise my gun.

"You still want to cancel the deal? We can always talk with your heirs."

They throw a furtive look towards the Krogans, and then they lower their weapons. It's evident that they could perhaps waste me, though that could prove to be difficult with my breastplate. But there is no way that only six of them can kill two Krogans in combat armor.

"We accept the transaction. The ship is yours."

They leave, dragging their long hoofs. They cheated me, and now I've fooled them. Before, they could kill me if I dared to resist, now it's us who can tear them apart. As grandpa Paco always said, that's tit for tat.

I feel an irresistible joy flooding my chest. I've recovered my ship. With my new allies I might even be able to repair it. I will be able to return home.

But I don't know how I'll explain to mom the two children-in-law she has now...

Buyers of the future

I'm looking at the space station's airlock behind which my starship is located. My only hope to return home with my mother. But suddenly I am wavering. My ship was stolen by some aliens that literally stank. They had it for weeks, perhaps months, since I'm not aware of the time that has passed. What could they have done with it? What will I find inside, once that I have regained it?

"Is something wrong, Tanit?"

I lift my head, looking at the kind of dinosaur that has addressed me. A female Krogan, about seven feet tall. She's still young, the equivalent of some sixteen human years. She's the female of the warrior at her side, an armored monster that is ten feet tall. Or perhaps I should say one of the females. Because I am the other one.

With eleven years, I do have a real talent to get into trouble. Of course, after the horrible accident that killed my father and the rest of the crew, I had to take care of myself, and I don't think that any other human being would have performed much better than me. I managed to get out of trans-lux with a ship that was ripped apart. I was able to contact with an alien species. I even managed to bring my ship to this huge space station, *Meeting Point*. But then everything started going downhill.

The Rokuz cheated me, and took away my ship. An alien stole all the money I had. Some other aliens, the Ching, cheated me again and made a criminal out of me. Then the Krogan at my side almost killed me, but he didn't do it because he found me amusing. Finally, he decided that the best thing was to marry me, though I honestly didn't have a clue what I was actually doing. He forced me to pass the Ragh-Ar-Khar, the Krogan rite of maturity, where I had to fight against some kind of tigers and dogs with teeth like knives. A Krogan also almost raped me, which probably would have also killed me. In short, I was completely thrown for a loss and I came out unharmed of all that by sheer luck.

The good news is that I now have a family. Well, something like that: I'm married with two ET. Luckily, no sex, as I'm still a Po'lai, an adult-who-is-not-an-adult. But let's see how I get rid of that little detail as soon as I grow up.

At least these two helped me to recover my ship. Because I might have an IQ that qualifies me as a genius, but up to now my adventures have been far from glorious. On this side of the galaxy, everything seems to work more based on force than on intelligence.

"I don't know what we'll find, Tara," I respond.

Then our male laughs, with that stupid cackle that sounds like coughing, while he releases the safety of the small cannon that he holds.

"Ke, ke, ke... Art'Ana, those stinking Rokuz cannot do anything that a real Krogan cannot dominate. Wait here while I do some scouting. Tara, on guard."

He filters himself through the wall while I sigh. Art'Ana. Now, that's another one. It so happens that I'm the matriarch of the nest. Like the head of the family. The leader of these two Krogans. On one side, that is good. It means that they will do anything that I ask them to do. That they will protect me at all costs, even with their lives. But I also know that it's a position for which the Krogan females can fight. And I hardly reach the breasts of the Krogan who is now inspecting the hall, her rifle ready. She could kill me with one single blow. If she decides to become the leader, I will not be able to stop her. To be honest, I won't even try. I'm not crazy.

We wait for quite a while until Groar filters again himself through the wall. It's a very strange spectacle to see how he appears from an apparently solid wall. The alien technology is sometimes very surprising.

"These Rokuz are biological waste," he states, deridingly. "They set up some mines against intruders, but they were so badly placed that half the station could have passed beside them without triggering them. I have deactivated them. Later I'll make sure that I set up some decent booby-traps."

So what causes his contempt is not that they placed mines, it's that they were so sloppy doing that. Krogans! They love everything that can disembowel somebody or something.

"Then let's go," I mumble, entering the wall.

The outer airlock of the *Moon Shadow* is open, and we enter. I close the outer door, and the lock starts its cycle to adjust the pressure. Suddenly I realize that the atmosphere inside is not exactly the same as that of the space station, though Groar should have already noticed it. Perhaps it's not adequate for my new family. I quickly explain that there is slightly less oxygen, somewhat more nitrogen and that the atmospheric pressure and gravity are slightly lower. They grunt, dismissing it.

"It's within the correct parameters," explains Tara. "Our world has also somewhat less oxygen, and the pressure is not a problem. It won't affect us."

The inner lock door opens, and I'm welcomed by a wave of pestilent air. The Rokuz stink, but I did not imagine that even the air conditioning would not be able to remove their stench.

The familiar corridors are empty. I try to advance, but the Krogan female retains me softly.

"First the warriors," she advises me. "We don't know whether the ship is or not empty."

It proves to be an unnecessary precaution, because there is nobody. But Groar goes in front of us, weapons ready, scouting the path that I am telling him. Tara, on the other side, walks behind me, guarding our rear. Krogans always march as if they are in hostile territory. I suppose that millennia of evolution cannot be changed just like that.

A sudden noise surprises us, and both aliens turn immediately towards the door that has opened, weapons ready. I am shaken when I see what has appeared in the door frame.

"Don't shoot!"

They hesitate, but then lower the weapons. After all, the cat does not seem especially dangerous. But they watch it with obvious mistrust, which is exactly what it's doing with them.

On the other hand, I am overwhelmed with joy. Massimo's cat has survived! When the Rokuz stole my ship, I supposed that they had killed her, or perhaps she had starved to death. But she has survived! At least there is another creature of my solar system here.

I crouch and extend my hand towards her. She snorts. I know that in a cat that is a sign that you better do not get too close unless you want a good scratch, so I withdraw my hand.

"Bagheera, it's me! Don't you remember me?"

A lot of time has passed, but she seems to recognize my voice, because she approaches with care, sniffing. I let her smell me and then she rubs against me and starts purring: she has recognized me. Carefully, trying not to make sudden movements, I caress her long hair. She purrs harder. Obviously, she has missed me.

"What is that animal?" inquires Tara.

"It's a cat... A pet."

"Pet?"

I realize that I've used a human word. Common does not seem to have a word for pet, I believe. It costs me some effort to explain them what I mean. The Krogans never had pets, though they did use animals for war along their history.

A brief noise makes the Krogans raise their weapons, looking for the possible danger. But Bagheera is even quicker: in less than a breath, she has jumped onto a kind of rodent that crossed the door and has killed it. One moment later, she starts devouring her prey. It's obvious that she's hungry and these animals —whatever they are— allowed it to survive.

"What is it eating?" asks Groar.

Tara inspects it briefly.

"N'Agu rodents. Rokuz consider them delicious. Probably they have escaped. We'll have to fumigate, these animals become a real plague."

So the aliens that stole my ship also filled it with mice or something like that. I feel that my anger towards them increases. I should have shot them when I had the opportunity. Not that it would have solved the problem, but I would have been very at ease. Well, at least Bagheera has survived because of them.

"Let's continue."

We leave Bagheera with her prey; there will be time enough to celebrate our reunion, now we have more important things to do. We continue sweeping the corridors, both Krogans alert, but we do not encounter any more surprises. It does not take us long to reach the command deck.

The bridge is dark when we arrive due to the automatic energy saving, but the lights go on as soon as we enter. The control terminals also start up. I'm surprised when I see the dates they show during their initialization: I've been in this alien space station for more than two months.

I unlock the computer terminals. Apparently the Rokuz that stole my ship have not been able to penetrate the system, because the computer recognizes me as the captain and activates the systems as soon as I give the order. Now, that's a great relief.

But my relief changes immediately to rage when the computer starts providing the damage report. I don't know what the Rokuz have done to my ship during these two months, but there are a lot of systems in red. Not only have these bastards not fixed any of the damage that the ship suffered during the accident where my father and the crew died, it seems as if they have caused new ravage to the ship.

I explain it to Groar and Tara. They shake their heads, a very characteristic Krogan gesture to indicate that it's not important.

"What did you expect? They have been trying to find out how you got here. The species that can dominate the galactic travel will have a technological advantage of decades, perhaps even hundreds of cycles. It's likely that they have disassembled some equipment so as to inspect it."

I sigh. Probably they're right, but that does not make me feel better.

"Let's see what they've done."

I had thought about taking the transport cart, but we have to go on foot because my new family is too big to fit inside. Well, Tara is about seven feet tall and could squeeze perhaps inside with little comfort, but the ten feet of our warrior make that any human device is far too small for him. He has to duck when crossing the doors, and in some secondary corridors he must bend so as not to hit the piping of the ceiling.

It's a long walk. We have to descend seventeen decks, walking along the whole ship, and the human stairs are very uncomfortable for Krogans, though they don't complain about it. It will be worse when we go up again.

It takes us half an hour to reach the engine room. The sub-light engines don't seem to be damaged, but when we get to the trans-lux engines, I feel like crying.

The Rokuz have been meddling with the systems. They have disassembled all equipment, or almost all, and they have plugged literally hundreds of cables to the flux transformer, so as to connect it to a bunch of machines. I have no clue of what these do. To fix this disaster can take us months, specially because neither Groar nor Tara understand the human manuals, and I'll have to translate them one by one.

Tara does not seem to share my pessimism. She has a look at the Rokuz machinery, inspects briefly the trans-lux system and then switches on some of the machines, looking at them with interest. She busies herself for a while with them. At a certain moment she tilts her head, with that gesture of curiosity that is inherent to all Krogans. She does some more things with the machines that I am unable to understand. But finally she turns towards me. I have the feeling that she seems satisfied.

"It looks worse than it actually is. I can fix this."

My heart seems to cringe for an instant due to my emotion. Will I be able to return with mom?

"Are you sure?"

Then she starts laughing, with that strange Krogan laughter.

"Ke, ke, ke... Of course I'm sure, Tanit. My specialty is space propulsion systems. They always fascinated me. However, unless there is something that I have not seen, this primitive propulsion cannot make the jump that you say that brought you here."

I irreversibly go down. Even if we're able to fix the flux injector, it will still take us one hundred fifty years to reach Thuis, where mom is waiting for me. I swallow hard, trying to overcome the despair overwhelming me.

"But it did!" I hiccup. "I don't know how, but it brought me here." I close the eyes while my breast contracts with my sobbing. "I want to go back with my mother!"

A huge finger touches my face and on opening my eyes, I see how Groar is looking at the tear that he has scooped from my cheek; he's contemplating it with obvious surprise.

"Water?" he mumbles.

You can't say tears in Common; to my knowledge that word does not exist.

"Water shed by sorrow," I explain, wiping my face with the back of my hand. "We call it tears in our language." I close again my eyes, while my sobs become louder and louder. "I won't see my mother back. I won't see her again."

Another huge arm is placed around my shoulder and presses me against a body, in such an affectionate gesture that I would have never expected it from an alien. But Tara is a female, and she knows what a wounded cub is. She knows that she has to comfort him, so she says nothing while I weep against her breast; she simply cuddles me.

"The Art'Ana should not show any weakness," growls Groar. "It does not matter how big the grief is."

I don't care. It's true that I'm officially the matriarch of our nest, but I'm still eleven years old. At my age I should not even be married with them, and I would not have been if I had known anything about alien habits when I reached this shitty space station. I am a scared little girl that has lost everything. That's just what I needed, that I could not even cry.

Tara at least understands it, because she hisses in a way that I know is a sign of reproach between Krogan.

"She's just a Po'lai, an adult-who-is-not-an-adult."

"She passed the Ragh-Ar-Khar!"

"Yes. She passed the rite of maturity. But she's only five cycles old. Don't expect her to behave like an adult."

Our male grunts; he does not seem to be convinced.

"Perhaps you should challenge her and become our Art'Ana."

Then Tara releases me, facing Groar. She bares her teeth and snarls menacingly, leaning forward, taking the combat position.

"Don't insult me! She's my Art'Ana! I accepted her as such! While she has honor and guides us with wisdom and honor, I will obey her. Even if she's a Po'lai. I will fight for her. I will die for her. You know that a challenge would be only justified if she dishonorred the nest or put it unnecessarily at risk. I also have honor! Or perhaps you doubt it?"

The huge warrior contemplates her for an instant; then he diverts his look.

"I do not doubt your honor," he admits. "But for an instant I wondered whether our leader was capable of guiding us."

"You accepted her as your mate when she was still a cub. Even before she passed the Ragh-Ar-Khar. Before she became your Art'Ana. She might be a Po'lai, but even before she became an adult you did respect her as if she were your equal. And now you ask whether she is capable of leading us?"

The huge warrior turns and looks at me. A long look. Then he bends, until his face is at the same height as mine. He extends his claws, and carefully wipes my tears.

"I offer you my apologies, Art'Ana," he says formally. "I did not intend to question neither your courage nor your honor. I simply forgot that you're a Po'lai. But you're my Art'Ana, and I will follow you until the end of the universe. If you want to return with your mother, I'll do the impossible to comply with your wish."

"So it is," confirms Tara, also bending until her face is also in front of me. "You're the owner of our nest. Command and we will obey you."

Contemplating the two monstrous faces in front of me, suddenly I feel much better. My mother may be far away, but these two are now my family. They will take care of me. They will protect me. And if there is a way to return with mom, then they will help me. They're weird. Very weird, closer to dinosaurs than to human beings, no matter how mammals they might actually be. But they're all I have now.

I wipe my tears and try to smile, though they obviously do not know what a smile is.

"I'm sorry. I... Well, I'm a Po'lai. I could not help it. I hope I did not disappoint you."

"You didn't," answers Groar. "It's understandable that you felt sorrow. You're the only one of your species in this part of the galaxy, and we don't know how you can return. But you have us. If there is a way to repeat your voyage, we will do it."

An alarm sounds before I finish opening my mouth so as to answer. It's an important signal that I immediately recognize. Collision alarm! I run to the closest terminal, wiping with the back of my hand the tears still blinding me.

"Report collision data!"

The computer voice almost seems petulant when it responds.

"Collision aborted."

I frown. Is it poking fun at me? No, that's not possible for a computer.

"Display object that has triggered the alarm."

A hologram appears. It seems as if it has been taken with the port cameras of my ship. It's a tiny spaceship, not more than five meters long, which was heading directly towards us. But it suddenly changed course and started navigating in parallel of the ship's hull, close to the huge cracks that extend along the whole port side.

I have to explain Groar and Tara what has happened; obviously they have not understood what the computer has said. The Krogan leans forward, inspecting the ship with interest. I then amplify the image, until the ship occupies the whole display.

"Problems," announces our male. "Those are Tloc."

"Tloc?" I wonder. "Who are they?"

"The buyers of the future," Tara informs me. "It's not good news that they're here."

I look at her, perplexed.

"They come from the future?"

"No," splutters Groar. "They're called like that because they hoard all new technologies. They buy or steal them. They'll corrupt anyone for that purpose. They'll murder anyone who interferes. Any new invention ends up in their hands, which gives them a tremendous technological advantage in front of the other species. They never sell anything, except that which is obsolete for them, and then they deliver it at exorbitant prices. If a species antagonizes them, they will deny them any progress. They buy the future of our species for their own advantage."

"We have spent three thousand cycles in stagnation," snarls the female, and it's pretty evident that she does not like the Tloc at all. "They don't allow for technological advances, as these might put at risk their supremacy. Their weapons are very powerful, and they're almost invulnerable. If they can't buy the knowledge, they will make sure that they steal it or that it disappears without any trace." She snorts with contempt. "They're not the buyers of the future. The Tloc are their masters, because they're denying it to us."

I look from one to the other. By the way they bare their teeth, I can see that they would be delighted to piece apart those Tloc. It's pretty evident that the species in question is not very popular.

"But they can't control the advances of so many worlds!" I protest. "There must be at least a hundred species in this station. At least one hundred different planets. How is it possible that they control all the technology?"

"No one knows," responds Groar. "They have obviously many spies. But their technology allows them to be informed about everything that occurs everywhere. No development escapes their attention."

"But... has no one ever tried to investigate in secret?"

"Of course. But the laboratories explode inexplicably, the scientists die of unknown causes. It has been almost two thousand cycles that nobody investigates; it's a very risky activity. And if they have any success, the Tloc will come and buy it... or loot it."

I look at the hologram. That ship is really tiny. But suddenly I feel a knot in the stomach.

"What do they want? This ship does not have any special technology. In fact, it's very primitive when compared to the ships you have here. Tara, you said that yourself!"

The other shakes her head, obviously dubious.

"Perhaps they only inspect the ship of a previously unknown species," she mumbles. "Or perhaps the Rokuz have not been too discreet and they know how you got here. If so, we're going to have a huge problem. Their technology makes them almost invincible. Nobody remembers the last time that somebody killed a Tloc."

"We'll have to prepare ourselves, just in case," grunts our male. "Tanit, how do you activate the armament of this ship?"

I stare at him, perplexed.

"The armament?"

"Yes, the weapons on the ship."

Suddenly I realize that I have my mouth wide open and I close it before responding.

"This ship has no weapons. Why should it? It's a colonization ship."

They look at each other. I could swear that they seem to be scandalized.

"But it should have weapons! How else will it protect itself from the pirates? From hostile species? All ships carry weapons!"

I sigh. It looks as if they're going to face a serious disappointment.

"Not this one. Groar, my species does not have any pirates attacking starships. And we've never met a different species. I... well; I'm the only one of my species that has ever met a non-human race."

They again look at each other. Then they stare at me, tilting their heads. That means that I've surprised them.

"You know what that means, Groar," says finally the female. "She was a cub in a damaged ship that yet managed to arrive here. She managed to learn Common on her own. For the first time in the history of her species, she made contact with a foreign race. She managed to survive until you met her. And you still doubted whether she was capable of leading us? How many cubs could have emulated her? Or even how many adults?"

The warrior growls.

"It seems I was wrong. She's a survivor. But it won't help us that this ship is unarmed."

I shrug, even though I know that they won't understand that gesture.

"There is nothing we can do about that."

He growls again, with evident disapproval.

"We'll see. I'm going to inspect the ship."

He leaves, while Tara starts examining again the space folding engines. She asks a million questions, and I tell her everything I know about the engines. After a while I have no alternative but to access the terminal, open the manuals and start looking for the answers: this is getting too technical for me. In the meantime, she busies herself with the Rokuz equipment. She seems very interested in the information that she's finding.

But finally I am fed up with everything. It has been a long day. I have passed the Krogan's rite of maturity, and I've not been the main meal of a kind of tiger by a pure miracle. Then I was attacked by something similar to a dog, with teeth like daggers. If that were not enough, I have almost been raped, I have received two marriage proposals, of which I accepted one, and I have shared telepathically a Krogan wedding night. Oh yes, I have also cheated some Rokuz, so as to recover the ship that they had stolen from me. I think that's enough for today.

Tara leaves her work reluctantly, but at least she listens to me, to my relief. I don't know how late it is, but I did not have lunch and I'm hungry. The Krogan nods when I tell her.

"Yes, let's eat something."

I suppose that she expected that we would return to the nest, but I'm not in a mood for that. This time I'll have a real lunch.

The kitchen is pretty cold, but I immediately turn the heaters on and the room warms up quickly despite the fact that the door to the canteen now actually leads to open space. I try not to look in that direction. That's where my father and the rest of the crew died.

I start up the oven and then I visit the hydroponic gardens. They're now a total disaster after two months of neglect, but to my surprise all plants have survived. I pick up a melon, bring it to the kitchen, and then go to my cabin so as to change clothes.

But when I see the bathroom, I cannot resist the temptation of taking a shower. There is no such thing in the station; the cleaning is electrostatic, which is obviously something totally different. I undress and let the hot water rinse my body. I close the eyes out of sheer happiness. How I missed this!

I am at the brink of jumping up when a huge creature looms through the door frame. But I should not have been startled. It's Groar. Then I notice that he is grasping a gun.

"What's the trouble?" I ask.

"I heard a strange noise," he answers. "Like a small cascade, with falling water." He makes a gesture, pointing at me with the gun before lowering it. "What is that?"

"We call it a shower," I explain. "Yes, it's like an artificial cascade. Our species like it."

He growls something and leaves. It's possible that the Krogans don't like getting wet.

I leave the shower and let the electrostatic field dry me; then I put on clean clothes. I suppose I'll have to bring some clothes to the nest, though the two months that I have been with Groar I was naked the whole time. In any case, after the shower and with clean clothes, I feel really great.

I return to the kitchen, where I left Tara, and take out the food. I prepare two jumbo steaks for her; I suppose she'll be able to eat those. She smells them, suspicious, and then bites the first one. She seems to like the taste, because she immediately eats them in a trice. But she does not use the cutlery that I've placed on the table. Probably she doesn't have a clue what they are being used for.

I, however, enjoy a civilized meal for the first time in months. A tomato soup. Fried chicken. Melon. I feel like as if I'm in heaven, I'm fed up with that brown smudge that the automatic kitchens of the station dispense me.

Bagheera appears when I'm almost finished, and I search for her food. She smells the meal suspiciously, as if she did not recall it, and finally starts eating it without much enthusiasm. It looks as if the rodents she has been eating until now were tastier.

After some time Groar returns, so I'm forced to cook again. No jumbo steak for him. I have to prepare a piece of meat that is so heavy that I can hardly carry if from the pantry to the furnace. However, when I get it out of the furnace, he smells it and starts eating it apparently with pleasure. It's my luck that these two are on my side: I suspect that they are some of the carnivores that buy meat in the station without asking where it comes from. I might have ended up on their plate, as far as I know.

"The taste is somewhat strange," says the warrior when he finishes. "But it was very acceptable. We have to provide the automatic kitchen a sample of this."

And that's how I find out that there are other ways to request our kitchen what you want to eat, apart from trying to imagine it.

"Did you find anything?"

"No. Let's return to the nest, we have to make plans."

I look around, but Bagheera has disappeared again: probably she doesn't trust the two huge monsters that are with me. Well, I'll find her later on. She has just eaten, so she won't starve.

We leave the ship, but to my surprise Groar tells us to go up in the lift, instead of descending. He wants to see from the balcony what the buyers of the future were looking at.

I didn't even know that there was a balcony in this space station. It's a huge room, with views onto space. When the window polarizes and allows us to see the outside, I remain literally open-mouthed.

The view of the sky in Mars is impressive, but it's really nothing compared to what you see when you are in orbit or traveling through the solar system. During my trip from Mars to Earth I spent many hours looking at the stars from the observation room of the *Moon Shadow*, almost incapable of assimilating so much beauty. But now I realize that it was... I don't know. Poor.

When I brought my ship to this space station, I did not return to the observation room and I therefore never saw the stars. The bridge filters the view by default, so as not to distract you during the navigation. There are no windows through which you can observe the stars, just some screens that show you exclusively what is important for the ship. And I never realized that I missed the most amazing stellar sky that a human being has ever seen.

You must understand this: Earth and Mars are about 26,000 light-years from the galactic center. But I am at the border of the Scutum-Centaurus arm, at just half that distance. The galactic center here dominates the whole sky, with millions of stars illuminating us as if it was plain day. I am unable to describe this. But I've never seen anything this beautiful.

It takes me some effort to look away from the immense sea of stars and gaze towards my ship, which glows in the starlight. When you look at it like this, it is really impressive, quite bigger than the other ships that I can see from here. I look at the three huge fissures running across the hull, twenty decks long. Obviously I had inspected them with the outboard cameras of the ship, but they're far more impressive when seen from this perspective.

"How could this happen?" I ask aloud. "And in trans-lux? Supposedly you cannot hit anything while in trans-lux!"

"Amazing," marvels Tara. "I never heard of anything like this. And I never saw damage like that. That does not look natural."

"It looks as if a gigantic claw ripped open the ship," growls Groar. "But the beast would have been gigantic. Nobody has ever heard of a beast like that."

"So what happened?"

He nods with his head, in a gesture that I know that means doubt for his species.

"I don't know. But we shouldn't be surprised that the Tloc are interested, even if they do not know what your ship did. This does not have a logic explanation."

Suddenly a slightly shrill voice interrupts us.

"Would you be interested in a Segean rifle? We also have disruptors from Feren..."

We turn towards the two beings that have approached us. They are bipeds, around six feet tall, covered by a brown skin. Their face is similar to that of the sea lion, except that they have a huge red crest on top of the skull. Some disproportionate hands, with four long fingers, hold a long device that by the looks of it is a weapon. But they're not pointing it towards us; it looks as if they're offering it to us.

"A Segean rifle?" both Krogan ask simultaneously. "Those are very difficult to get by!"

"Impossible to find, I would say." The beast with the crest looks pleased. "I see that you're interested."

My new family looks at the rifle that they're being offered, I'd say almost reverentially. Krogans! They're like little kids when you talk about weapons. I finally get bored by the sales pitch of the merchant and look around. There are others like him close to an automatic kitchen, talking with each other, but otherwise we're alone in the balcony.

I throw a glimpse towards Groar and Tara, who are inspecting the weapon. To be honest, I'm tempted to tell them to leave that old crock and return to our apartment, but they seem very enthusiastic. I sigh. Well, I'll let them play around a bit. After all, they helped me to recover my ship. Let's not spoil their fun.

I head for the automatic kitchen. I didn't drink during dinner, and suddenly I'm thirsty. The melon was drier than normal; otherwise I would not have abandoned the company of my nest, knowing that you have to be very careful in this space station. But what the heck! I'm an adult here. After all, I passed the Krogan rite of maturity. I know how to take care of myself.

There is about a dozen of aliens similar to those that are negotiating with the Krogans standing there, but they polity move to one side when I approach. Then, while I am still extending the hand to make my order, one of those beings grabs me as I pass at his side, holding me by the waist, and starts to run. I suppose that he thinks that, being much smaller than he is, I won't provide much resistance.

But I'm not a delicate flower. In reality, I'm pretty strong for an eleven year old girl. As I have been living for three years at a gravity of 1.3 gees as a training to be able to travel to Thuis, with my mother, I have far more muscle than what a girl of my age would have on Earth. And on Mars, with its lower gravity, I broke the arm of a much bigger boy for going too far. It would not have been a problem to do it also with an adult. There I was literally three times stronger than any of my friends.

The ET certainly does not expect the punch in the face that I give him. He releases me, recoiling with a scream that I suppose is of pain. As far as I am concerned, my knuckles are hurting now; I have hit him with all my forces. Of course I don't waste time. Taking advantage of his surprise, I grab his arm, toss him over and throw him to the floor. On this side of the galaxy, they don't have the slightest idea about martial arts; on the other hand, on Mars I was champion in my category and I competed against boys who were four and even five years older than me. But then, I was also the only girl that had ever finished the colonist training. He cries out very satisfactorily and remains on the floor, moaning.

Obviously the other aliens have seen what has happened, and jump towards me. They're in for a surprise: I not only learned martial arts on Mars. Here Groar made me undergo a tremendous Krogan training so as to be able to pass the Ragh-Ar-Khar, the rite of maturity. These beasts are not as tough as a Krogan, and within an instant I have knocked out three or four, with some broken bones.

But there are too many of them. One ET grabs my arm from behind. A moment later several of them have grabbed my other arm. I kick the one trying to retain me, and then the rest of them bring me down to the floor. One of them bends over me, holding something that I suppose is to tie me down, but he never manages to do it. Because suddenly a big boom rumbles through the room and he no longer has a head.

That headless beast falls on top of me, while his companions release me hurriedly and grab their weapons. What a delusion! None of them is a rival for a Krogan, much less for two of them. Within one minute everything has ended. Those that are not dead have fled, and Tara is helping me to get out from under the corpse that is spraying me with a sticky orange blood that strongly smells like ammonia.

"A good fight," she comments while she lifts me. "You fight like a real Krogan."

"Groar trained me," I explain, looking at my tacky clothes. "How disgusting!"

"I didn't teach her that," corrects me the warrior. "It's an interesting way of fighting. Are you all right?"

"Yes," I answer while both look around, their weapons ready. "You arrived just in time."

"It was my mistake," objects Groar. "We should not have left you alone. Why did these Sneog try to kidnap you?"

"I don't know." I try to unglue my clothes; they finally release with a strong and ugly suction noise. It's disgusting, and it also stinks. "Perhaps they wanted to sell me as meat on the market."

But the two Krogans don't seem very convinced.

"No. It was too professional. Too elaborate. And they tried to distract us. There must be much easier preys than one who is escorted by two Krogans. Not to forget that the Sneog are famous mercenaries. They were going after you, Tanit. And they wanted you alive."

For an instant I totally forget the sticky concoction that covers me. Suddenly I'm anguished.

"Why?"

They briefly look at each other. Even though they are aliens and I'm incapable of reading their expressions, I detect concern.

"We'll find out. But now let's return to the nest. We're exposed here."

We return to our apartment, but Groar lets us wait outside while he inspects it, just in case that somebody entered. Probably it's a bit paranoid, but I'm not going to object, after they tried to kidnap me. As soon as we enter, I stand on top of the white surface which is the toilet, and the remains of blood —or whatever they are— slowly detach from my clothes, falling to the floor and sinking into it. They don't have showers here, but this is equally effective. As soon as the clothes are clean I undress, so that the system also removes that goo from my body. I'm not concerned by the fact that they see me without clothes: after all, we are married, and Groar has seen me naked for about two months. In any case, even if I was an adult, for them I would be as sexually exciting as a giraffe, or some other equally weird beast.

When I exit the toilet, they have also undressed; it's a Krogan habit that you are not dressed inside the nest. Pretty weird. Perhaps it's to show the family that there is nothing to hide. They are sitting facing the door, their weapons close, just in case. I sit beside them, also looking at the door. Groar has trained me well; suddenly I realize that, without really being conscious about it, I have picked up my small gun and placed it also at my side.

"Why would they want to kidnap me?"

Tara growls.

"The only reason that I can think of is your ship."

I look at her, surprised.

"Why would anybody want my ship? It's totally busted!"

The warrior puffs; his snorting is worse than a bull's bellow.

"Tanit, your ship traveled almost one fifth of the galaxy in fractions of a cycle. There is no starship capable of doing that. That knowledge is worth a huge fortune, and there are species that will do anything to get hold of it."

I think about that. It's true, I never considered that.

"But I don't know what happened! My ship was not supposed to be able to do that!"

A hologram of the galaxy materializes in front of us and Tara points at it. There is a small line from the Solar System pointing towards the Dorado constellation. But when it reaches Gliese 163, which is where

Thuis is located, the line swings away, forming a curve that ends in the Scutum-Centaurus arm, very close to the galactic center. Fifteen thousand light-years away from home.

"But it did. It might seem impossible, but it did. This is your ship's navigation profile, I retrieved it from the analysis that the Rokuz made of your trans-lux engine. You have crossed a distance that no other being has ever achieved."

I look at the thin lines. Yeah, I knew it, but I can still hardly believe it. What did we hit in trans-lux mode? What made me jump to where we are now?

I must have spoken my question aloud, because the female responds immediately.

"Tanit, the collision did not cause you to arrive here."

I look up, perplexed.

"What?

Then she zooms into the image, until it shows the exact collision point and the location where the straight line sheers off to the curve that brought me here. Her claw marks one of the points.

"Do you see it? Here there is a strong perturbation of the engines; you can see it because the trajectory oscillates somewhat. This must be the crash that killed the crew. But you continued cruising for some time. Until here."

I look bewildered to the point that she is showing now. It's the Gliese 163 system. My destination. Thuis. Mom. I had arrived! I had returned with my mother! So why did the ship jump suddenly to the other end of the galaxy?

"But... what happened? I only left trans-lux..."

"I do not know what happened, Tanit," says the female. "But you moved six thousand six hundred light-cycles in just nanocycles." She does something with the controls, and some symbols appear. "Observe the time scale."

I scrutinize the symbols, but they don't tell me anything; I don't know how to read the Krogan writing. But she's talking about nanocycles. That is, in the order of one or two minutes. I remain open-mouthed. Have I traveled fifteen thousand light-years in one minute?

"Impossible!" I manage finally to mumble.

"This is serious," mutters Groar. "Tanit, we have to find out what happened, and we need to do that quickly. To be able to travel at those speeds will make that any race that obtains that technology becomes the dominant species. It's not surprising that they wanted to abduct you. Your ship and you are worth more than anything else in the universe." He rises. "Let's mine the ship's accesses. The Rokuz will try to return."

I think about the stinking penguin-bats that stole my ship and I shiver.

"Do you think that they're the ones that tried to kidnap me?"

"It's very likely. They have these data. They know what happened, and they will try by all means to get hold of you and your ship." He points to the female. "Tara, don't leave her alone even for a nanocycle. She's in danger. I don't think that the Rokuz will divulge this information if they know what's good for them, but they can hire mercenaries to capture her. The Sneog did not work on their own behalf; somebody hired them. The Rokuz, on the other hand, are too coward to expose themselves."

The Krogan nods and gets up, her weapon ready in her paws. Suddenly she looks very dangerous.

"You know that I will protect her with my life."

The warrior starts dressing. Then he fastens his breastplate, puts on a helmet, and starts collecting a great variety of weapons from a cabinet that I did not know existed because it was hidden in a wall. When he finishes, he is really frightening. The way that he's equipped, he could win a war all by himself.

"Take whatever you need from the armory," he insists, heading for the door. "Tara, make sure that Tanit has a complete armor. A simple breastplate might not be enough for what we are facing."

He opens the door, the weapons ready. After quickly inspecting the alley, he jumps immediately outside. Then I stop seeing him because the door closes.

I turn towards the Krogan female. She is lowering a huge gun; apparently she had pointed it to the door the moment it opened. Looking for an instant to the armory, as if wishing to inspect it, she leaves her arsenal on the floor and touches my shoulder, making me stand up.

When Groar made my breastplate, I thought that he had sacrificed hours of sleep to manufacture it, but apparently it wasn't so. The nest has the most amazing 3D printer that I have ever seen. Tara makes me stand up to take measures, and my body suddenly lightens up with different colors while something scans me. My friend lets me stand on my toes, bend, squat down, raise my arms and legs, turn my hands and feet, flex my fingers... Actually, she makes me carry out any possible movement that a human being can do, including many that are so weird that perhaps I'd do them only once in my life. The computer of course is recording all this, it analyzes my movements, the tension of my muscles... With all this and the schema that Tara has fed into the computer, the printer starts to manufacture me an armor.

It takes hours to start even producing something that looks like a pair of boots, and that despite the fact that the movement of the nozzles is so quick that I am incapable of tracking them; I only see some flickering shadows. However, the boots seem very complex, as they consist of multiple layers of many materials, and I could swear that they have circuits embedded in them.

Eventually I end up being bored by the whole thing, but Tara is not in the mood to give me conversation. She is examining the armory, and she looks like a kid with new shoes, admiring each artifact as if it was a world wonder.

"A Nexx neutralizer!" she cries out with joy. "I only knew them from the stories in the nest! How did you get this?"

I shrug. Honestly, I have no clue about what that gadget does, but knowing Krogans it is certain that it must be something that is tremendously explosive or deliciously deadly. Even though I have weapons of my own, I am sure that these must be like toys besides those used by our male.

"I don't know. It belongs to Groar."

"It's unique!"

I sigh and go to the automatic kitchen. Trying to imagine my dinner, I get again a shapeless dough with a strong mixture of flavors. That the alien machinery can read your mind is awesome for many things... but not if you do not know how to explain to the computer how to prepare human food. At least it's not poisonous. I remind myself that I need to bring some food samples from my ship the next time I go there.

Tara comes to prepare her dinner by the time I am finishing. She is better at this: the kitchen provides her with something that looks like an extra-extra-big raw steak. Of course, with her size she needs to eat much more than I do. Then she sits behind me, back to back, as Groar usually does. This way, nobody will be able to attack us while we eat. Krogan history is so violent that they have a lot of such silly mores.

It takes her exactly half a second to lift the small cannon that she left at her side when the door starts to open. But she should not have worried. It's Groar, obviously pointing at us with his gun. He lowers it as soon as the door closes.

"Ready," he boasts. "There is no living being except us who can enter that ship."

Honestly, I don't care a rat's ass. I'm yawning, so I go to bed. Half asleep, I hear them... well, do their thing. At least I'll skip that detail of our matrimony. Groar has promised to respect me until I'm eighteen years old; advantages of being a Po'lai. I fall asleep with that thought.

When I awake it is dark, and two huge bodies cover me, forming a dome that protects me against any possible enemy. This is how Krogans protect their cubs, sheltering them against the many beasts that roamed their home planet. Anybody wanting to reach me will have first to kill them both. In a way, it's comforting, though slightly claustrophobic.

"What is claustrophobic?" asks a voice in my mind.

Turning my head, I see the blue and yellow eyes of the huge warrior contemplating me in the darkness. I did not know that he was telepathic. Then I remember that he talked to me with his mind when we welcomed Tara into our nest, when we shared her N'aga, which very crudely we could translate as her wedding night. I feel a chill. Though I never had any sexual experience, I did share telepathically theirs. It was something really disturbing.

"Don't worry, little Gal," reassures me Groar. "You know that it won't occur again. Not until you have the appropriate age for your species. What does claustrophobic mean?"

I explain it quickly, grateful to change the subject.

"Fear of small spaces. Some members of my species have that trouble."

"Surprising." He sits up while the lights go on, and one instant later Tara is also straightening. "Let's eat something and then we go training."

"Training?" I protest. "I already passed the Ragh-Ar-Khar! Why should I continue training?"

Then that armored monster growls, threatening.

"Art'Ana, you should know that the safety of the nest is the most important thing to safeguard. You saw yesterday that we have to be prepared for anything. That requires training. Until now you simply learned how to survive. Now you must become a real warrior."

"He is right, Tanit," the female supports him. "We still have a lot to learn."

I sigh. My hope was that I had finished with that darn training once I had passed the rite of maturity, but it looks as if that is not the case. Of course, after the kidnapping attack yesterday, I'm more receptive to the idea. The respect of life does not seem to count much on this side of the galaxy.

Groar organizes a little skirmish between Tara and me in the gym. Obviously he knows my abilities very well: he trained me. But Tara has just married us, and he wants to see her weaknesses.

She's very good, I must admit. I am far faster and agile than she is, and even so she's able to defeat me in most of the close combat fights. Tara is also very good shooting, much better than I am. But though her aim is superb, she has not been trained to handle all kinds of weapons. The female despairs when her training harness beeps, stating that I have killed her for a fourth time.

"It's not possible!" she screams. "I was completely covered!"

Groar and I laugh. I surprised him with the same trick a few weeks ago, and since then he has practiced this new tactic himself.

"It's that I have not used a projectile weapon," I explain. "I used the laser."

"So what?"

"A laser forms a beam of coherent light. It goes in a straight line, but it will be deviated by any reflecting surface. That's the advantage of a laser: You can shoot hidden enemies, provided that you can change the beam's direction with a light reflecting surface, so that they are hit from the back or any other unprotected point. It's basic optics."

She looks around. Then she stares at me.

"Surprise," she declares. "You cannot reach me from where you are. There is no reflective surface that you can use."

I start laughing again.

"Obviously I did not use one single reflecting surface. I used three." So I point out the three points, one by one. "That's where I shot, the beam bounced there and finally there. The last surface did not reflect very well and the laser lost a lot of power, but even so I killed you."

She looks at the three points, traces the path with a claw and then looks at me with a gesture that I suppose is of admiration.

"Very smart... I never thought about using a laser that way. I always thought that it was not very useful. It can only generate brief pulses and heats up very quickly."

Before I can answer, an alarm sounds. Both Krogans lift immediately their heads, instinctively changing the weapons that they hold from training to combat mode.

"What happens?" I ask, also changing the mode of my laser. Now the gun I hold in my hand will really kill. No more war games.

"One of the mines I placed on your ship has exploded," informs our male. "Somebody tried to enter." He releases an indulging grunt. "Whoever it was, he's now dead."

"Well."

I don't know what else to say.

"And the damage?" inquires Tara.

"I don't know. It can't be too bad, I was very careful placing the traps. We'll have to go and see."

So we get dressed. Tara insists that I put on my breastplate, since the complete armor is not yet ready. To be honest, I don't feel like it, but Groar decides that we will all wear our breastplates, so I eventually place it on my T-shirt. I suppose it will look a bit weird to walk around with a breastplate through the corridors, so I decide to put on a blouse on top of it.

"Why do you think it is weird?" asks Tara, while she finishes fastening hers. Honestly, I don't know why Krogans use breastplates, as their skin is so tough that a bullet will probably ricochet against it. But of course the front of their bodies is softer than the back, where it is almost impossible to wound them.

"Well... I don't know. It looks weird to me."

Both look at each other, but they do not comment. Probably they think that I'm the weird one, because I don't want to go armored everywhere.

We leave, armed to the teeth. Or to be precise, they are armed to the teeth. I only carry a gun with incendiary bullets, my laser and the dagger they gave me when I passed the rite of maturity. Actually, in theory, it is a dagger, but due to its size I use it as a sword. It's the only thing that I can carry, all the armament that Groar has is too big, too heavy and unmanageable for me. My mate has told me that, now that I'm an adult, I will have to equip myself with heavy armament. Krogans seem to think that, the more firepower you have, the better. Keeping in mind what I have seen the two months that I have been here, I tend not to disagree.

We take the lift. The first time that I got on one I almost got killed: I fell in free fall God knows how many floors, because I did not know that you must think about whether you want to go up or down. Now I know, and we raise slowly four floors until we reach the docks. The corridors are pretty crowded, but all aliens move quickly out of the way when they see us. Actually, it's when they see the Krogans, because I don't seem to be even a fraction as dangerous as these two armored monsters.

We get to the huge hall from which we can access my ship's airlock, but suddenly Groar stops. Tara also halts and both raise their weapons, looking apparently uneasy around them.

"What's the trouble?" I ask.

"Something is wrong," snarls Groar.

I also look around. There is nothing strange around us. Well, there are more aliens than the last time I was here. Some are looking down from a lateral terrace. I frown. They are very similar to the ones that tried to kidnap me. Yes, it's the same species. Sneogs. This may not mean anything, but...

A sudden movement draws my attention towards the floor level. There are more over there. And they're pulling out hidden weapons. I open my mouth to scream a warning, but the two Krogans are much faster and start shooting before any sound comes out of my mouth. I try to grab my laser.

But I never manage to draw it, for something hits my chest and throws me violently backwards, slamming me brutally against the wall. Probably I have fainted from the impact, because the next thing that I see is Tara's face above mine, looking rapidly around. Then I realize that she is wearing me in her arms. Even so, one of her paws holds a gun.

"What has happened?" I ask weakly.

She doesn't look at me. She is inspecting our surroundings. I also look. There is a collapsed wall, where Groar and Tara must have been shooting. The terrace has come down due to the fire of the plasma cannon that our male employs and the explosive shells that Tara likes to use. The ravage is immense. And there are corpses buried among the rubble.

"They shot you. Can you walk?"

"Yes."

She leaves me carefully on the floor, and immediately she sheathes the handgun and takes the heavy rifle that she carried on her back. Performing a complete circle, she makes sure that there is nobody around us; if there was, he must have run away. There is only one thing that is worse than a furious Krogan, and that is several furious Krogans. Groar and Tara did really dispatch things; the hall is in ruins. I take out my gun with incendiary bullets.

"You say that they shot at me?"

"Two explosive bullets. Your breastplate stopped them."

I look down at my breast. My blouse is ripped apart where the two projectiles hit me. But the breastplate below it has only two notches. I knew that Krogan armor was really tough, though I never supposed it would be this much. But it has obviously saved my life. That, and the fact that Tara insisted that I should put on the breastplate below my clothes. If they had shot me in the head... I suddenly feel as if my legs are made out of jelly. Someone has tried to kill me!

"They tried to kill me?" I stammer, trying not to come down. "Who? Why?"

"Let's find out," growls the warrior, approaching carefully the rubble, weapons prepared. Tara follows him, but walking backwards, protecting our back so nobody can attack us from the rear. I have trouble moving the legs, I'm trembling without control. Tightening my fist around the gun, I also take out the laser. This gives me some courage, but even so it does not stop the shakes. Someone has tried to kill me!

There are about eleven or twelve ripped-apart alien bodies, but one seems to be still alive by the way it is moaning. It's a miracle that he has survived, keeping in mind how expeditious both Krogans have been.

Groar doesn't tread carefully. He grips the Sneog by the crest on top of its head and lifts him as if he was weightless. The ET tries to resist, but he's hanging three feet above the floor and his arms can do nothing to be released by the huge paw that holds him.

"Who has contracted you?" asks our male.

"I will not say anything!" squeaks the other alien. "The code forbids it!"

Groar pulls out the claws and slowly drives them into the leg of the one who has attacked us. Then he starts lowering the paw, tearing apart the leg, while his victim screams of pain, screams that make me shudder.

"I'll ask again," he grunts when the leg is little more than some shreds of meat through which the bone is visible.

The Sneog whimpers pitiably. He must be suffering a lot.

"The code forbids giving that information!"

"Wrong answer."

The Krogan changes the hand that is holding his enemy and takes out again his claws, lifting the paw. I am hardly able to raise my voice: between the shakes that I still have and the spectacle that I have just witnessed, I am ready to faint.

"Groar, you can't do that!"

He turns halfway and tilts his head, with that gesture of curiosity that is inherent to all Krogans.

"Of course I can!"

"He's wounded!" I argue.

He and Tara look at each other. It's pretty evident that they don't know what I'm talking about. The mentality of this species is very different from that of the human race.

"So what?"

"You can't..." How the hell do you say torture in Common? I have no clue. "It's not honorable to hurt so as to force somebody to confess something!"

Now they're both looking at me with their heads tilted. I perceive their incredulity.

"Why would it not be honorable?"

"Because they can't defend themselves!"

They again look at each other. Then Groar growls.

"All right."

He releases his victim, but before it can fall, he nails the claws from both sides into the skull, with a movement that is faster than the eye. I feel that I am on the verge of passing out due to the impression. I had thought about letting him go, but it is evident the Krogans have a very special way of making war.

"You should not have killed him," I splutter while he drops the body.

"Why not?" he inquires apparently surprised. "He was an enemy. He tried to kill us."

"Because..." To be honest, I can't come up with any justification that can satisfy them. The rules of human behavior don't apply here. Then inspiration comes. "We could have followed him to his boss. To find out who sent him."

"That's not a bad idea," approves Tara. "We'll try to leave one alive next time that they attack us."

"Next time?" I ask weakly.

"They will try again," snarls Groar. "We'll have to be prepared. Let's go to the ship, we're exposed here."

I glimpse something in my peripheral vision and turn. The female Krogan, however, is faster: her paw moves like lightning through the air and closes around something that is very small. For an instant I had the impression that it was a fly.

"A spy eye," she informs us. "Somebody was watching us."

The warrior approaches.

"You have it?"

"Yes."

"Perfect. We'll analyze it as soon as we can. Let's find out who wants us dead. Wait here."

He turns and filters himself through the airlock wall, weapons ready. Some minutes later, he pulls his head out. It's really a weird spectacle to see a tyrannosaur head coming out of an apparently solid wall.

"Secure. You can enter."

It might be secure for us, but when we enter and advance through the corridors, we find a real slaughter close to the cargo airlock. Groar had not exaggerated when he said that they would all be dead with the traps that he had set up. To be precise, they've been blown to pieces, to the extent that I can't say how many they were —though they had to be many— nor to which species they belonged. The whole corridor is full of entrails and a sticky brew that I imagine is blood or something similar. I feel like as if I'm going to vomit.

The Krogans don't seem to share my feelings. Actually, Tara congratulates our male on how elegantly he placed the traps, as the damage to the ship is only minor. And it's evident that he takes it as a compliment. I suppose that's the mentality they have.

We reach the bridge and I switch on the systems. Tara is right: the damage is negligible. Groar then asks me to switch on the external cameras and points out where he has placed additional traps, in case that they should try to enter through the other airlocks or the breaches in the hull. He seems very satisfied of himself; he actually seems to even relish the idea of dispersing the guts of some additional intruder.

"Why did the Sneog say that the code forbade to say who had contracted him?" I ask, trying to change the subject.

Our male puffs.

"They're mercenaries. Their code of conduct forbids them to reveal who contracted them. But it's well known that those animals are cowards. He would have spoken if you had allowed me to finish, Art'Ana."

I feel how a shiver goes down my spine. Anybody would talk if they ripped away the flesh from the leg to the bone. But I'm not ready to allow torture, no matter how normal that might seem to them.

"It was not honorable," I state, and that finishes the question. Honor is everything for a Krogan. They will never do anything that will sully their honor.

I look for Bagheera, but can't find her, and the computer is unable to detect her. Finally, I shrug. She has survived for two months; I imagine she'll be all right until we return. Because Tara is in a hurry to return to our apartment, so as to inspect the spying device that she has captured.

We leave after Groar has placed a few new traps. I really hope he knows what he's doing and they won't affect us when we enter or leave. He assures me that there is no danger, but I'm only half assured. I wouldn't like to be blown to pieces.

We filter ourselves through the station's airlock, both Krogans obviously with the weapons in their paws. I thought that was an exaggeration, but as soon as I exit I also grab my gun and the laser.

They're ten. Black, between five and a half and six and a half feet, they have flattened heads similar to those of the praying mantis. They are bipeds, with legs and arms that look very disproportionate because of their length. Their hands have six fingers; these finish in long nails from which some liquid seems to drop. The skin looks very tough, but it's difficult to see because they wear a kind of uniform fitted with many devices that I don't recognize. A faint flickering surrounds them, as if the air around them was vibrating.

"Alarm," warns Groar about the effect that they have on us. "Declare your intentions."

Both the cannon that he holds as well as Tara's weapon are pointing to the bizarre beings, and I know that they are ready to shoot on the spot. So am I. These things are very disquieting, especially because of those red eyes that seem to burn like coal.

"There is no reason for alarm," reassures one of them, with such a deep voice that it sounds outright gloomy. "We are unarmed."

Groar makes a gesture, and Tara approaches these strange ET, briefly inspecting them one by one; she never stops pointing at them. Then she moves to one side. If we end up in a firefight, these bugs will have a tough time to get out of our crossfire.

"They don't seem to be armed, Art'Ana."

So she's passing me the ball. After all, I'm the group leader. Well, I suppose that I don't have any other option than talk with these startling beasts. Though I feel a knot in the stomach. For some strange reason I feel that these aliens are very, very dangerous.

"Declare your intentions," I repeat the words of our male.

But the one that had spoken before ignores me and looks at us, one by one.

"Who is your leader?" He turns towards Tara. "I suppose it is you. The Krogans are usually led by females."

Tara makes a gesture in my direction, without lowering her weapon.

"She's our Art'Ana. Our leader."

The alien turns towards me and inspects me from head to toe.

"Surprise. She's not Krogan."

That annoys me. It almost sounds like an insult.

"I am now." I lift the pendant that I am wearing around my neck, the one that Groar gave me as a gift when I married him. "I belong to the K'Raugh clan. This is my nest."

"Surprise. The Krogans have sometimes welcomed females from other species, but we know of none who has steered a nest."

That vermin is starting to get on my nerves.

"What do you want?"

"The Rokuz have told us that you stole that ship."

"The hell we did!" I explode. I realize that I have stated it in Spanish and change to Common. "That is incorrect. The Rokuz took away my ship, and then I recovered it in the same way. The ship was mine when I arrived and it still is."

They remain silent for a few seconds.

"Confusion. The Rokuz sold us the ship. Then they informed us that you seized it."

Ok, so he's taken aback. That's not surprising, if the Rokuz have swindled them. Well, I personally am very pissed off with those penguin-bats that tried to steal my ship. I'll have to say that explicitly, the intonation does not mean anything in Common.

"Rage. The Rokuz cannot sell what is not theirs. The ship is mine. It always was. If the Rokuz have tricked you, that is not my problem."

He seems to think for an instant; then he advances in my direction. I move sideways, lifting my weapons. If this brute thinks that he can hurt me, then he's going to get an incendiary bullet into his skull. I've never shot at an intelligent being in my life, but, during the Krogan rite of maturity that I had to pass, I wiped out a few beasts that intended to kill me. This won't be all too different, this being looks like another animal to me.

But he didn't come to attack me. He simply advances to the wall and places his hand on the airlock. But the hand does not cross it; the lock remains solid, as if it was a normal wall. Then I get it. Only the legitimate owner of the ship can cross it. That's why the intruders did not enter through here, but rather through the cargo airlock in open space, before being blown apart.

"Rage. The Rokuz have deceived us."

So now he's furious. Tough luck, boy. It seems that those Rokuz are even bigger cheaters than I thought. I'm not the only one that they have swindled.

"I told you."

He turns towards me. Suddenly he seems very dangerous, so I make sure that he can clearly see that, if he attacks me, he's going to find himself with a few holes in the skin, apart from being burned alive. But he does not pay any attention to my weapons.

"We Tloc are not used to be cheated."

So these are the Tloc. The buyers of the future. It's not surprising that they made me feel uneasy.

"This time they did."

I have the feeling that he wants to grab me, but he must realize that I am still pointing at him with my weapons. Groar is also looking askew at him, while aiming at his friends. Tara could also shoot him from her position.

"We'll buy your ship. You can be assured that we'll be very generous."

No way. This ship is my only hope to return with my mother. With some luck we'll be able to find out what made me get here.

"No."

He clenches the jaw. As far as I can see, he has no teeth, but the sound is very displeasing.

"We'll pay you twenty times its value."

"It's not for sale."

Then he bends towards me. I lift the gun until it's only inches away from his face, but that does not seem to preoccupy him.

"Be careful, little creature," he hisses. "The Tloc always get what they want. The wise thing would be to sell this ship while you still can. It is dangerous to refuse."

"It's not for sale," I repeat. "And it's even more dangerous to face some Krogans." I gesture towards the pile of debris at one side of the hall, not all too far from where we are. "Ask them."

He does not say anything, but looks at me one last time. His eyes seem to glow as if he wanted to drill me with them. However, he leaves and joins his mates. They talk together for an instant and then they leave. I lower my weapons while they move away.

Suddenly Groar pushes me aside so hard that I roll over the floor, making that the bullet fails and drills through the air where I was just an instant ago. The Tloc have turned and it so happens that they *are* armed: they're shooting at us.

Our male jumps through the airlock; there, he's safe, as the Tloc cannot enter. Tara makes a huge leap towards the debris, barricading herself behind a massive block of the collapsed terrace. Hastily, I follow her example between the buzz caused by the ionization of the air due to the lasers that are trying to hit me. I shoot three times towards the closest enemy, but the incendiary bullets simply ricochet, hitting the wall, where they organize a nice bonfire.

So I try the laser. No way, the light beam simply deviates from its target. These Tloc have a kind of energy shield that makes out weapons worthless. I have to duck when several lasers start to point in my direction. One instant later I have to cower in my hideout, as light beams and explosive projectiles are impacting all around me. If I move, I'm dead.

I look around, towards Tara. She's making gestures, but I don't get what she wants to tell me. Then she does as if she's shooting the slab in front of her, extends her claws, touches the block and touches her chest. Afterwards the does as if she's falling backwards. Finally, she points to one side. I look. There is a reflecting area on the wall, I can see there how our enemies are approaching.

OK, I got it. She's telling me that I should use my laser trick. When I nod, she raises the paw with four claws. She folds one. Then a second one. A third one.

On the count of four. As soon as she folds the fourth claw, I shoot the mirror on the wall. The beam rebounds, hitting one of the Tloc. Of course it does not hurt him because of his shield, but all turn to see from where this unexpected attack comes. I take the opportunity and leap towards another piece of wall that offers more protection.

Tara has also taken advantage of the opportunity and is firing an uninterrupted stream of explosive bullets against one of our attackers. She does not seem to be doing anything to him, as the bullets rebound, but suddenly the air surrounding him becomes violet; sparks appear. One instant later, the shield overloads and the Tloc's body shudders when several explosive bullets hit it, ripping it apart. He has not fallen yet when Tara has already changed her target.

The Tloc turn towards her and start shooting, forcing her to hide again behind the big terrace block. Then a kind of explosion floors them all. Groar has exited the airlock and has fired the plasma cannon that he carried with him. He reloads and a second shot impacts at the center of our attackers. As far as I can see, he has not injured them, but at least he has left them dizzy, they're all over the floor.

Now, I know that the plasma cannon is now useless; that device heats up a lot and you can only make two shots with it. But Groar knows that also. He has jumped forward, grabbing one of the Tloc. It does not help the poor fellow that he has an energy shield; the Krogan simply grabs him by the feet and uses him as a mace to attack another one. This shield is excellent to stop bullets or lasers, but it does not seem to work against a simple punch.

I'm firing, but my bullets ricochet against the shields; the Tloc simply ignore me and concentrate their fire on Groar. His breastplate is starting to be affected by the impacts; it won't take long before they really wound him.

I stop firing for a moment; after all, it does not seem to do anything, but there is something that is nagging at my mind. Something related with a Tloc who is firing at our male while on his knees.

Shit! I know what it is! The Tloc is showing me the boot soles, but these do not seem to have the slight flickering of the air that indicates the presence of the shield. Could it be that...?

I point carefully and the Tloc screams of pain when my bullet impacts and his feet are suddenly wrapped in fire. Forgetting about him, I search for another target. Yes, there is another one in the same position. Seconds later, another Tloc is burning.

Tara is looking at me with surprise. Pointing to my feet, I then make a gesture as if I fired at them from below. After that, she turns towards the enemy: She has understood it. She starts firing at the feet, as that's the weakest point of the force shield. The explosive bullets don't penetrate the field, but their force is such that the enemy ends up stumbling; I use that instant to place an incendiary bullet in the boot soles.

After a few minutes everything has finished. One of the Tloc managed to escape, but the others are dead. Tara has wiped out two aliens, and I've left four of them burning. Groar has finished off two simply by hitting them; he also tore one's head off. These ET finished their fight in the worst possible way.

I notice that I am panting, and I'm pretty upset. It's not the first time that I have fought for my life: when I passed the rite of maturity, I had also to kill some beasts that wanted to kill me. But until now I had never shot at a sentient being. Of course, the Tloc also look like beasts to me; if they were anything like humans, by now I would be really in shock. But when you're fighting for your life you don't think too much. Even so, I don't feel very well.

"Good trick," praises Tara and, to be honest, I take it as a compliment. "Now we know how to kill them, those shields make them almost invincible."

"Grrrr..." growls the warrior. "They're not worth much in the melee. But they're a problem for remote combat. How did you manage to pierce their shields?"

"Tanit discovered that the boot soles don't have a shield," explains the Krogan. "It must be because it prevents to walk properly or perhaps the field cannot form adequately on the ground."

"And Tara has discovered that the shield can be overloaded with sustained fire," I hurry to add, so as to make sure that we share the merit. "The energy must be limited and the shield heats up in excess when so much kinetic energy is generated."

"Well, I've found out that the shield is worthless once you have grabbed a Tloc," points Groar out. "Because it does not protect them from my blows. So the Tloc are not as invincible as they want others to believe." He growls with evident satisfaction. "Good fight. Today we honored our clan."

Unfortunately, his complacence is premature. Something has grabbed me suddenly from behind, lifting me from the floor. One of the Tloc was not dead and has taken the opportunity to attack me. I feel how a weapon is pressed to my side, in the gap that the breastplate does not cover.

"Rage," I hear him say. "You should not have attacked us. Drop your weapons or I will kill your leader."

I see that our warrior lifts a heavy gun and points carefully. Though I know that he shoots really well, I hope that his pulse will not shake. I am trembling myself. This vermin is using me as a shield, if Groar is not careful, it will be me who will be hit by the projectile.

Then I scream of pain. The Tloc has driven his nails into my leg. Nails like knives.

"Lower the weapons," he commands. "Or I'll kill her."

I hear the buzz of the magnetic generator driving the projectiles in the Krogan weapon and the Tloc falls backwards, while I'm being showered with leftovers of his brains. But instantly a horrible pain hits my side; I hear my own scream of pain one second before the darkness surrounds me.

I recover the consciousness due to the jolting of Tara's steps, who is carrying me in her arms while she runs through the corridors. My right side hurts with a horrible pain, and when I look I see that they have removed my blouse and the breastplate; I'm wearing only my undershirt, which is soaked in blood. I'm injured: the Tloc managed to shoot me before he died.

The pain in my side is beyond all bearing. I try to touch it, but then it seems to increase, despite the fact that I was convinced that this was impossible. I can't avoid a scream. I don't know how the wound is, but it must be serious.

"Don't touch it," commands Tara. "We'll arrive soon."

Arrive? Where to? Probably they're bringing me to a doctor, but how is a doctor going to cure me? There is no other human being closer than fifteen thousand light-years.

I whimper of pain and try to clench my teeth, doing the impossible to ignore the wound in my side. But my leg is also hurting, there where the alien clawed me. And it seems to hurt more and more.

"This way," I hear Groar say, and I turn my head to look at him. He's running in front of us and he finally stops at what seems to be a shop. He makes some gestures and then places the claw on top of a black plate. He's paying something.

We enter. There is a kind of huge white table in the center of the room, with a massive head from which a lot of arms protrude. Tara lays me with care on the table, and the mechanical arms start moving one instant later.

Within seconds they have removed my undershirt. Or to be more precise, they have cut it from my body. A robotic arm tries to take away with care the cloth that is sticking to the wound, but I pass out again when it does. Actually, it's my luck, as I can't stand so much pain.

But the pain does not cease when I open my eyes again; no, it's far worse. My leg is also hurting a lot. I look. I'm only with my briefs; they have also removed my pants and shoes. My leg is terribly swollen, of a horrible blue color. The nails of the Tloc apparently had some kind of poison. I pant, knowing that I'm sobbing of pain. It's evident that I'm going to die.

"What do you mean that the auto-doctor cannot cure here?" is Groar roaring. "If she dies, so will you!"

"It's not my fault!" defends itself a little creature that is hardly five feet tall; he has a somewhat simian look. "The machine does not recognize her species! It will take us at least one cycle to analyze her! And we have no clue about the toxin that she has in her lower extremity! We can't prepare an antidote without any data! Where does that venom come from?"

"A Tloc clawed her. He probably had that poison in his nails."

"A Tloc?" exalts the doctor. "How do you want us then to find a remedy? We don't have a sufficiently advanced technology to counter their venoms!"

"No," suddenly Tara says at my side. "But they do."

Groar lifts his head, looking at us.

"You mean...?"

"There is no other option." A claw is raised above me, pointing to the doctor. "Close the wound as best as you can. She must not lose more corporate liquids. And do something so that she does not feel so much pain. Hurry!"

The arms of the machine start moving, approaching my side. I feel another vivid pain, and again I fall into the darkness.

When I wake up again, I'm no longer lying in the doctor's office. No, I am attached to Tara's back with a kind of harness, my head right beside hers, looking over what would be her shoulder in case she had one. She's firing; I can see how the bullets are impacting the force field of a Tloc. Then the field overloads, disappears, and the explosive ammunition converts the alien into a shapeless mass of meat.

I moan of pain and Tara turns her head towards me while she reloads her weapon.

"Are you all right?"

It's evident that I am not, the pain is unbearable.

I must have said it aloud, because the Krogan growls, irked.

"They have injected you a painkiller so that it won't hurt that much, but it will still take some time before it acts. There was something more effective, but we were not very sure that it would not be poisonous for your metabolism. What they have injected you is compatible with most species, but it's slow."

I close my eyes for a moment. My side is still hurting a lot, but I no longer feel the leg. I'm not sure whether that is good or bad. Probably it's bad; it must be a sign that the poison has advanced so much that I no longer feel the pain.

"I'm dying, isn't it?"

She growls a low and prolonged sound.

"Not if we can do something about it."

There is a tremendous explosion and she jumps forward, running for a new cover. Then I see Groar. He's surrounded by a lot of fallen Tloc in the middle of a smoking area, and he's killing them one by one. He breaks their ribs by kicking them, rips away their limbs with a simple yank or simply crushes their skulls. The force shield that in theory makes them invulnerable is useless for those poor bastards. Within two minutes he has finished off the twelve that had faced him. The last one managed to stand up and shoot him, but the Krogan breastplate is almost as good as the force field. The monstrous warrior approaches the terrified Tloc, takes out his dagger and slowly inserts it into his enemy, as if the force field did not exist.

"The trick is to stick the weapon slowly," he coldly explains Tara, taking out the immense knife from the body while this falls to the floor. "The shield only rejects the higher energies, but allows anything moving slowly to enter, like the air. If that were not so, they would asphyxiate."

"Good to know," acknowledges the female. "Let's proceed. We need to find an auto-doctor as soon as possible."

"But it did not work!" I mumble. "I heard it; they have not cataloged my species. They can't cure me."

The Krogan approaches. His huge paw touches my face with a surprising softness, almost with tenderness, if these aliens are capable of that.

"Don't worry, little Gal," he reassures me with a soft voice. "We'll find a Tloc auto-doctor. Those are far more advanced than the ones we have. They'll cure you." He snarls menacingly while he recovers the huge plasma cannon that he was carrying on his back. "Or we will not leave any living Tloc on this station."

He starts to advance, with Tara following him with caution at a certain distance. This is how Krogans fight: the warriors perform the frontal assault, while the females provide cover fire. These armored monsters are almost impossible to stop without heavy weapons.

"Where are we?" I ask, trying to ignore the pain in my side. It seems to be less; perhaps it's true that the painkiller that they have given me is starting to act. But I am slightly dizzy.

"In the Tloc zone of the station," responds Tara. "They have tried to stop us, but they were not very effective."

Yeah, she can say that. The hall where we are is in ruins. Krogan's don't do things by halves when they fight. Their technique is as simple as ferocious: they simply destroy everything that is in their way. There are not many species that can face them. They're professional warriors who evolved on a planet where the fight for survival was plainly brutal. If you add to that a very tough skin and a tremendous ferocity, you have the same probability to stop one as to do it with a furious rhinoceros. Or the tyrannosaur that they resemble somewhat.

I don't get to see the enemies, so quickly does Tara jump into cover, with an incredibly agile movement for such a huge creature. But the jolt makes me cry out of pain. She ignores it: she's already firing.

"Green circle!" shouts suddenly Groar. "Hold your fire!"

Tara lifts her weapon and stops shooting. But she does not stop pointing at the three aliens that are approaching, holding a green plastic circle between them. I assume it must be the equivalent of a white flag. They show their empty hands so as to show that they are not armed, though probably they have them hidden; Tara was not capable of detecting them when we met this species.

"Declare your intentions."

I feel a burst of pain and moan, so I miss the answer of the Tloc. Probably they've asked why we're attacking them, hearing the answer of the Krogan.

"Our Art'Ana has been wounded by Tloc. We want you to cure her."

"We deny having wounded a Krogan."

Krogans don't know how to lie; they consider that dishonorable and they would prefer to die before dishonoring themselves. However, they do know what a lie is, and I could swear that I can recognize despise in the voice of our male, even though I am incapable of capturing alien emotions.

"You did it in front of us. One escaped, but the other Tloc are dead."

That seems to worry him. I remember what Tara said, that nobody remembered the last time that someone had killed a Tloc.

"It's not possible to kill a Tloc!"

The warrior laughs.

"Ke, ke, ke... Really?" He points towards the center of the hall. "And what are those that? N'Agu rodents? Perhaps they were, at least they were not much more difficult to kill. It's obvious that you Tloc are greatly overestimated."

The black being looks towards the remains of what possibly were his friends, in the middle of the smoking debris of the hall. He turns towards the others of his species and they talk something between each other. Then he turns to look at the Krogan.

"What some Tloc individuals have done is not the responsibility of all of us. We don't know anything."

Then Tara intervenes. I have the impression that she's very pissed off.

"Rage. The Tloc are biologic waste, but it is well known that they remain in constant contact with each other. You cannot ignore this attack. Either you cure her or you will all face the consequences. You are all responsible."

I'd swear that the other looks at her with despise. He does in any case not seem very impressed. Anyhow, I'm starting to stop paying attention; the pain is returning and I feel more and more dizzy.

"We reject your threat. The Tloc do not obey lower creatures."

"In that case," snarls Groar, "we will continue killing Tloc until there is no-one alive on this station. We'll see who the lower creatures are when we have exterminated you."

The Tloc makes a disparaging noise.

"You two want to kill all of us?"

Tara then releases a menacing growl.

"We have already killed twenty seven of your species. We can kill many more. And when the rest of the Krogan join us..."

The other creature seems alarmed.

"Why should the other Krogans attack us?"

Then Groar laughs.

"Why? Ke, ke, ke... You have attacked the K'Raugh clan. From now on, all K'Raugh will start exterminating Tloc. And because of our alliances with other clans, they will also enter into a war with you. Soon it will be all Krogan against the Tloc. Your technology will not save you. Not against Krogans. You have already seen what two Krogans alone can do."

The Tloc talk excitedly among them. Then their leader turns towards the huge warrior.

"We have never attacked the Krogan as such! You cannot pretend to let an individual confrontation degenerate into a global war!"

Groar points at me.

"You attacked her. And she's the Art'Ana of the Maart'Ing nest in the K'Raugh clan. Our leader. When you attacked her, you have attacked all of us. If she dies, you will all pay it with your lives."

The pain surrounds me again and I release a moan, closing my eyes for an instant. I know that I won't last much more, but I try to pay attention.

"Is she wounded? Why did you not place her in an auto-doctor? You cannot blame us if you have not taken care of her properly!"

Our male then releases the growl that precedes the challenge. The Tloc must have recognized it, because he recoils a few steps.

"The auto-doctor cannot cure her. It does not recognize her species. You have also injected her poison for which the auto-doctor cannot synthesize an antidote. She will die very soon. And you will die with her." With a swashing gesture he reloads his monstrous gun and points it towards the Tloc. "The truce is over. I want the Art'Ana to see how her murderers die before she does."

"Wait!" screams the Tloc. "Wait a moment!"

He turns towards his companions and they start talking with each other in their language, which I am unable to understand. I close my eyes again. This is the end. I notice that I am slipping again towards unconsciousness, but then I feel how Tara is shaking me.

"Tanit! Hold out! Endure! Don't surrender!"

I open my eyes and look at the strange face that I have in front of me. To my surprise, for an instant I have the impression that it's my mother who is talking.

"What for?" I mumble, feeling how my forces are abandoning me. "I'm dying. Leave me now. It hurts too much. Let me die."

"No!" screams the Tloc. "We'll bring one of our auto-doctors! We can cure her!"

"I don't care," I whisper, closing my eyes. "Let me go. Let me die in peace."

Then I slip for the last time towards the darkness.

When I finally awake, both Krogans are my right, their weapons ready in their paws; to my left there at least five or six Tloc. They seem even more anxious than my nest.

"What happened?" I muse.

"We almost lost you," snaps out Tara. "But this auto-doctor is far more advanced than those we have. We made it."

Touching the location of the wound, I only manage to feel the smooth skin. There is nothing, and it also does not hurt. I straighten and inspect my abdomen. There is no sign that I have ever been wounded there, except the blood-tainted briefs that I still wear.

Looking at my leg, I realize that it has again its normal color. I breathe with relief. For an instant I was convinced that I would die. If I have narrowly escaped death, it's because of my new family. They might look like monsters, but once again this proves that the beauty is inside.

I look around. I'm lying on a kind of platform, at approximately four feet from the ground. Contrary to the other auto-doctor, this one does not have any kind of arms; it looks like a common table.

Sitting down, I move my feet over the edge. I feel great. Actually, I have the feeling that the machine has done much more than simply removing the poison and curing my wounds, because I feel phenomenal. I even have the impression that I can see better than before.

"We saved her. As you can see, we have complied with our part of the deal. It's your turn now."

"Deal?" I ask, jumping to the floor.

"We negotiated in your name while they were curing you," explains Tara. "It was necessary. But you won't like it. However, you will have to accept it."

I look around, then at her.

"Why?"

"Because if you're incapacitated, I'm the Art'Ana of the nest and I pawn the word and the honor of the nest if we reach an agreement during a negotiation."

Suddenly I feel as if something cold is running down my back. I don't know what Tara has agreed, but it's evident that it will disgust me and yet I will not be able to do anything about it. Not if she and Groar have accepted it. Not if the nest's honor is compromised if we break the deal. Thus are the Krogans: Honor is everything. Even life does not matter if you lose your honor. They will force me to accept it, whether I like it or not.

"And what have you agreed?" I ask in a small voice.

It is Groar who intervenes.

"Your cure as a compensation for the attack, as well as a personalized force field for you, so that nobody can attack you again by treason. Also the auto-doctor, as it is the only one that can cure you. In addition, we will keep all weapons and equipment of the dead Tloc as our war booty. In exchange, both parties commit to cease all hostilities."

I nod. It seems like a good deal, actually we're getting a lot out of this agreement. What I don't see is why I would not like it.

"That sounds OK to me."

"There is something more," joins in the Tloc who seems to be the leader. "You will sell us your ship."

I look at him with horror.

"What? No!"

"Your companions have closed the deal. You must accept it. The payment is very generous."

I turn towards the Krogans, incensed.

"How could you accept that? It's my only hope to go home!"

Then Groar bends, until his head is at my height, looking me in the eyes.

"Listen well, Gal," he says softly in his language, so that the Tloc will not understand him. "That ship is dangerous. It traveled across half the galaxy, doing something that no other ship ever did. As soon as the word gets out, all species will try to get hold of it, at any price. Your life is worthless while you have that ship. And an unarmed ship is an easy prey."

"But..." I protest, looking for words. My knowledge of the Krogan language is still very basic. "If I sell it, I won't be able to go back!"

"Tanit," interrupts Tara. "I inspected thoroughly the engines of your starship. It's impossible that they could perform that trip. Something else caused it, but whatever it was, it's not on your ship. We'll find out what made you travel so far. But now you have to get rid of that ship; we're in danger while you own it. We can protect you from the Tloc. We can protect you from assassins. But we cannot protect you if absolutely everybody is trying to kill you so as to get hold of your ship."

I breathe in deep, trying to calm down. They are obviously right. If I have traveled fifteen thousand light-years in a matter of weeks or perhaps even within minutes, then that is a technology that everybody will ambition. One for which every species will be willing to kill, and life is not worth much around here. I will last only days as soon as the word spreads. If I'm lucky. I don't want to imagine what they will try to do with me if they capture me alive. I already saw how Groar tried to extract information from a prisoner.

"All right," I state in Common, turning towards the Tloc. "If the nest has agreed to sell the ship, I will not dishonor my nest by disowning their accord. But I want to retrieve my personal belongings. My... an animal that belongs to me. And some food."

"That is acceptable," they respond. "But you will not remove nor modify any equipment on the ship. The technology must not be altered. We will accompany you all the time, so as to ensure that you do not change anything."

I shrug. Once the decision is taken, I don't care a damn what they do with the ship.

"Very well."

We go all together to the docks and I open the ship's airlock. I have to explain the Tloc how it works; they get it immediately, it's very rudimentary for them. Then Groar deactivates the mines he had placed and all accompany me to my cabin, observing while I retrieve my things and place them in the suitcase. I take the opportunity and dress. Yeah, I know that these ET don't care a shit about the fact that I'm half naked, but I do. Then I continue packing.

Having emptied the closet and the drawers, I start putting away what I have on top of my desk when they ask me to inspect the holographic cube with the photographs of my parents. They return it soon enough: it's obvious that this is not a secret technology.

My father's cabin is very close. I have not entered there since... well, since he died. Too many memories, and too painful ones at that. With the Tloc following me closely, I enter. For an instant I fear that they will not allow me to take anything, but the holocube with my photograph on the table convinces them that these are part of my personal belongings. It's not that I take much. The cubes that dad had of mom and myself. His paper diary, which the Tloc don't consider even worth a second look. The two model ships that he was finishing, together with the drawings. I have to show them to the Tloc, clarify them what a model is and then explain them how the drawings correspond to those of the ships. By the way they look at me, I'd say that they think that the humans are crazy. But they allow me to wrap everything and place it carefully in the suitcase, which has been growing in size as I placed all my stuff inside. By now it has a very respectable size. Actually, it is bigger than I am.

With the suitcase following me, I first go to the hydroponic gardens and then to the kitchen. I fill another suitcase with food. The extraterrestrial automatic kitchens might be very good, but my culinary creativity is nil and I always get something with a really disgusting aspect. Edible, but you better don't look at it. Given that the machines can reproduce samples, I prefer to eat something that at least looks like human food. In addition, I don't have a clue of what Bagheera eats, and it's obvious that the cat will not be able to ask a machine for the food it likes.

Finally, I call Bagheera. It costs me less than what I expected; the cat comes immediately when I call it, though she looks mistrustful at all the aliens accompanying me. I take her in my arms. To my surprise, she does not resist but instead snuggles in them. She must have missed me a lot while she was with the Rokuz; before that, she was quite surly. Or perhaps she thinks that I'm going to protect her from all the monsters surrounding us; it's possible that the Rokuz tried to hurt her.

"I'll give you access to the on-board computer," I tell the Tloc. "But it only understands my language."

"That is not necessary," they respond. "It's a very primitive system. Let's carry out the transfer."

They extend a black plate in my direction and I touch it with one hand. One instant later I know that my personal account has been increased by sixty-four billion credits, an incredible fortune. The bad news is that in exchange I have lost everything that tied me to my home.

I look around one last time. I feel like crying, but I won't do it in front of these insects. Followed by my suitcases and the two Krogans I go to the airlock, and exit to the space station.

"It was necessary, Tanit," clarifies Tara, who must have understood my mood. "This ship could not help you, but it could destroy you."

"I know," I mumble. "Can we go to the balcony? I'd like to see it one last time."

But when we get to the balcony, I'm surprised to see that there are a lot of small vessels hustling around my ship. Then I notice that it is moving.

"Tugboats," explains Groar. The Tloc know that they have to take away the ship as soon as possible. They won't be safe either while the ship is here."

Slowly, but increasingly faster, the starship starts moving, turns and draws off until it disappears in a starry background like they've never seen on Earth. I feel the lump in my throat and strongly embrace the cat that I still hold in my arms.

"Meow?" she asks.

"Yes, Bagheera," I respond. "Now there are just the two of us left."

And two aliens, I should add. I don't know what I will do now. But it's very likely that I will never return home.

Rescue in Hell

Do you know what happens when you have sixty-four billion credits in the bank and you're married with two aliens that look like dinosaurs? That you bore yourself to death.

Let's make it clear, I'm not complaining about being married. Though on Mars or on Earth this would be a no-no at my age, at fifteen thousand light-years from home these things are very different. Officially, I'm a Po'lai, an adult-that-is-not-an-adult, as I passed the dangerous rite of maturity and I survived. A Po'lai is officially an adult, with the only inconvenient —advantage from my point of view— that she cannot have sex until the matriarch of the nest allows it. Which, by the way, that's also me. Obviously I'm not ready for that: with eleven years I'm not old enough to have sex with a man, much less with an alien that is ten feet tall and some four feet wide. But by the time I become eighteen, I will have a serious problem, if I have not returned home. And right now that seems quite difficult, if not outright impossible.

Even so, to be married with two Krogans is a gravy train, as they've saved my life several times and nobody dares attacking me when I'm with them. The Krogans belong to a warrior species, and they're as difficult to stop as a battle tank. That's good because law and order don't exist in this part of the galaxy. Well, actually they do exist. Each species has its own laws, and if you're in their territory you better comply with their laws to the letter, they're not exactly very lenient if you infringe them. But outside a planet, it's worse than the mythical Wild West. Why? Because the habits of the different races are so different that it has proved to be impossible to reach a common behavior, so everybody does what he sees fitting.

For example, at home we have laws against murder. But here there are many species —including the Krogan— for which killing many adversaries is a matter of prestige. There are even predator races, which don't find any inconvenience in eating other intelligent beings. If they don't do it continuously it's because they want to trade, and it's not a good policy to eat your customers or suppliers. But if somebody kills somebody else in public, the most likely thing that will happen is that everybody stops by to enjoy the show. Nobody will move a hand, claw or tentacle to prevent it.

Yeah, and trade is also terrific. Apart from the fact that the concept of value is something very subjective, it's universally accepted that if you have been cheated in a deal then it's your fault; you should have negotiated better. And that is assuming that they don't simply steal it from you: there are species that don't understand the concept of property, and they will take everything you own without even asking. On the other hand, they will not say a word if you steal whatever they have. There is a Law of Commerce, but these are very lax laws and nobody worries too much if you break them. The only place where it is mandatory to comply with it is this space station, *Meeting Point*, and only because it establishes some basic behavior rules that at least set some order. By the way, those rules don't specify that you can't kill anyone, only that the bodies of the dead will be used to provide energy to the station. Assuming somebody does not eat them first, of course. There is a quite busy meat market, and nobody asks where the meat comes from.

Meeting Point is huge, the size of a small moon; it even has its own gravity field. Nobody knows very well who built it; apparently it has been here for quite a few millennia, and that detail was somehow lost in the fog of history. But it's the main commerce center of this crowded part of the galaxy, where in a radius of fifty or sixty light years there must be around a hundred species. I've lost count of the amount of aliens that I've seen so far.

Escorted by the other female of our nest, Tara, I have visited part of this artificial planetoid. They say that the souk of Port Deimos on Mars is the most complicated and convoluted structure that human beings have ever built. Well, I've been there, as I grew up close to that place. And it's pure geometry when compared to this station. You can get lost in a matter of minutes, unless you know where you're going.

Whoever built this station created flat decks, straight corridors and rectangular halls. But in the millennia that have passed, they have done so much mischief that by now there are no longer drawings of the station. There are terraces in holes that they have opened across several decks and the corridors twist like earthworms, dodging shops, workshops and hovels of varying kinds, assuming they don't return to themselves. Dozens of species roar, groan, squeak, tweet or whistle in their respective languages, or communicate with each other in the universal language that they have, Common. This, which is totally based on logic, is also sometimes very difficult to understand, as everybody pronounces it with his own intonation.

At least I understand the shops and the banks. By now I also identify the medical centers, though for me they are totally worthless: as they do not have cataloged the human race, they could do nothing for me if I become sick or I'm wounded. The bars are also easy to identify; after all, I worked in one when I arrived at this station. I'm also capable of guessing what some of the workshops do. But there are many premises of which I have no clue what their purpose is, and I steer well away from them unless I'm accompanied by somebody from my nest. Once I almost entered something that proved to be the equivalent of a Roman circus... as a gladiator. I realized on time what I was entering because they were taking out the corpses of the combatants. I get the shakes every time I think about it.

While I try to distract me, our male tries to get hold of a ship. We had a tremendous firefight with an alien species, the Tloc, during which I almost died. Afterwards we reached an agreement with them. I survived thanks to the pact that Tara negotiated, as at that moment I was agonizing. She managed to get some magnificent concessions. The bad news is that, in exchange, we had to sell the ship that brought me here to the Tloc. It's true that they paid very well. Not less than sixty four billion credits. An immense fortune. But that deal left us stranded on this station. Unless we can get hold of a starship, we won't go anywhere. Unfortunately, whoever arrives here with a starship also needs it to leave, so it's not easy at all to find one.

And Groar insists that the ship must be heavily armed. Now, that's understandable. Our fight with the Tloc resulted in a big pile of corpses. My new family ravaged as only Krogans can do: they basically fired at anything, whether it moved or not. The station management passed us the bill for the damage, the whooping sum of seventeen million credits. We did not discuss and paid without questioning it; that amount was mere pocket money when compared what the Tloc paid for my ship. Even so, the station management is not very happy with us. Despite having reached an agreement, the Tloc would be delighted to see us dead. And I bet that there are a lot of aliens on the station who must think that we have much more money than we deserve and that they should have part of it. For many species piracy is an honorable profession, so I get the point that our male is making: we are not very popular, so our ship should better be capable of defending itself. Unfortunately, such a ship is difficult to get and our warrior spends a lot of time outside.

While Groar searches for a ship, I'm bored to death. I brush or play with the cat that survived the accident that brought me here, but the animal gets soon tired of it. There is nothing else to do, and this space station does not have much entertainment. Actually, it has, but the entertainment is so strange for me that I am unable to understand what pleasure the aliens take from it. Apart from the four or five hours of daily combat training, I have nothing to do. Sometimes I switch on the equivalent of the television, but except the news —which are quite boring— most of the time I don't understand anything of what they're emitting. And if I understand it, it's even worse: It goes from the repugnant to the horrible.

Tara entertains me from time to time, teaching me the Krogan language or telling me stories of her species. Sometimes we go out and she explains me the different places and facilities that we visit. But most of the time she's grappling with the problem about how I arrived here; apparently she made a copy of all the records that the Rokuz made when they stole my ship and she's analyzing them. Though she does not seem to make much progress.

"Is something wrong with you?" she asks when I sigh for the umpteenth time.

I hesitate. Common does not have a word for what I want to say, at least as far as I know. And if the Krogan language has one, I still ignore it.

"Grief due to inactivity."

She tilts her head in that gesture of surprise that is typical of her race.

"Is it possible to grieve because you do nothing?"

I nod.

"Yes. My species calls it boredom."

"Then do something. What did you study? Or does your species not teach anything to their cubs?"

"Of course they do. Actually, I finished..." Shit, the concept of university does not exist here. "Some advanced studies. Astrobiology. The knowledge of beings that are foreign to our home world."

She bends again to continue addressing the problem that she's so intensively studying.

"Then try to learn something about all the species that there are in this station. It will take you quite a while."

I straighten in surprise. Of course! Why did I not think about it? I studied Astrobiology at the university so as to be able to help mum with the flora and fauna of Thuis when we would meet again. That was the only way that they would allow me to travel to that colony, while still being a girl. It was not sufficient to be a genius; it was also necessary that I could do something useful for the colony.

Well, I might have to wait for some time before I return with my mother. But I have an opportunity that no other human being ever had, as I've been the only one that has met aliens: document intelligent extraterrestrials. When I get home —assuming I can get back— I will be not only the youngest astrobiologist in history, but also the most famous one. I'll return with a knowledge that human beings have never dreamed of. The idea fills me with enthusiasm; I'm eager to start.

I need something to capture images, take note of my comments and if possible perform biologic analyses. Tara accepts reluctantly to interrupt her work and accompany me to find such a device; I have no clue about the alien technologies, but she is at least familiar with most of the species, their technical capabilities and where to find what I'm looking for.

It doesn't take us long. The Krogan knows an adequate shop close to the place where she went to look for weapons, and I find a mixture of recorder and biologic analyzer used by the alien doctors. It has sufficient memory to store the information of more than a hundred thousand patients and it is also encrypted with my brain pattern, so that nobody else will be able to use it. A real marvel. Of course, Tara insists on entering the weapons store, where she buys herself a kind of portable cannon that throws incendiary grenades. These Krogan are like kids as far as weapons are concerned. She also purchases me an electromagnetic rifle of my size with cryogenic projectiles. So, if I shoot somebody, I'll freeze him. It must be to compensate her grenades. Though being honest, I am far more thrilled by my recorder.

We return to our apartment and I convince her to be my first record. She endures with forbearance while I photograph her in three dimensions and then in different stances, so as to finally scan her internal organs. Then she leaves for the training area to test out her new toy while I look in wonder at the scientific treasure that I have just captured. To my joy I also find out that the device comes with factory information about slightly more than a hundred species and is capable of identifying and labeling the different organs, as well as their functions. And, since it can read my mind, I see the information in Spanish.

Now, that's too much: Tara has two hearts. I suppose that, being so big, she needs it for the blood circulation. She has a backbone that is far stronger than those of human beings, and her ribs are so strong that it looks as if they were designed to stop a bullet. On the other side, the lungs and stomach are similar to those of the human beings, though in-between there is an organ that I am unable to identify. The label that the device shows indicates something like 'booster'. I take note that I have to research what that is.

The rest of her anatomy, to my surprise, is pretty common. She could have evolved on Earth; except that strange organ and the two hearts, she does not have anything that is especially weird. Well, except the shape, but on Earth we had some dinosaurs that could have evolved towards her shape if they had not become extinct. But of course the dinosaurs were not mammals.

Tara obviously is one: her breasts look similar to those of a human woman, though obviously they are much bigger. I can even detect the ducts for the milk. On the other hand, the internal sexual organs look more like those of the orangutans. What the heck, if they did not have here those auto-doctor machines, I could even act as her midwife the day that she has cubs. When I made the colonist course on Mars they showed me how to assist in childbirth, and Tara's would not be very different.

Groar returns and it's his turn to be examined. He does not like it, but I make my authority as the matriarch of the nest prevail and he ends up accepting it grudgingly. When he finally goes for lunch, I have duplicated my data. There is not much difference, except what you would expect because they have different sexes. The most outstanding fact is that he has some additional ribs on his back, in addition to an especially tough skin. He is literally armored there. I would not be surprised if you fire a bullet there and it ricochets. I don't dare even to image in what kind of environment the Krogans have evolved so as to need this kind of armor. Even the rhinoceros on Earth did not have that kind of protection.

He finishes eating and enters the training area. Probably he'll spend a lot of time admiring Tara's new toy, so I get dressed and leave. Of course, I first put my breastplate below the blouse. I have already seen how things work around here, and having that protection saved my life a few days ago. In addition, I'm armed and I've put on the energy shield that we got from the Tloc. If somebody wants to mess with me, he better should come with heavy weapons. With all the combat training that my alien husband has subjected me to, I can even take on a Krogan. Something which, by the way, I already did during my rite of maturity.

It's when I enter an elevator that I notice that I'm being followed. Krogan. About a dozen. Usually I would not have noticed them as we're in the middle of the Krogan neighborhood, but I saw two of them when I went out with Tara to buy my recorder. I recall them because they have some scars that must be the result of a tremendous fight. It's not easy at all to wound beings as armored as they are, and much less to cause scars like those two have.

While I raise through the lift tube, I look down. Yes, they're also entering the tube. I go up six decks to one of the main station avenues, exit the tube and pretend to stroll around, looking at the shops. After a while I enter into a shop and buy a device they sell there. I have no clue of what it does, but it allows me to see that they are waiting at a certain distance, pretending that they are not looking in my direction.

I frown. There is something weird here. It does not seem as if they want to do anything in public, but perhaps they're waiting until I enter a less crowded area of the station. In that case, I'll be in real trouble. If necessary I can bring down a Krogan, I've done that before. But I can't handle a dozen of them.

Pretending that I don't see them, I pass at their side, again in the direction of the lift. I enter the elevator, and I deliberately try not to think about whether I want to go up or down. That's what happened to me the first time that I entered one: if you don't indicate what you want to do, you drop like a rock.

And that is exactly what happens: I go into free fall. However, as I am prepared for it, I command the elevator in my mind to stop me at the proper floor, and I exit hurriedly, looking up. The Krogans are descending, but much slower. I just managed to get well ahead of them. So I start to run.

I enter hastily into the nest, and both Groar and Tara rush out immediately from the training area as soon as they hear me, the weapons in their paws. Panting from the effort, I report my small adventure. I know that they will protect me from those enemies. But, to my surprise, they start laughing with that weird laughter that sounds like a cough.

"Ke, ke, ke... Tanit, they were not trying to ambush you."

I suppose that I now look pretty stupid.

"They were not?"

"No. They belong to our clan. We have hired them to escort you when you go out. In case that the Tloc contract somebody to hurt you despite our agreement with them. They will need a real army to fight so many Krogans."

Now it's sure that I'm looking stupid, though probably they are not able to recognize that expression.

"Why did you not tell me?"

"We did not want you to be worried. After all, you're a Po'lai."

Then we hear the noise on the other side of the door. Growls and a scream as if they were killing somebody. Immediately the two Krogans are again with the weapons in their paws, pointing to the door. Without even being aware of it, I have also taken out my small gun with explosive bullets. Tara makes a gesture towards the door; the camera is activated and we see a hologram of the outside.

The Krogans are standing around a kind of marmot that is about five and a half feet tall. Most of them are pointing at him with weapons of different shapes and sizes. Now, that's not very smart: If they start shooting, they will kill each other. Others are playfully nicking him with their sharp daggers. Well, it's what Krogans call playful. The marmot is bleeding from different wounds.

"Stop that!"

Groar and Tara look at each other and open the door, their weapons ready. An instant later, the marmot is thrown at my feet.

"He was trying to enter," clarifies one of the Krogans with scars. "We have not killed him in case you wanted to do it yourself."

"Good work," praises Groar. "Return to your lookout positions."

The Krogans leave, evidently very satisfied with themselves, and Tara closes the door. The marmot is moaning on the floor. To be honest, I feel sorry for him.

"Bring him to the auto-doctor," I command. "Then we'll see what he wants."

"Let's see first whether he wears arms," growls Groar, quickly searching him.

He does not seem to be armed, as the Krogan lifts him immediately and brings him to the next room, which is where we have the auto-doctor that we got from the Tloc. Within minutes the machine has cured the wounds of the alien. However, it does not repair his torn uniform.

Finally the marmot gets up. He has a light brown fur with a quite beautiful hair. A very amusing mustache. His eyes are very normal, he has small ears and a dark snout. And that is all the similitude with a marmot. He has hands with five fingers ending in very sharp claws. Because of his teeth, it's also very obvious that he's not a rodent. Just the opposite, because of the shape of his canine teeth, I'd guess that he's a carnivore. He could perfectly be an animal from Earth, except for the slight detail that he is taller than me and it is an intelligent being.

Despite his peaceful aspect, I don't put my trust in him. By now I have already learned that the aliens are unpredictable. I continue with the gun in my hand, just in case. And Tara does not even try to hide that she's pointing at him with her new toy. I'd rather have that she did not do that. If she fires that junk, her incendiary grenades will make us all burn.

"I did not think it was so dangerous to see you," mumbles the marmot.

Groar grunts, clearly amused.

"We are dangerous. All our enemies know that."

"I am not an enemy."

The warrior snorts.

"We'll see. Identify yourself."

"I am..." He states an unpronounceable name, so full of gees and jays that I am tempted to clear my throat, so complicated is it. "I represent the Kanil species. I come to contract your services."

We look at each other. Even though I still cannot recognize Krogan expressions yet, I know that those two are trying not to laugh. It also takes me some effort not to laugh aloud. Contract us? That's really funny. With what the Tloc paid us for my ship, we have more money than what we'll ever be able to spend. Not less than sixty four billion credits. Of course we're not going to be so stupid as to say that. It's not convenient to state that you are rich when you are surrounded by beings that would be delighted to kill you so as to get hold of your riches. I might be a girl, but I was not born yesterday and I've been already sufficiently chastened.

"Why us?"

"Because we know that you fought against the Tloc. That you have killed many of them. Nobody has been able to kill a Tloc in an individual fight for hundreds of cycles."

I glimpse at Groar. He's looking at me. I know he's proud. More honor for our clan, though the death of the Tloc was in reality a desperate attempt to save me. He was successful and now he can boast of having done something that nobody ever achieved. Krogans love to show off.

"So you're looking for warriors."

"I'm looking for somebody who is capable to perform a rescue where others have failed. Somebody exceptional, capable of doing the impossible. If you have successfully confronted the Tloc, then probably you are what we are looking for."

Tara then intervenes.

"And why do you think that we will help you? We are not mercenaries. Your money is of no interest to us."

"We know that you're looking for a ship. A well armed ship. We will give you a ship of those characteristics if you're able to perform the mission."

Groar grunts deridingly.

"A Kanil ship? They're so weak that they surrender as soon as a pirate approaches. If it were not for your fleet, your world would by now have starved to death. Only the escorts keep the pirates at bay."

"A Xebu warship."

Both Krogans straighten. Then they look at each other, tilting their heads. I know that's their way of showing surprise.

"You have a ship from the Xebu?"

I am unable to distinguish the Kanil voice tone, but I could swear that he's gloating with the interest that he has raised.

"A pocket battleship. We captured it during the last war with the Serelens, thirty-two cycles ago. We don't know how they got it. It has been repaired, but it's very uncomfortable and of little use for the Kanil."

Groar's voice sounds suspicious. I know that, after so many weeks in his company I start capturing his emotions.

"It will be too big for us."

"It only needs a crew of two, though it can lodge up to one hundred assault troopers. You can man it. And it's very well armed."

Groar and Tara look at each other. Even though they don't say a word, I know that they're keen to accept the offer. I don't know what kind of species the Xebu are, nor how their ships look like, but it must be something impressive. Then they look at me. Of course, I'm the Art'Ana, the matriarch of our nest. The decision is mine.

"How is that kind of ship?" I ask in Krogan, so that the Kanil does not understand us.

"I've never seen any. But it's very powerful and very fast," responds the warrior. "With a ship like that we would not have to worry about most of the threats."

I stare at him in doubt.

"We don't know in what state it is."

Then Groar grunts with contempt.

"No matter in what shape it is in, we can repair it. We have sufficient credits to do it. It's impossible to get a ship like that by normal means, it simply is not for sale."

So I look at Tara.

"But the mission must be very dangerous. Or they would not offer anything like that."

They both laugh.

"Ke, ke, ke... More dangerous than the Tloc? Tanit, you're already in danger. The Tloc agreed not to attack us, but soon they will put a price on your head. You know too much. They will want to be the only ones to know about the galactic jump. They have your ship, but they will want to make sure that nobody gets what might be in your head. Unless we can get a very powerful ship, we will be an easy prey for the bounty hunters. Soon a dozen Krogan will not be sufficient to protect us. Not if the price for killing you might reach hundreds of millions. The Tloc can pay that."

I sigh. I suppose that they are right. But I'll be dammed if I look forward to such an adventure. Groar has trained me well and I have the protective shield that we got from the Tloc, but I still remember all too well that not so long ago I almost died in a firefight.

"Very well," I snap out to the Kanil in Common. "Let's hear what it is. Perhaps it might interest us."

He makes a few turns around the subject, but eventually he tells us everything. There was a small ship in transit towards their planet that for unknown causes has crashed on a world halfway to its destination. We have to rescue the survivors. As simple as that.

Or perhaps it's not that simple. It sounds funny even to me. At least it does not look normal that a starship should crash on a planet. How could that happen? Supposedly a starship cannot hit anything while in trans-lux. Well, I know an exception: the accident that brought me here. But crash on a planet? Apart from leaving trans-lux, the ship would need to have the normal engines damaged. Even a minimum operation should have allowed placing the ship in orbit. And if the engines did not work at all, it would have crashed onto the surface at the speed of a meteorite, assuming that it had not been burned by the atmosphere. There would be no survivors.

I mention it to my nest in Krogan so that the marmot does not understand us, and they both agree. There is something strange here. I turn towards the marmot.

"How is it possible that it crashed on a planet? Did the engines not work?"

He makes a strange squeak and opens the hands, in a gesture that I suppose means something similar to a shrug.

"We don't know. The ship is damaged, but we cannot inspect it from the planet's orbit and we have not been able to get sufficiently close so as to know what happened."

"And how do you know that there are survivors?"

"The communications of the crashed ship still work, though not very well. There are two survivors, the rest of the crew is dead."

"Did you not attempt a rescue?" joins Tara in.

"Of course. Several times. But we were not able to do it. That is why we need a special team. Somebody capable of doing the impossible, to have success where we failed. The planet is dangerous."

Groar growls suspiciously.

"What kind of dangers are on the planet?"

"Extremely strong winds. Volcanic eruptions. Dangerous animals."

Both Krogans snort with obvious contempt.

"That is nothing special. We have that also on our planet."

"That's why we are resorting to you. Our rescue teams did not survive."

We look at each other. Shit! Perhaps he has slipped it out, but the Kanil has said too much. It's not that they have failed; it's that their rescue teams died in the attempt. The planet in question must be quite dangerous. But if they have sacrificed several rescue teams, it must be a real VIP.

"Who are the two survivors?"

I am unable to read the expressions of the aliens, but it's evident that he has doubts because of the time it takes him to respond.

"I am not authorized to say it."

Well, he might not be authorized to tell us, but we are not that interested in this rescue, Xebu ship or not. And in addition... risk our lives without even knowing why? As far as I am concerned, that marmot can go to hell.

"Then start looking for somebody else," I state, turning around. "I am not going to risk the lives of my nest for a nobody."

"He's a cub!" screams the Kanil behind me.

I turn, perplexed.

"A cub?"

The alien extends his arms, as if begging me.

"He's only one cycle old!"

Groar grunts, obviously irked.

"In that case, he's dead. A cub of that age, no matter how quickly his species matures, cannot survive alone."

"He's with his mother. She is wounded, but she can still take care of him. They are still alive. But their time is running out. Their supplies will run out in twenty-six microcycles."

I make a quick calculation; it's pretty complicated, but I was always good in math. A cycle in Common is approximately a hundredth millionth of the time that it takes the galaxy to make a complete turn, slightly more than two Earth years. A microcycle is a little more than nineteen hours and a half. Twenty-six microcycles are therefore about twenty-one Earth days. Now, that's not much. Not if we have to travel to another solar system.

"Then the rescue is impossible," I answer. "We would never reach the rescue location on time."

"We have a scout ship here. It's the fastest ship that we Kanil have. It will take us thirty-five microcycles to get there and carry out the rescue."

"And will the cub survive nine microcycles without food?" inquires Tara.

"He will not be without food."

I frown. There is something amiss here.

"Did you not say that they will run out of supplies in twenty-six microcycles?"

"Yes." I don't know why, but his voice suddenly sounds strange. And what he says afterwards gives me the shakes. "But his mother is available. As soon as we know that the rescue is imminent, the cub can start with her. Her body will give him at least twenty microcycles more. Sufficient time for the rescue."

"You mean...?" It costs me even imagining it. "You mean that he will eat his mother?"

He simply looks at me.

"I heard that you're female. If your body was the only food supply, would you not be ready to give it to your cub?"

I feel how a shiver goes down my spine. Of course, I never thought about having kids, not at my age. Probably I would do anything for them. I know my parents would have done that for me. But to be eaten! I suppose I can't think like an alien.

"And could she not stop eating for a few microcycles? So that the cub would have more time before... starting with her?"

I'd swear that he is wavering.

"I suppose she could. But only if the rescue was imminent."

I think furiously. It's a baby. An alien, but an alien baby. And his mother loves him so much that she's ready to let him eat her so that he will survive. I feel a knot in the stomach. This is too much for me. But I feel that I cannot allow that this baby and his mother die. No matter how dangerous this might be.

"There is something weird here," snarls Groar. "What are you hiding? Who is that cub? Why would you want to give a warship in exchange for that cub?"

It takes the Kanil some time to answer, as if it did cost him to say it. Finally, he seems to take a decision.

"He's the Light of Heaven," he states in a low voice.

By how the Krogans tilt their heads, I know that they're surprised. Though I did not understand anything.

"The Light of Heaven?"

"Their living God," explains Tara. "It's not surprising that they are willing to pay anything in order to rescue him! They believe that a curse will fall upon them if the cub dies."

"The bad news," points Groar out in his language, so that the marmot will not be able to understand us, "is that this places us in a very difficult position. If we fail, the Kanil will kill us for having let their God die."

"And they will kill us also if we refuse to save him," objects the female in the same language. "As if we did not have enough with the Tloc, now the Kanil will also want to finish us off."

I inhale deeply. All options are bad. It's evident that I have a special gift to get into trouble. Well, if we survived the Tloc then I imagine that we can rescue that baby. At least I have two armored warriors with me. They will protect me, so I suppose that I'll be safe. I hope. And we need that ship. Groar is right: The Tloc will not allow me to live.

"Then we don't have any alternative, do we?" I ask in Krogan.

They simply look at me, but it's not necessary that they say anything. It's obvious that they think the same thing. In any case, I'm the Art'Ana. The decision is mine.

"All right," I sigh, turning towards the Kanil. "We will go with you. You said that you are still in contact with the crashed ship?"

"Yes."

"Then tell the mother that she must stop eating eighteen microcycles before our arrival So that the cub has sufficient supplies until we get there. We will try to save them both. Where is your ship?"

"Deck three hundred and eighty, lock seven hundred and four."

"We need our weapons," warns Groar. "Go and prepare the ship. We' will arrive in forty nanocycles. Be ready to leave."

"We will be waiting for you."

While the Kanil exits the nest, with Tara still pointing her weapon at him, Groar moves to the armory and starts pulling out sufficient weapons for a small war. I grab for my breastplate, but Tara shakes her head.

"We need our armor. We do not know what we will face."

To be honest, I've never used my armor before. Tara needs to help me putting it on, though I don't put on the helmet. Then, while I pick up my clothes and other things that I want to take with me, she puts on hers.

"We cannot bring with us the auto-doctor that we obtained from the Tloc," informs me Groar, while putting on his own armor. "Even if it is the only one that can cure you. But we'll take with us a static capsule, so as to bring you back here in case that you're wounded."

I wish he had not said that. A static capsule is a kind of wrapper where time almost stops. It's horribly expensive, but we can afford it. Actually, we even have two. It's something that is very useful if you need to transport a wounded, because it gives you a lot of time to bring him to a place where you can cure him without bleeding to death. But it's not funny at all that Groar reminds me that I could get hurt. I almost died only weeks ago, when we battled against the Tloc.

"Let's take the two capsules with us," I respond.

He growls something.

"I had thought about leaving your pet in one of them. We cannot take it with us."

I doubt for an instant, but then the female intervenes.

"Tanit is right, we might require both capsules in an emergency. I'll take care of the cat."

Tara programs the cooking machine so that it will take out Bagheera's food several times a day; this way, the cat will not starve. As she also knows that it needs to poop on the white surface that absorbs the excrements, we don't have to worry about that either. She will probably miss me, but there is nothing I can do about that. I caress her before we leave.

"Take care, Bagheera."

She mews mournful, or at least it sounds like that to me. She must understand that something is happening. But then she gets onto the bed and lies down there. When we leave through the door, she's still looking at us. I really hope she's OK.

We raise quite a lot of excitement while we march through the corridors of the station, but all aliens move quickly to one side when they see us coming. It's logical: When a Krogan carries a breastplate, he is not exactly in a good mood, but when he wears a combat armor then he is looking for a really big fight. In addition, after word has spread about our battle against the Tloc, nobody wants to have a quarrel with a Krogan.

We reach airlock seven hundred and four and they are waiting to provide us access. Filtering ourselves through the wall, we get aboard. They have hardly closed the lock behind us when the ship starts moving. We have not even reached our cabin when the ship is already accelerating, even though this scout ship is very small. Only hours later, after we have left behind the gravity wells of the solar system where we are, we change to trans-lux mode. Folding the space for the stellar jump. From that moment on, we can only wait until we reach our destination. However, this time I won't get bored.

Groar trains me during the whole trip on how to use my personal armor. Well, they call it armor, but in reality it's a mixture of armor and spacesuit. It's incredibly complex, the 3D printer of our nest took two full weeks to manufacture it.

If anybody thinks about the medieval armor that we used on Earth, then he's totally wrong. A Krogan armor looks like the medieval armor as much as a starship looks like the old sail ship models that my father made. For starters, it adjusts to my body like a second skin; actually it's more comfortable to be naked than dressed inside the armor. It's not rigid; it adapts to my movements in such a way that sometimes I have the feeling that I'm not wearing anything. And it is very, very strong. Groar proved it by shooting two explosive bullets at me. The armor contracted immediately at the impact point, dissipating the force of the explosion, and the bullets did not even cause as much as a scratch on the surface. It is intended to resist the impact of micro-meteorites in space. As these travel at a speed of hundreds or thousands of miles per hour, they would release as much kinetic energy as a bomb when impacting the armor.

But that's just the armor part. It is also a spacesuit, and the spacesuits that we humans use are a joke beside it. Of course it has oxygen bottles, but it could work even without them, regenerating the atmosphere while I use up oxygen and exhale carbon dioxide. It recycles my waste, converting it into water and... well, something like food. Eating your own shit might sound weird, but I could survive for almost three weeks without having to open the suit, before the unavoidable losses would make me truly eat shit.

Of course it has also a propulsion system, so as to be able to maneuver in space. The energy is provided by a small fusion reactor and, should it ever have no reaction mass, it can use the biological waste that it cannot recycle into food. There is no such thing as waste. You can actually even collect space residues, place them in a gap of the suit, and convert those into reaction mass. You will never run out of energy.

Logically, it resists both heat and cold. Actually, it is very resistant. I could be at the absolute zero or in a furnace at fifteen hundred degrees and within the armor I would still continue with some comfortable seventy degrees. I can pick up a red-hot iron or bath in liquid nitrogen without any problem. And it has sensors to see hundreds of miles away at almost any frequency.

But its use is really complicated. You must understand it: It can safeguard me from almost anything. They would have to throw me into the sun or attack me with heavy weaponry so as to be able to penetrate my armor. But the intelligent systems it has also require intelligent instructions. Because the armor itself can also kill you if you do not use it properly.

Almost all alien devices are managed with the mind, but apparently that is not true for the really critical systems. This is due to the fact that in a critical situation your mind might be occupied with resolving the problem you face, while many mechanical actions can be performed almost instinctively. However, the instinct can be obtained by means of an exhaustive training.

And you can bet that I train. Groar trained me in basic combat, so that I could pass the Krogan rite of maturity. Now, I thought that was tough. But when he hooks up my armor to a combat simulator, that's when I find out what is really tough. During the thirty-five microcycles —some twenty-eight days— that our trip lasts, he literally pounds away at Tara and me. Of course, by the time that we finish the training, we are both sure that we can face whatever they might throw at us.

We notice it when the ship leaves trans-lux. It is a very strange feeling, as if your brain stretched and shrank again for a second. Knowing that we have traveled between the stars by folding space, it almost seems logical.

Obviously we go immediately to the bridge, to see where we are. It will still take us a day or two to arrive there, but we are impatient to know about our destination and the Kanil shows it on a screen: a dark planet where huge yellow-red lights burn, joined by rivers of the same color. And it looks as if there are explosions on the surface.

"What is that planet?" asks our male. "It looks as if it is volcanic."

"It is," answers the pilot. "This is a very young system and the planets are newly formed. We are in the Renero system, very close to the Krogan worlds. You know it as Ren-Ar-Reo. This is the fifth planet of that system."

Groar and Tara then look at each other. By now I know them sufficiently well so as to detect most of their emotions and I'm detecting concern.

"You know that planet?"

"Yes." The voice of our warrior tries to downplay it, but I already know how to recognize the tone of his voice. "It's a volcanic planet. A very dangerous one. We Krogan know it as the Fesk Nar-Lorin."

My knowledge of the Krogan language is still not very good, but I know how to translate it. It means the place of the damned souls. What we humans know as Hell.

We return to our cabin and organize what my family calls a war meeting. In the Krogan language, so as to make sure that the marmots don't understand us.

"It's going to be very dangerous," warns Tara. "It's not surprising that they searched for a special team."

"Will our armor resist?" I ask with ingenuity. "The temperatures must be very high and there seems to be a lot of lava."

"I'm not worried about the armor," grumbles the warrior. "It can withstand even the lava for several microcycles. But the eruptions launch both ashes and stones up. That is very dangerous. And there will be extremely strong winds due to the air convection. We are going to face a lot of trouble simply to land."

Then Tara starts laughing.

"Ke, ke, ke... Groar, I was the best pilot of my nest since I was six cycles old. I can assure you that I do not care how strong the convection currents might be, I can place any ship right beside the shipwreck. If that is not enough and we cannot land there, I can sustain the ship above the wreck while you rescue that cub and his mother. However, if we are hit by a volcanic bomb while we are in the air, then we're going to be in serious trouble."

"Has anybody ever landed on that planet before?" I ask.

"Yes," grunts Groar. "Some fools did. Most of them were never able to take off again. Tara, are you sure that...?"

Then the female hisses, in a clear signal of reproach.

"I am the best! Do you doubt it?"

"No. Art'Ana?"

I inhale deeply. The decision is mine. On an impulse, I approach the intercom and contact the bridge.

"How many rescue missions have you sent?"

I could swear that the pilot hesitated for a moment before responding.

"Four."

"And why did they fail?"

This time there is no doubt: he hesitated before responding.

"The air currents are very strong. It is also necessary to land at a certain distance, the accident area is very rough. The terrain is dangerous. There are aggressive animals. None of the rescue missions were able to return."

I cut the intercom and drum with the fingers on my leg, doubtful. I have a strange feeling. As if there was something else that they have not told us.

"What do you think?" I ask my new family.

Both growl at the same time.

"It's too late to back down," mumbles Groar. "If we refuse to land, they will kill us. Not by something as stupid as attacking us. But they could for example open our cabin to the outside, to the void."

"We can attack and take control of the ship," suggests Tara. But we would have to kill them all, they will fight until death to save their God. And the Kanil will then put a price on our head. They will never forgive us if we let their God die."

I sigh. So we either go down or we murder the whole crew, becoming also outlaws in the bargain. Well, I don't think that the Kanil are more dangerous than the Tloc. But it disgusts me to carry out a mass murder so as not to take risks. In any case, the following words from Groar close the discussion.

"But it would not be honorable to do so. Not when we have accepted the mission."

There is nothing more to discuss. Honor is everything for the Krogans. They will rather die than disgracing themselves. Tara and Groar are going down, I am sure. And nothing of what I say will convince them otherwise. I could stay, but I know that I will not do that. They are now my family. They saved my life several times. Under no circumstances will I abandon them. No matter how dangerous this might be.

"When we can only perform the mission. Our honor requires it."

I might have spoken like a real Krogan, but to be honest I am scared shitless. However, no matter how scared I might be, I will go with them. I'm not invulnerable, but my armor will protect me from almost anything. And I also have the energy shield I got from the Tloc. It's even possible that I am the one who has most possibilities of us three to get out unscathed.

To my surprise, there are many ships orbiting the planet. Huge ships. Even Groar is amazed when we see from the bridge how we are going to dock against one of them.

"At least half the Kanil fleet must be here," he tells us in his language, so that the ET who is piloting our ship cannot understand us. "It must be true, their living God must be down there."

I look towards the planet which by now dominates the whole sky. It does not exactly look reassuring. The place of the damned souls. Hell. A very appropriate name. Despite everything, I can't avoid a shudder.

"I suppose we won't go down with this ship?"

"I don't think so. This is not an atmospheric craft. There are very few starships that can land on a planet, and even less on this one."

We enter a huge hangar by filtering our scout through the ship's airlock. Within minutes they have transferred us and our equipment to a smaller vessel in the middle of an enormous expectation. And when I say enormous I do not exaggerate at all: there are at least five hundred marmots around the hangar watching us in silence.

Tara sits immediately down in front of the ship's controls. The seat is slightly small for her, but she does not seem to notice. She quickly inspects the controls. Then she turns to look at me.

"No problem at all. I can pilot it. It's just a shuttle, and an obsolete one at that. Nothing special. Art'Ana?"

I breathe in deep and sit in the co-pilot's seat. Shit. I can't even see the window. So I stand up again.

"Let's go."

The nice thing about the alien ships is that they manage gravity so well that you don't even realize that they're accelerating. Suddenly we are crossing the airlock and moments later we are again in space.

I look at the ship that we have just abandoned while Tara maneuvers towards the planet. It's really huge. A warship, by the looks of it. Human ships are ridiculous by comparison. But Groar does not seem impressed.

"Kanil battleships are like biologic waste," he comments deridingly. "Even a Krogan frigate has more firepower."

Tara laughs while she quickly descends towards the atmosphere. Meanwhile, I wonder how brutal Krogan warships must be if they consider this to be a shit.

We enter the atmosphere and a tongue of fire wraps around us due to the air friction as we're coming in so fast. But as we descend and reduce the speed, we recover our vision. It's a way of speaking, because we are in the middle of thick clouds of black smoke. Our female has to navigate blind.

"Arriving at rescue area."

Suddenly we exit the clouds. Groar gets closer to the cabin windows and looks outside.

"Those Kanil excrements fooled us."

I also look out of the polarized window. The aspect of the planet is terrifying. There are lava rivers everywhere. Volcanoes erupt all over the place. And worst of all, there are at least forty ships that have crashed around the landing area. Our warrior is right: they have tricked us. There are far more rescue attempts than they told us. And all finished with catastrophic results.

I feel that my hair is bristling. There is something strange here. It's not normal that these ships crashed, no matter how strong the air currents might be here. Suddenly I have a weird feeling.

"Tara, pull up!" I command on an impulse. "Now!"

If Krogans have something good, it's that they don't dispute an order from their matriarch. Instantly our pilot puts the engine to full power. That is a good move, because almost immediately a fireball passes just below us.

"Evasive maneuvers!" roars our male, jumping into the co-pilot's seat. "Activating armament!"

"No!" I scream. "Don't shoot! Gain altitude and avoid the fire, but don't shoot!"

The huge warrior turns towards me, obviously surprised.

"What?"

I'm looking through the window. There are some strange shapes coming out of the lava. They look like giant worms. Or perhaps these are the necks of creatures that are immersed in the molten rock. One of the beasts turns the neck in our direction and spews a fireball towards us. Luckily Tara is aware of it and the incandescent meteorite does not hit us.

"Shooting is not an option," I explain to Groar while exploring the terrain with a look. "Those ships had also weapons, and the only thing that they achieved is being shot down. Let's try not to piss off those animals."

"They have stopped shooting," reports Tara. "But they are watching us. Gods, there must be at least seventy!"

I lean out, looking down. It's true, the lava rivers and lakes are infested with necks peeking out of the molten rock and turning towards us. And every moment more appear. There must be already over a hundred. It's impossible to land here. We will be shot down as soon as we try it.

A metallic reflection catches my attention and I look in that direction. There are ships on the ground and they don't seem to be damaged. They are in the crater of an extinct volcano. Of course! These beasts live in the lava. There is no lava in that crater and its slopes hide the ships from the projectiles.

"Tara, turn right. Thirty degrees. Land in the crater where the other ships are."

She looks while our shuttle turns.

"You know that we'll be in the line of fire of those animals while we land."

"Approach from the opposite side of the crater, so as to be a target for a shorter time" commands Groar. "Then land performing evasive maneuvers. If those ships were able to land, I don't see why we could not do that also."

Out pilot lifts the ship's nose and turns in a wide circle that will make us approach the crater from the opposite side. I continue observing the creatures in the lava. They are tracking us with their heads, but they no longer try to shoot us. Actually, when we descend to land in the crater, they don't fire at us, even though we are well within their range. There is something very weird going on here.

"Pffff," puffs the Krogan while switching off the engines. "I thought that we would not make it."

The warrior points to the other ships surrounding us. There must be about half a dozen.

"They made it also. It was obvious that it is possible to land."

I don't say anything, but I am thinking furiously. Now, the place where all the crashed ships are seems to be a site that the beasts in the lava defend as much as they can. But this place does not seem to preoccupy them, as they did not attack us or the other ships that landed here. Why?

Tara grunts something while she stands up.

"For what it's good for... Those ships are abandoned. They are all dead."

Then I see the movement close to one of the ships and point.

"Not all. There is one survivor"

Both Krogans arm themselves to the teeth while the lonely figure approaches our shuttle. I close my armor and activate the energy shield we got from the Tloc. Though, to be honest, I don't expect that the survivor will attack us.

He enters the airlock and we wait patiently while the system equals the pressures and ejects the poisonous gases. Then the alien enters and removes his helmet.

It's a Sneog. He's biped, around six feet tall, covered by a brown skin. His face is similar to that of the sea lion but he has a huge red crest on top of the skull. I frown. Sneog are not exactly lovable. They are mercenaries and I already had a few bad encounters with them. First, they tried to kidnap me. Then they attempted to kill me. In short, my encounters with this species have been everything except peaceful. Luckily, the Krogans are with their weapons ready.

But soon it becomes evident that he is not coming for a fight. He is wounded and begs us to bring him outside the planet. He is the last survivor of another rescue mission.

I let Groar perform the questioning. Apparently the Sneog were also hired for this same contract and they went do111wn to the planet with five shuttles, in a demonstration of force. Only one survived the attack of the beasts, and by then their fuel reserve had been so depleted that it was a miracle that they could even land. They asked the Kanil for help, and these responded that they only would assist them if they rescued the Light of Heaven. The twelve that traveled in the shuttle gave it a try, but they did not even manage to approach the Kanil ship.

The lava beasts literally fried them; he escaped because he was walking slightly behind and was able to tumble behind some rocks.

Groar generates the area map, making him point out his course and the location of the massacre on the hologram. I frown, surprised. They passed beside several lava rivers, but the beasts did not attack them. Only when they approached the area where the crashed ship is, were they assaulted. Our warrior also notices that detail.

"Did the beasts in the lava not attack you while you marched?"

"No. We were preoccupied, but they just observed us. But suddenly they assaulted us. Only I survived. Can we leave now?"

"No," I respond. "We first need to save that cub."

"It's impossible!" shouts the Sneog.. "Didn't you see how many of us tried? And they are all dead!"

"So will we if we try to take off without the cub," mutters Tara. "The Kanil will not allow us to abandon our mission. If we try to take off, we will join those wrecks over there. Two of them were shot down by missiles, the damage is very different from those of the other ships. They must have tried to reach again the orbit."

The wounded sits down, obviously dejected.

"Then we are dead."

Groar grunts deridingly.

"We are Krogan. A Krogan never surrenders. If we have to die, we will die with honor."

I would have preferred that he had not said that. But his species is like that. Death is just a slight inconvenience, the only important thing is their honor. I sigh. We better start moving. Let's see how we get away with the worms. Because we do not have many options.

I put on again the helmet that I had removed while we talked with the Sneog. All take the hint, even the visitor, and put on theirs. On impulse, I attach the biologic recorder that I bought in *Meeting Point* to my spacesuit. I don't know whether I'll get close enough to the worms so as to be able to analyze them, but you do never know and those beasts are really very interesting. Then I grab my gun. This is not a tourist tour; I might actually need it.

The shuttle is somewhat outmoded, and they also saved in the manufacturing. The airlock of most alien ships is a wall through which you can filter yourself but that does not allow the passage of air. Not this one. It has two doors, like the human ships, and we need to squeeze in a reduced space while the inner door closes and the cycle starts to recycle our atmosphere and replace it by the external one.

It takes an eternity before the lock finally opens. I am nervous, checking continuously my armored suit. Until now I had only tested in a safe environment. But what if it does have a crack through which the air escapes? Through which the poisonous gases might enter?

It's silly, of course. Groar made us check twice our suits, and then he has verified them personally. There is nothing to fear.

In any case, I check out the atmosphere as soon as the outer door opens. There is a higher pressure than the one to which I am accustomed, about 1.2 atmospheres. To my surprise there is a lot of water vapor in the atmosphere, and even more oxygen than on Earth itself, almost thirty five percent. But there is little nitrogen and a lot of sulfur, apart from many ashes. Despite so much oxygen, I would suffocate in an instant if I was not wearing a spacesuit.

Well, actually that would be if I was not cooked first. The temperature is around two hundred fifty degrees Fahrenheit. This is not exactly a cool place.

Suddenly I realize that Groar has already exited, followed by the Sneog. It's my turn; the Krogan habits state that the warriors go first, with the females in the rear. But the Art'Ana, the matriarch, goes in the center, heading the females. Tara is already looking at me as if asking herself what I am waiting for. She has her incendiary grenade launcher ready and it is then that I notice how worthless that weapon is going to be. Incendiary grenades are going to be here like a refreshing shower. At least I carry my cryogenic rifle, which is capable of freezing anybody. Though I wonder whether it will work at all with all the heat around us.

I carefully go outside and I am greeted with a slap of noise. It's a continuous roar, sometimes interrupted by what seem to be huge explosions. I have to adjust my suit to let it attenuate the volume of the external noise. The atmosphere is very dense and this infernal noise is very well transmitted at great distances. Then I look around.

OK, it's the crater of an extinguished volcano. No surprise here. While I still lived on Mars I visited a lot of dead volcanoes. I even visited the greatest volcano in the solar system, Olympus Mons. Obviously I had to go in a spacesuit because it is fourteen miles high and it peeks almost outside the atmosphere, no matter how terraformed Mars might be. Now, that crater was really impressive, as it is thirty-seven by fifty miles wide and two miles deep. This crater is not even fair; it must have less than half a mile in diameter.

I look at the ground. Solidified lava, and there are not even fumaroles. This volcano is well extinguished. Not that I'll complain, it's just what we needed, that it would start an eruption right now.

"Let's go."

Groar opens the way, followed by the Sneog, with Tara in the rear. The route is difficult, as the terrain is very irregular. We have also to climb the crater walls. These are very steep and I am panting from the effort, even before we are halfway of the slope.

When we finally reach the border of the volcano, we stop for an instant, looking at the amazing spectacle in front of our eyes.

There are thousands of volcanoes. Literally. Volcanoes up to the horizon, and most of them are active. Some simply churn out lava, but others continuously spew ashes and rocks into the sky. If Hell really exists, it must be very similar to this.

There are lava flows everywhere, and what seems strange is that there is solid rock between so much magma. I suppose that the molten rock eventually cools down with the air. Because there is a lot of wind. The lava heats up the air, which obviously ascends, dragging downwards cold air from the stratosphere. This convection effect creates a very uncomfortable wind that is continuously jostling me around. Perhaps the Krogans are not affected so much, as they weigh a lot more than I do, but I am a girl and weigh less than a hundred pounds. I don't know whether I can fly away, but just in case I manipulate my armor so that the soles remain anchored to the ground. That's a characteristic of my spacesuit for when there is no gravity; it prevents you from flying away when you walk. It will also prevent me from running, but I am not going to risk to be carried away by the wind.

A huge neck then rises from a lava river flowing close from where we are and turns towards us.

"Don't shoot!" I shout, as all have by instinct raised their arms.

They all obey, even the Sneog, and I observe the worm, or whatever it might be. What kind of creature is that? I know that lava is molten rock, and if I recall well, it's at a temperature between thirteen hundred and over two thousand degrees Fahrenheit. How is it possible that this creature lives at those temperatures?

Life is very resilient, capable of surviving in really extreme environments. We humans have found organisms surviving at temperatures very close to the absolute zero. We found bacteria within rocks, even in the reactors of nuclear plants. The abyssal fishes on Earth survive without light under tremendous pressure. But live inside the lava? During my Astrobiology studies I analyzed animals living in really strange environments, especially those of the Zeta colony. But I've never heard of superior organisms living at such extreme temperatures.

Starting the biologic recorder, I commence to register the data of this creature. Well, I actually record what I can; at this distance I will not be able to identify its internal organs. I'll check it later, but I have the impression that the skin is like porcelain. Black porcelain. It must be a thermal coat protecting its internal organs from the tremendous heat. My teachers at the university would have given an arm to be here and see this.

A second neck appears from inside the lava and also turns the head towards us. I cannot see eyes, but I could swear that they are observing us.

"They will kill us!" extols the Sneog. "I'm getting back to the ship!"

I don't respond. If they wanted to kill us, they would have already done so, as we are within the range of their fireballs. But they do nothing. They simply inspect us during approximately one minute and then one of the animals swims away while the other dives again.

Despite myself, I breathe with relief. They did not seem aggressive, but over forty ships have crashed here. Those ships did something that angered these animals. We also did. Perhaps they are afraid of flying things, but we look harmless when on the ground.

"Let's go."

The Sneog has fled, to the contempt of the Krogans. We, on the other hand, start advancing slowly in the direction of the accident location. It's not difficult to see, the white ship contrasts clearly against the black mountain against which it crashed. It's complicated to walk on the volcanic terrain, as the rocks are very irregular. Luckily, my boots can anchor themselves to the ground: with the strong wind gusts and the arduous terrain, it's more than likely that otherwise I would have fallen more than once.

While we advance, we start seeing more worms, or whatever they are; I'm pretty funky, but they ignore us, even when we pass very close to them. I have no clue why they attacked the Sneog, but we don't seem to be very important to them. We have walked for almost one hour, advancing slowly, and they still dismiss our presence. One of them even passed around eighty yards away, as if we did not exist at all. It is huge, it must be at least twenty yards outside the lava. I have no clue about the total size of that beast, but I would not be surprised if it was sixty or even seventy yards long. I hope that my biological recorder has captured everything.

A rock drops suddenly from the sky, at less than a hundred yards from where we are, causing a huge racket and raising a big cloud of ashes and small rocks. I am petrified for an instant. That volcanic bomb must weigh at least a ton. If it had fallen on us... But Groar simply looks up to the sky, checking that no further rocks are falling down, and continues walking. I follow him after a slight hesitation. It does not matter whether I walk or stand still; if something like that falls on us, we won't live to tell it, no matter how strong our armor might be. To my relief I see that in front of us there is a totally flat plain that is more than half a mile long. At least we'll be able to walk comfortably for a while. Then I notice something.

"Wait."

I stop. All the beasts in the lava have turned towards us and are approaching. They have not yet launched their fireballs, but it's obvious that they are ready to attack us. Until now they have ignored us; however, their behavior has changed. There is something here that they are protecting.

I think furiously. I studied Astrobiology at the university, as that was the only job that would convince the authorities to allow me to join my mother at the colony of Thuis. One of the subjects was Animal Behavior, and this aggressive demeanor by gregarious animals is very typical when they are protecting their young.

I straighten, suddenly excited. That's it! For whatever reason, we have entered the hatching area of these animals. They live in the lava, but perhaps they put their eggs on the ground, in the same way that there are sea animals that place their eggs on dry land. The turtles on Earth, for example. Or the caleros of the Zeta colony.

"What happens, Tanit?" asks Groar.

"I think that I just found out why these beasts attack everybody that approaches them. Give me a few nanocycles."

I look carefully at the esplanade. It does not seem to have anything special. To me it looks like natural rock. Then I start distinguishing a slight movement, as if something was moving with the air currents. It looks as if there is something like weed, of a color that is very similar to that of the rock. Only that it is not weed. These must be the larvae of the worms living in the lava. Their colors camouflage them so much that it is almost impossible to distinguish them from the rock where they are lying.

The conclusion is pretty obvious: these larvae must not be capable of resisting the high temperatures of the incandescent magma. When they tried to land here, the ships switched on their jets. Assuming that they would not burn the larvae, they would crush them, so the worms shot them down. When they landed in an area where they would not cause any havoc, the worms stopped caring. But when the crews disembarked and tried to pass here, stepping on the larvae, the adults intervened again.

I change the helmet visor so as to show me only the infrared light, but it's a disaster: there are no many heat sources that I am almost blinded. Then I change the filter to ultraviolet light. And indeed, now I see clearly that on the rocks there is something that looks like long thick branches. They move very slowly. Somebody who did not guess what these are would assume that these are simple plants and step on them. He would kill the larvae, attracting the wrath of the lava worms against him and his companions.

Are these worms intelligent? I have no idea. It could be, as they do not attack deliberately unless you get too close. But that kind of behavior is also typical of some animals protecting their herd. In summary: there are insufficient data to be able to answer the question. What seems to be clear is that if we try to cross between the larvae, the worms are going to bombard us with their fireballs until we are not more than ash.

I adjust the helmet visor to return to normal vision, though overlaying the ultraviolet image. Thus I will see the larvae without losing sight of the terrain.

I look around. The whole plain in front of us is covered with larvae. But to the left there are some rocks, and the path seems to be clear. We'll have to take the hard way.

Groar and Tara are surprised when I explain them my findings. But as soon as they inspect the terrain with ultraviolet light, they quickly reach the same conclusion. We humans tend to believe that some huge monsters like them should not be very smart, but that is not so. I don't know whether the Krogans are especially intelligent, but these two are.

"Good deduction, Art'Ana."

I feel that I'm bloated with pride, especially because Tara has said it so formally. It's not only that I did it well; as she has used my title as the matriarch of the nest, she is recognizing at the same time that I am a good leader. Keeping in mind that the Krogan females do fight for the leadership, she's also confirming that she is willing to obey me. As she measures twenty-four inches more than I do and weighs at least five times as much, that is very reassuring.

"That way."

We climb the rocks, trying to stay as far away as possible from the larvae. And it works: the worms continue to watch us, but they do not attack.

We then reach another lava river. Shit! The crashed ship is on the other side, we will not be able to cross.

"Let's use the propulsion," states Groar.

I had completely forgotten that our spacesuits have propulsion systems so as to maneuver in space. Within an instant we are climbing into the air.

And I almost end up in the lava. The air turbulence over the river of molten rock is tremendous; even Groar and Tara seem to have problems to stabilize their flight, and I am much lighter than they are. Within seconds I have climbed over a hundred feet due to the ascending air. Then I start flying over solid ground and I carefully reduce the power of my propulsion until I finally make a soft landing. I breathe out with relief as soon as I feel that my feet touch the ground again; I did not like my first flight at all, despite the fact that the suit is supposed to stabilize automatically my flight path. It's not a good place for flying.

We climb the rocks and finally reach the crashed ship. It is small for a starship, hardly seventy yards. We surround it slowly, looking for the airlock. But then both Krogans halt. They take their rifles from their backs and look around with suspicion.

"Is something wrong?" I ask.

Then Groar points towards the vessel.

"See for yourself."

I look. That side of the ship has been ripped open, with metal sheets bent outwards. It must have been where they hit something.

But then I frown. If it had hit something, the sheets would be bent towards the inside, not towards the outside.

"There was an explosion inside the ship?"

"A bomb or a penetrating missile," grunts the warrior. "But it did not explode correctly. If a complete charge had exploded, the whole ship would have been pulverized."

I feel a shudder go down my spine.

"Somebody tried to kill them?"

"Yes," confirms Tara. "Let's be careful. The survivors might want to defend themselves. And the murderers will try to prevent the rescue."

I unhook my own rifle from my back and release the safety. Then I look around. You would have to be crazy to come down here to kill the survivors. No, if somebody wants to finish the job, he will try it while we attempt to get out of here.

Groar grunts with approval when I state that aloud.

"You start thinking like a Krogan. We will have to be careful."

Finally, we find the airlock: it's on the top forward side of the ship. It's likely that it is in reality a side, but the vessel is almost capsized. At least it is intact. Well, more or less. The front part of the ship is intact, the rest is clearly damaged.

Groar and Tara grab me by the arms and switch on their propulsion systems, lifting me to the top of the ship. I greatly appreciate that. I am too light to fly alone with these strong winds. They obviously noticed it also.

The airlock is what you would expect, a wall that is permeable to the bodies but which does not allow the air to escape. Despite the fact that I have seen this for months, this technology which makes that materials behave differently depending on what is interacting with them still surprises me. I stop Groar when he is going to pass through it.

"No," I command. "I will go. The Kanil are small. You could scare the survivors."

"They are bigger than you," he objects.

"That's why I know that I will not scare them."

I descend through the airlock into the ship. While I do that, I still hear how Tara tells our male:

"It's obvious that our Art'Ana does not lack valor."

I cannot help but laugh. Valor? What for? But the laugh chokes me one instant later. Something that looks pretty much like a weapon has been placed against my helmet.

"E ne rejj-es efff?"

I turn slowly, trying not to make abrupt movements. There is a Kanil of about my height with a device that does not exactly look like a welcome present.

"We come to rescue you," I respond in Common, hoping that she does not notice the funk I have. My armor is supposed to be able to resist several direct impacts, but even so, I prefer not to put that to test.

She lowers the weapon and drops onto what looks like a seat; it's only then that I notice the bloodstained clothes that she is wearing.

"Save... save the Light of Heaven."

Then she falls backwards, as if her forces have abandoned her.

I immediately call Groar and Tara, who jump through the airlock weapons in paw, as if they had to come to my rescue. They briefly inspect the room and then lower their rifles.

"Are you all right?"

"Yes." I point. "She is wounded. And it does not help that she has not eaten for eighteen microcycles."

"Well," grunts Groar, unhooking the package that he was carrying on his back. "That's why we brought the static capsules."

He deploys the capsule, which looks like a bag, and carefully we place the wounded inside. I hope that it's not too late, she seems to be in a very bad shape. Then Groar presses the activation switch and the bag becomes rigid, presenting us a smooth silvery surface. Within it, time has almost stopped. If she has not died, the Kanil will survive until we can cure her.

"And the cub?"

We look around, but there seems to be nobody else here. Then Tara points to one side and I turn to see what it is. I notice some very small eyes peeking from below what seems to be a pile of fur.

"Over there."

I approach it, speaking softly in Common, though the cub has probably not learned that language yet. Carefully, I move the pelts that cover him to one side. He's cute, like a cotton teddy the size of a two-year old. Really adorable. But then he opens a mouth full of sharp teeth and bites the hand that I am extending towards him.

Well, he bites the spacesuit. My luck, if I was not wearing my armored suit, he would have hurt me quite a lot.

"Now come on! Naughty! Don't you have any manners?"

He must be very scared, because he continues to try biting and clawing me. Now, that's an adorable teddy! Luckily, Tara grabs him and unceremoniously places him in the second static capsule. An instant later, this also shows us its silvery surface.

Groar then starts to hang the first capsule onto his back.

"I'll carry the mother," he declares. "Tara will carry the cub."

I don't protest. It's obvious that they, being far more massive than I am, are more suited to transport the survivors. While they load their burdens, I take the opportunity to walk around the room. Behind a console I then stumble onto the remains of something.

I start staring at it as soon as I realize what it is. Probably cannibalism does not have for them the same moral implications as for the human beings. But it's very evident what their provisions were. And the mother would have been the next plate on the menu if it had taken us longer to get here. I feel how a shiver goes down my spine.

We have a tough time to get out again. The ship is tilted and the airlock is above us. We have to climb, as we cannot use the propulsion of our suits in such a restricted space. It takes us almost twenty minutes to exit, but finally we are again in the open air.

"Look!"

I look in the direction in which Tara is pointing. There is something in the sky, and the worms suddenly seem to be alerted. I make that my helmet zooms into the image. It's a kind of bird. No, it looks more like the prehistoric pterodactyls. My helmet reports its dimensions: it's huge, it must have a wingspan of at least sixty five feet. And more are approaching behind it.

I jolt when one of the worms spits out a fireball. Instants later, all are attacking the flying creatures. Some fall, shot down by the projectiles that the worms are firing. Other pterodactyls however dodge them, launching themselves towards the ground. Towards the plain where the larvae are. The fire of the worms becomes more intense. It's obvious that they are protecting their brood with all their forces.

Suddenly, to my great anguish, something grabs me firmly and lifts me into the air. Within a moment I am dozens of feet above the ground. I look up. It's one of those pterodactyls; it has grabbed me and is probably bringing me to its nest to have a banquet at my expenses, without realizing that it will not be able to penetrate my armor without boiling me first in the lava for fifteen minutes.

I react instinctively, Groar has trained me well. Lifting my cryogenic rifle, I shoot it in the body. One instant later it is covered with ice. The bad news is that we then start to fall like rocks. Luckily, the harsh training that my male has subjected me to shows; again I react by instinct, switching on the jets of my spacesuit. My fall starts to reduce speed, but not fast enough. Within a few seconds I'm going to fall into a lava lake. Shit! I'm going to get fried! My armor will last a few minutes in the lava, but not sufficient to reach the shore. I feel that I am suddenly paralyzed with fear.

Then a huge dark shape emerges from the molten rock, immediately below me. Seconds later, I hit something. The shock absorbers of my boots soften the impact, but even so I lose my balance and fall on my ass. Once on the ground, the spacesuit jets switch off by themselves and I breathe out with relief, knowing that I have escaped by a whisker.

Unfortunately, that's not exactly true. I hear the bellow above the noise of the explosions and I turn my head, staying paralyzed with terror: there is a huge neck coming out of the rock on which I am sitting, and the head has turned towards me. I thought that these were worms, but apparently they are similar to the plesiosaurus that swam in the oceans on Earth, back in the Jurassic epoch. Except for the little detail that these beasts swim in the lava and launch fireballs. Oh, and I'm sitting on it.

I don't know whether it is looking at me; it does not seem to have eyes. But it is evident that it is conscious of my presence; the head is pointing towards me. Will it throw a fireball in my direction? I don't know whether my armor will resist it, but in any case I'll end up in the magma and I'll be cooked.

Could I shoot it? It worked with the pterodactyl. But in the best case, I'll freeze it and it will sink. Unfortunately, in that case I'll sink with it. I stay very quiet, waiting to see what the beast will do.

To my surprise, the animal turns its head, looks forward again and starts advancing slowly through the lava in the direction of the shore.

"Tanit!" I hear over the radio. "Use your jets! Reach the shore!"

Good idea. I had completely forgotten about the propulsion of my spacesuit. But I hesitate. Apart from the fact that this hellish wind can throw me again into the lava, the flames of the jet are going to hit the animal as soon as I switch on the propulsion. I don't think that it would hurt a creature swimming in the molten rock, but perhaps I might scare it and then it will hit me with one of its fireballs. Let's wait somewhat. For now it has not tried to hurt me, though it had the opportunity. However, I am ready for takeoff if it goes under or tries to attack me. On an impulse, I switch on my biological analyzer. If I am able to get out of here, I'd like to know something more about these animals; I never thought that a superior organism could live at these temperatures.

We reach the shore and the beast places its head on the rocks, then staying very quiet. Is it perhaps inviting me to get off its back? I hesitate for a moment, but then I walk carefully along its neck, and trying to keep my balance, I manage to safely reach the shore. I hardly have descended from the beast when the head goes up and approaches me to less than one foot away. It could cut me apart in one single bite, but it does not make any attempt to attack me.

On an impulse, I extend my hand and caress the huge head. I have understood it. These beings are intelligent, or at least semi-intelligent, and have understood what we came to do here. They have also noticed that we took an exquisite care not to hurt their brood. And probably they have also understood that the pterodactyls that attack their larvae are also our enemies, hence that they have saved me.

"Thank you," I say, though I am perfectly aware that it cannot understand me.

Then I have a strange sensation, as if somebody hugs me. It's so real that I even turn around to see who it is. But there is nobody. I look back, and the alien is sinking again into the lava. It's then that I understand that it was him. Telepathy or something similar. We cannot understand each other as we are too different, so it has transmitted me an emotion.

Both Krogans arrive running, ignoring the heavy packs on their backs. I could swear that they are preoccupied. Who would say that, knowing that they are a species of intelligent dinosaurs. Though I know that they have feelings, and their concern seems genuine.

"Are you all right?" asks Tara, in what sounds as an anxious tone. "We were ready to shoot, but with so much wind we were not sure that we would not hit you."

"I am OK," I answer. "Don't shoot. They are intelligent and they know that we are not enemies. Let's simply avoid stepping on their larvae."

"All right," confirms Groar. He points. "That way."

The path across the rocks is a nightmare, but we carefully avoid any flat area. I am not very sure that with the ultraviolet light we will be able to detect all larvae, so we better do not take any risks. It takes us almost two hours to return to our ship. The Sneog immediately leaves his as soon as he sees us coming.

"I see that you were successful. Will you help me to get out of this planet?"

I don't even see his weapon until Groar and Tara shoot him at the same time. The impact of the explosive bullets is so strong that the body is thrown some twenty yards away.

"Amateur," snarls Groar, evidently very pleased with himself. "You never attack a Krogan in the open, and much less when he wears armor. He should have waited until we were in the shuttle and we had removed our helmets, then using a grenade."

Tara growls her assent.

"The Sneog were never great strategists."

I look at the corpse to our left. The spacesuit is clearly torn apart. It the shots did not kill him, he is certainly dead now. I sigh. It makes no sense to recover his body; I would not know what to do with it.

"May his soul rest in peace," I mumble. I suppose that even aliens must have one.

Then we cross the airlock. We have to take turns; the two Krogans occupy so much space with the capsules what it is impossible that we enter all at the same time. Tara goes in first, weapons in her claws, just in case somebody managed to enter. Being smaller than the warrior, she can move better. Then it's me who enters. Tara is already removing the static capsule with the cub from her back.

"Is he OK?" I ask.

She simply growls.

"I don't see why not, the capsule is intact. I'm going to contact the Kanil."

I look at her, puzzled, why she takes the pilot's seat.

"Why?"

"To tell them that we have their living God aboard. So that they will not shoot us."

I nod, while Groar enters and starts removing his own pack. Tara is already talking through the communications system.

"They've told us to wait. They will escort us. An honor escort."

Suddenly that makes me feel very uneasy. I don't know why, but I have a strange feeling. As if something was amiss. And I am starting to trust my forebodings. They have saved already my life several times.

"Tara, I don't want an escort."

Both Krogans turn to look at me.

"Why?"

I think for a moment. Then I realize what is wrong.

"Somebody sabotaged that ship. It had to be a Kanil, nobody else would be granted access to that ship. And it had to be somebody who is very well placed. Somebody with a lot of power. Somebody who knew what ship their God would take and managed to introduce a bomb, despite all the security measures that you would expect in a case like this."

They both nod at the same time. I said it already, these two monsters are nobody's fool.

"And who could make sure that somebody from the escort shoots us." Tara is already switching on the systems. "We won't wait. Let's get out of here."

She takes off abruptly. Immediately she turns the ship so that we won't fly over the worm brooding area and starts gaining altitude. Then we hear a brutal explosion and our shuttle is savagely shaken. Groar peeks out of the window.

"Well," he comments calmly. "The volcano is active again. Somebody has dropped a great caliber bomb onto our landing location. Tara, evasive action. Get into the ash clouds, they won't detect us there."

"You know that we can hit one of the rocks that the volcanoes are spewing into the air."

"Better than a missile. Oops. It looks as if they have started shooting at each other."

I feel that my legs are like jelly and sit down on the floor, while Groar takes the copilot's seat and switches on the Comms system to talk with the Kanil. He expresses himself very creatively. I thought that Common could not be used for insults, but for five minutes our male uses that language to describe some Kanil habits that probably are impossible, but which make your stomach revolt simply by hearing their description.

They respond from different sources, giving contrary instructions, but the signal is suddenly drowned by an extremely strong emission.

"I am the Poggher. Stay covered until we finish off those traitors. Don't respond to any communication except mine."

Tara looks at our mate.

"The Poggher?"

"Their supreme priest."

"Shall we listen to him?"

Groar snarls impatiently.

"We have no option. This shuttle cannot perform a stellar jump, and they have a whole fleet in orbit. Let's stay hidden for now."

"No problem."

We continue flying, hidden in clouds of ashes. Sometimes we see something like a meteorite pass close to us, but Tara seems to a have a sixth sense to avoid those volcanic bombs. After a while, I start to calm down. I get up and stand between the two, looking to the outside. Though there is nothing to see, just a wall of gray ash. Tara is flying blind.

After many hours, while our pilot is making a sudden turn to the right to avoid another incandescent rock, the Comms system thunders again.

"I am the Poggher. Get into orbit and dock at our flagship."

"How do we know that it is him?" I ask naively.

They both growl, amused.

"With such a strong signal? It must come from the flagship. And if that ship has been conquered by the other side, we are dead."

We finally exit the clouds of ashes and we start to see the stars.

"I believe that we have just gotten into a civil war."

Yeah, Groar can say that. There are remains of spaceships everywhere. Many are falling towards the planet, disintegrating in the atmosphere. Here they had a real battle.

"Let's hope that the correct party won," mutters the female.

I look at the tremendous disaster that we have in front of us and shudder. Thousands or even tens of thousands of Kanil must have died in this fight.

"How do we know if it is the correct party?"

Our male laughs at my innocent question.

"It's the correct one if it does not try to kill us and pays us for the rescue."

I look again at the huge massacre.

"Do you really think that?"

Then his voice changes to a tone that I know he uses when he's being serious.

"Art'Ana, the Kanil religion and government are none of our business. We do not intervene in that fight, among other things because we would be unable to understand their reasons. They have been fighting for millennia due to theological disputes. If they were not able to solve their differences, neither will we."

He is obviously right. Even if we knew for certain that one of the parties is better than the other, what moral right would we have to intervene?

Tara is avoiding the remains, jumping from one derelict to another. Initially, that surprises me, as she does not head directly to the flagship, a huge monster that clearly exceeds in size all other ships. Then I understand it: She's using the wrecks as shields, in case that there still is somebody willing to kill us.

But her precautions are apparently excessive; nobody tries to shoot at us. I sigh of relief when we enter the ship's hangar.

Contrary to the last time, now there are only five Kanil in the hangar. Big, dressed in blue and yellow garments. One of them carries a staff and has a very sophisticated cloth hat that is almost two feet high. I suppose it is the high priest. They do not utter a single word until we place the two static capsules in front of them.

"Is the Light of Heaven there?"

"Yes."

The priest points to one side. There is an auto-doctor there.

"Place him in the auto-doctor."

Groar growls and lifts his weapon.

"First our reward. We risked our lives to bring him here."

The Poggher simply contemplates him, with a gesture that I suppose is of contempt. But then he must realize that it is a bad idea to piss off a Krogan. He nods to our right.

"There it is."

I turn. On one end of the huge hangar there is a strange ship of around hundred twenty yards. It's stylish, not at all like the classic stellar ships, which have protuberances all over the place. It almost looks like a fish. It even has something that looks like fins.

Groar grunts with delight.

"A Xebu ship. I never saw one, but I have heard about them."

"As you can see, we comply with our part of the deal. Now bring the Light of Heaven to the auto-doctor."

"The cub is all right. It's his mother who is seriously wounded."

The look that the high priest throws me is clearly mocking, and that despite the fact that I cannot read the facial expressions of these marmots.

"It's only a female. She is of no further importance. Let her die."

He steps on the capsule opening button and the silvery surface disappears. The female is heavily breathing; it's obvious that she will not last for long. I feel that I am invaded by indignation when the Poggher orders our male again to take the cub from his capsule and place him in the auto-doctor. On an impulse, I take the cryogenic rifle from my back. Immediately both Krogans also grab their weapons.

"What is this?" rages the one with the hat. "Fury! Do you dare to disobey me?"

"I am also a female," I snap out to that idiot. "And the life of this mother is worth much more than yours. She was ready to sacrifice herself for her son. That is much more than what you would do. Groar, cure her."

"I'll do it," offers Tara, squatting down and taking the female in her arms. I don't know how she has done it, but she's still holding her grenade launcher. She slowly recoils with her precious cargo until she reaches the auto-doctor and deposits the female on the platform. Even before the arms of the device start moving she is already handling her weapon with both claws.

"You are crazy!" screams the Poggher in my direction. "Let her die! Don't you see that her influence on the Light of Heaven is a heresy?"

Then I get it. The mother must be an inconvenience for the priests. She must object to the fact that the cub is manipulated by these characters in blue and yellow clothes. Now, that is a good reason to save her.

"If she managed to give birth to the Light of Heaven, then she is herself a blessing," I reply, and by how they straighten I notice that I have hit the target. It's true, the mother is an influent person and the priests want to get rid of her. One more reason to protect her. She will not only do the best for her cub, she will also keep at bay the ambition of the priestly caste. Because I don't like these characters at all.

The priests look at each other, but they know that we'll shoot them if they move, and they are unarmed. They wait in silence while the auto-doctor cures the wounds of the female. Finally, this sits down on the auto-doctor platform. She looks around, obviously confused.

"The Light of Heaven!" she shouts. "Where is the Light of Heaven? Where is my cub?"

We lower the weapons and I point.

"Here."

She runs to the capsule and deactivates the static field that slows down the time. As soon as she sees her baby, she hugs him with all her forces. The cub hugs her also and mutters soft words to his mother. Now he really looks like a teddy.

Then there are two small explosions and the high priest and another one fall dead. It seems that some of the priests did have weapons concealed below their tunics. I look at them, perplexed.

"But... what happens? What is this?"

One lifts his gun, pointing at my breast. Not that it worries me much; I am wearing a Krogan armor, which will stop one single bullet without any problem. And we will shoot ourselves before he can fire a second one.

"Rage! Don't you understand it? Enough of those ridicule superstitions! The Light of Heaven must die. Thus, all will know that their beliefs are worthless! That he is not a God and that nothing will happen if he dies! The rule of the priests must end!"

So, what happened in reality is a kind of coup. A revolution. And we went straight into it. We were supposed to fail and the baby was supposed to die. As the initial attack would have looked like an accident, the revolutionary could have stayed in the shadows, subverting the established order. Unfortunately, against all odds, we succeeded.

Then Groar snarls threatening.

"Do you really think that you will be able to kill us? Kill Krogans? With that toy?"

"We don't have to kill you."

I know what he is going to do even before he finishes speaking. While he turns his weapon, I jump towards the baby, covering him and his mother with my body. A second later, my energy field starts deflecting the shots. I really hope that Groar acts quickly, this field will not resist a sustained fire.

But I should not have worried. The huge warrior has surged forward at the moment that they started shooting at the baby, or at me, to be precise. He has grabbed two of the rebel Kanil and has knocked their heads together with so much force that one of them has split open as if it was a nut. In the meantime, Tara has ripped off the head of the third one. There is nothing worse than two pissed-off Krogans.

"Are you all right?" asks the female Krogan when everything has finished. "For a moment I thought that they were going to kill you. I did not remember that you were wearing the Tloc shield."

To be honest, neither did I. Actually, I had trusted my armor. But the energy field is far more efficient.

"Yes." I look around. These shots are going to draw the attention of somebody. Soon we will be in a big mess. Nobody will believe that we did not kill the high priest.

"You have to leave," says suddenly the Kanil female in Common. "Take a ship. I will entertain them as much as I can."

"What about you?" I ask, while both Krogans are already turning away. "And your cub?"

I could have sworn that the marmot smiled.

"He is the Light of Heaven; I am his mother. Nothing will happen to us. And I will help him to change our people. There are many things that need changing."

"Tanit!" shouts Tara behind me.

I nod. It's obvious that we have to get out of here as soon as possible.

"I wish you..." How the hell do you say 'good luck' in Common? I have no clue. "Favorable odds."

She crosses the palms of her hands and bows. I do the same thing and start running. I manage to filter myself through the airlock of the Xebu ship at the same time that a huge Kanil contingent bursts into the hangar.

And I instantly get lost. This ship is very strange and it takes me almost half an hour before I find the bridge. Tara is seated in the pilot's seat and the Kanil fleet is clearly withdrawing. No, it's us who are moving, they continue around the planet's orbit.

"They did not shoot at us?" I ask naively.

"No."

I look at her, perplexed.

"And they do not pursue us?"

"No."

I stare at the screen. This is unbelievable.

"But... they must believe that we have killed their high priest. I suppose that the mother of the cub must have told them the truth."

"Even so, they would want to see us dead. We know that somebody tried to kill their living God. We have seen that the heretics have infiltrated the highest ranks of the priesthood. They will not want us to tell it."

I think an instant about it. It's evident that she is right.

"Then why do they do not persecute us?"

"Actually, Groar has asked himself the same question. He went to investigate."

"And I already know the answer," responds our male, entering through the door. He seems very satisfied of himself. "They had placed a nuclear device."

My mouth falls open.

"A nuclear device? And how did you find it?"

Then Groar laughs.

"Ke, ke, ke... Because they are morons. There are five locations where it is possible to place a nuclear device on a ship where it cannot be easily detected by something as simple as a radiation detector. Four of them require a significant disassembly for which they had no time. The fifth is the reactor itself. Though anybody wanting to place the artifact there will receive such a dose of radiation that he will die immediately, even with an antiradiation suit. But the Kanil are cowards. None of them is willing to sacrifice his life so as to eliminate us. So they hid the nuclear head in the only location where it would not look to be out of place."

Tara tilts her head, surprised.

"The armory?"

"Yes. It was obviously activated. It would have exploded in forty nanocycles, vaporizing the ship and us with it."

I pale on hearing that. They have tried to kill me before. But use an atomic bomb to do it! It's obvious that aliens have very different principles than us.

"I suppose that you have deactivated it?"

He makes a gesture that almost looks as disdain, though I am sure that he would never do that in front of his matriarch.

"Of course."

I sigh. Once again, I have dodged death thanks to my new family. But it is obvious that we will have to tread very careful in this hostile universe. There are now at least two species that want us dead.

"So what are we going to do now?"

"We have to return to *Meeting Point*. There are a few things that we have to retrieve from the nest. Your cat. Also the auto-doctor, as it is the only one that can cure you. The equipment that we took from the Tloc. And then we have to convert our bank account into negotiable goods, load them into our ship and get away. Soon there will be a price on our heads. If the Kanil don't place it, the Tloc will. We have made too many enemies."

I throw a look at the main screen, looking at the gigantic cloud of stars that form the galactic center. In such a great universe, where will we go? Where will we able to hide?

"And then?"

"We will arm this ship until we can face any vessel that wants to attack us. And once we are sure that we have an adequate defense, we will go for our true objective."

I turn and look surprised at the huge warrior.

"Our objective? What objective?"

He shows his teeth. Though others might see it as a menace, I know that if it is not accompanied by a growl, it is actually how his species smiles.

"To bring you with your mother."

I am fifteen thousand light-years from home, on an alien warship, with two huge intelligent dinosaurs. But suddenly I almost feel at home.

About the series "In strange orbits":

"In strange orbits" is a collection of short novels about a little girl that due to an accident on a starship is lost in interstellar space and tries to return with her family. Individual stories are only available in e-book format, but every five stories are bundled into a single volume, which is published both as an e-book and on paper. The stories of this series that have already been published or will be published soon in English are:

Volume 1:
1. The lost girl
2. First contact
3. The Krogan's nest
4. Buyers of the future
5. Rescue in Hell

Volume 2:
6. Krogan honor
7. The sacred amulet
8. At the other side of the impossible
9. Revenge of the Tloc
10. The ship that sang

Volume 3:
11. Echoes from Earth
12. Heart of Paradise
13. The goddess of Chaos
14. The Light of Heaven
15. In search of the Gods

"In strange orbits" was originally published in Spanish. Further work on the series is on-going.

As a self-published author, most of the reviews come directly from my readers. I would greatly appreciate it if you could leave a review of this story at Amazon or Goodreads. Thank you for reading this book!

Contact the author:

This author loves that his readers write him with comments, suggestions or simply to chat. You can contact with him on:

Twitter: @RamonSomoza

E-mail: ramon@somoza.name

Facebook: https://www.facebook.com/ramon.m.somoza

LinkedIn: http://es.linkedin.com/in/ramonsomoza/

The author also invites you to leave your opinion about this book at Amazon, Goodreads or any other book review site.

Note to my readers:

This book was translated by me, and I am unfortunately not a native English speaker. Though I have done an extensive review, I apologize for any potential mistakes or typos in this book. I am a self-published author and cannot afford a professional proofreader. Should you find an error, I'd be very grateful if you could email me so that I can fix it, rather than mentioning it in a review.

About the author:

Ramón Somoza (1956) was born in La Coruña, Spain. He writes since he was 15, when he was living in The Netherlands.

He has a university degree in Computer Sciences, but his experience covers many fields. He has worked as a translator; he has developed software, including simple web applications, desktop or corporate systems and even airborne software (Eurofighter). He has also worked in Manufacturing and Customer Services, as well as the A400M transport Final Assembly Line (FAL). His experience covers data modeling, contract negotiation, program management and even business intelligence and business development. He currently works at Airbus Defence and Space.

Ramón Somoza has also worked in standardization groups dedicated to both software and integrated logistic support aspects. He has participated in at least a dozen of these committees, and has chaired two of them at the Society of Automotive Engineers (SAE) and two at the AeroSpace and Defence Industries Association of Europe (ASD). He is currently the European chairman of the ASD/AIA SX000i, Integrated Logistic Support Guide and S5000F, In-service data feedback.

Nevertheless, his favorite hobby is writing. Given that he travels a lot, he writes most of his books during his trips. He speaks fluently five languages.

If you liked this book, you can visit the author's website at:

http://ramon.somoza.name